Daniel Wadsworth

Diary of Rev. Daniel Wadsworth

Daniel Wadsworth

Diary of Rev. Daniel Wadsworth

ISBN/EAN: 9783337019433

Printed in Europe, USA, Canada, Australia, Japan

Cover: Foto ©Raphael Reischuk / pixelio.de

More available books at **www.hansebooks.com**

DIARY

OF

REV. DANIEL WADSWORTH

SEVENTH PASTOR

OF THE

First Church of Christ in Hartford

WITH NOTES

BY THE FOURTEENTH PASTOR

HARTFORD, CONN.
Press of The Case, Lockwood & Brainard Company
1894

PREFATORY NOTE.

IN the exhumation and rearrangement of the possessions of the Connecticut Historical Society incident to the enlargement of the Wadsworth Atheneum in 1892 was brought to notice a Diary kept by Rev. Daniel Wadsworth during the larger part of his ministry as seventh pastor of the First Church of Christ in Hartford. Mr. Wadsworth sustained this relationship from September 28, 1732, to his death on November 12, 1747. His Diary, however, was only begun on the 5th of May, 1737—nearly five years after his settlement—and it ends with his last feeble entry sometime in February, 1747, nine months before he died.

The Diary is essentially a dry, prosaic, and commonplace one. The writer of it was all his life a valetudinarian, and apparently at no time a man of keenness of observation or pungency of expression. He was a timid, cautious, sincere-hearted pastor, distinctly evangelic in spirit and inspired by a conscientious if not strenuous desire to do a good part in his time. His time, however, was rather a dull one in his church's history save for two features, one of lesser and one of far larger concern. The matter of lesser importance was the building of a new church edifice, the second one in the church's history, to take the place of the old one erected by the first fathers on this soil. The other was the episode in religious affairs marked by the preachings of George Whitefield and his followers and known as the time of the "Great Awakening." In his relation to this passage of our New England story Mr. Wadsworth—and with him the great body of his church—took a conservative attitude.

And for readers outside of Hartford associations it is doubtless this feature of the present Diary which will lend it most interest. The observations made by its writer upon this most memorable portion of the history of his time are indeed painfully lacking in the racy and picturesque qualities we might naturally look for; but they avail, nevertheless, to show clearly the perplexities and struggles of a class of devout and sincere Christian ministers, of whom Mr. Wadsworth was only one among many, who were not able to sympathize with the new measures introduced by the Great Awakening, and respecting whom, for that reason, some of their contemporaries and many of their posterity have formed a perhaps too severe judgment. These pages will at least show that if these more conservative men and churches did not do exactly what might have been wisest, they were conscientious in what they did, and in the way they thought best were earnest and faithful workers.

The mortuary records in this Diary, though of a most meager quality, supply in some measure a real lack in the written annals of the time in which Mr. Wadsworth exercised his ministry in Hartford ; his official church-record, while minuting most church actions, taking no notice of the deaths of his parishioners or of others in the community.

But, such as these annals are, it has seemed to the present writer best to rescue them from their century and a half of oblivion. Impelled primarily by a desire to illuminate as far as possible the history of that First Church of Christ in Hartford, toward which object he has hitherto made sundry endeavors, the editor of these Wadsworth memorials has lovingly studied out these tracings of the hand of a predecessor in the pastoral office, and endeavored to bring that predecessor and the events among which he moved to some degree of life again, so far as the very dusty materials at command would allow.

To do this, however, it has not seemed necessary to print absolutely every daily entry in the Diary, nor in all cases every word of such entries as are made. It did not seem expedient to reproduce every instance of perpetually recurring phrases like the following: "This day in Studying, rainy weather," "This day visiting, nothing remarkable occurs," "Laboured under much indisposition, little study," "Little done, pleasant weather," "O yᵗ god might help me in my duty," "O yᵗ my heart might be quickened by divine grace." Expressions of which these are examples, constituting the only entry for a day, occur very frequently, and often for several days together. Enough of them probably are retained to satisfy any reader of the following pages that some scores or perhaps hundreds of such expressions have been properly omitted altogether.

A few transcribed passages from books Mr. Wadsworth was reading — passages not apparently illuminative either of his character or situation, but probably copied by him to fix them in his memory — have also been left unreproduced in this publication.

With these exceptions it has been the aim of this transcript to give the Diary just as Mr. Wadsworth left it; carefully preserving all references to events, places, and persons mentioned, and retaining the contractions, spellings, punctuations, and non-punctuations of the original autograph.

As to the personal history of the author other than as it is indicated in his Diary it must suffice here to say:

Rev. Daniel Wadsworth was born in Farmington, November 14, 1704. He was great-grandson of William Wadsworth, an original settler in Hartford; a man prominent in all public affairs of the little commonwealth till his death in 1676. William's son John—a brother of the Joseph who hid the charter—settled in Farmington, and there John's son, John, and his grandson Daniel were born.

Daniel was educated at Yale College, graduating in 1726, in the same class with Elnathan Whitman, son of his Farmington pastor, and destined to be his associate in the Hartford ministry as pastor of the Second Church. Young Wadsworth seems to have been employed to some extent after his college course as a surveyor of land, memoranda indicative of this fact remaining in various forms among papers left by him. He was employed in 1730 on the survey of the contested boundary between Farmington and Wethersfield; and in 1730 and 1731 he was one of the Deputies for Farmington in the General Assembly.

He probably secured the chief part of his theological training —and if so doubtless in companionship with his college-classmate and boyhood companion Elnathan Whitman—under the supervision of Rev. Samuel Whitman, the Farmington pastor. His ministry in Hartford began in some service of assistance occasioned by the failing health of his predecessor, the venerable Timothy Woodbridge, who died April 30, 1732, after a ministerial connection with the First Church of forty-eight years and eight months. His ordination to the pastorate took place September 28, 1732. The procedure on the occasion he himself inscribed on the church record as follows:

"The Rev⁴ M⸴ Whitman [of Farmington] began with pray⸴ and preached a Sermon from Matt. 24. 45., the Rev⁴ M⸴ Edwards made a pray⸴ and gave yᵉ Charge, the Rev⁴ M⸴ Colton gave the Right hand of fellowship."

Mr. Wadsworth followed the establishment of his ecclesiastical relations by the formation of social ones, marrying, February 28,

1734, Abigail Talcott, daughter of Governor Joseph Talcott by the governor's second wife Eunice (Howell), widow of Rev. Jabez Wakeman.

Mr. Wadsworth died November 12, 1747, lacking two days of forty-three years of age, having filled a pastoral term of fifteen years and two months. He left a widow and six children.[1] He was one of the trustees of Yale College from 1743 to his death, having apparently been elected in the place of Rev. Samuel Woodbridge of East Hartford. The numbers admitted to fellowship with the church in his ministry, seventy-five to the Covenant and one hundred and three to Full Communion, do not appear to be large for the Great Awakening period, but the proportion of one to the other indicates a healthful condition of the church, and a sound view of things that made for its welfare in the pastor.

Personally Mr. Wadsworth was very clearly a man of kind heart and strong pastoral and family affections. He was nervous and as he himself says "bashful." He seems to have been curiously afraid of accidents, lightning, and fires. Though apparently a dyspeptic and semi-hypochondriac he was after his method a laborious and industrious man. Several hundreds of his manuscript sermons, written fine and complete on little four-by-six folios of paper, remain in the possession of the Historical Society, attesting at once his constancy in this kind of activity and also his timidity in apparently on no occasion speaking without fully written notes. He was a man of considerable property, leaving an estate valued at above £4,000. His library compared favorably with those of ministers about him in like situations, though very small measured by some nearly contemporary Boston pastors, and above all with those of Increase and Cotton Mather.

He built a house on the site of the present Atheneum building founded by his grandson, the ground in the rear being his garden. His widow survived him nearly twenty-six years, dying June 24, 1773, in her 67th year.

Mr. Wadsworth sleeps beside those who occupied his pastoral office before him in the old Hartford burying-ground.

GEORGE LEON WALKER.

HARTFORD, 1894.

---

[1] Abigail, b. January 28, 1735; Eunice, b. August 31, 1736, d. July 23, 1825; Elizabeth, b. June 19, 1738, d. November 15, 1810; Daniel, b. June 21, 1741, d. November 3, 1750; Jeremiah, b. July 12, 1743, d. April 30, 1784; Ruth, b. July 1, 1746, d. December 27, 1750.

Jeremiah married Mehitable Russell, and became father of Daniel, the founder of the Atheneum, and of Catherine and Hannah. With this Daniel, who died in 1848 without children, the name of Wadsworth in the direct male line from Rev. Daniel Wadsworth became extinct.

A DIARY BEGAN MAY 5th. 1737.

Some years agone I began and kept a Diary[1] for some time but being unsettled in ye world and my business often calling me from home and out of Town and other difficulties occurring I at length dropt that, and then kept a weekly Journal till sometime after my settling in ye ministry, but I have now for sometime neglected that also, but being sensible of many Conveniencies y^t may accrue from private memoirs or minutes &^c I now resume and purpose to continue a Diary.

May 5. this day much indisposed for study or close application to any business. Entertained thots about projecting some scheme for ye reforming ye young people of my parish and endeavouring to bring y^m to a more serious concern about religion. I pray god to direct me in it.

— 6. This day spent in Studying a Sermon. I find difficult satisfying people discoursing about y^r Spiritual state; y^y want to know y^y shall be sure y^y believe, y^t y^y Love god, y^t y^y are in ye right way, are sincere and ye like. its difficult bringing y^m rationally to think or speak of these matters

— 7. This day under much perplexity as to w^t subject I should prepare a Sermon upon w^c is many times ye case with me, but yⁿ I would remember those words go I will be with thy mouth &^c.

— 8. Lords day. this day I preached A:M. from psal. 78. 34-37. P. m. from 1. Joh. 3. 8. a very warm day. baptized 3 children, 2 persons made publick confession of scandal, & owned ye covenant, god grant y^t y^y may bring forth fruit meet for repentance

— 9. this day not very profitably spent, so y^t I may almost say, diem perdidi. Some attempts at making a sermon, made little progress

---

[1] A fragment or perhaps the whole of the diary to which Mr. Wadsworth here refers, extending from Nov. 15, 1728, to April 23, 1729, remains. He was at this time pursuing his theological studies at his home in Farmington, and so far advanced as once at least, January 12th, to preach for Mr. Whitman. He was not, however, apparently accounted a clerical person, as the last few entries of the diary relate to his service on a jury at Hartford; an occupation which he characterizes as "unprofitable employment."

— 10. this day spent not yᵉ most profitably   warm, pleasant growing weather, nature revives, may grace do so likewise, as the face of the earth is renewed, so may yᵉ face of yᵉ moral world.

— 11. this day in composing a sermon studying nothing remarkable.

— 12. This day General election in this Colony   Governour, Deputy Governour and other officers[1] all chosen as in yᵉ year past, viz the same persons. Mʳ Colton[2] preached yᵉ Election Sermon. from Joshua 24. 20

— 13. This day in reading, conversation and impertinence

— 14. this day as yᵉ former —

— 15. Lords day Mʳ. Burr[3] preached for me in yᵉ forenoon from Joh. 17. 17. and Mʳ. Hosmore[4] in yᵉ afternoon from Sam. 4. 3. 4. a very warm day

— 18. This day took a Journey to Farmington and returned. Very warm, windy &ᶜ.

— 19. this day spent in reading, Conversation &ᶜ. No great profit. a refreshing rain in yᵉ evening.

— 20. Spent in perplexing thots. dies sine linea

— 21. a plentifull, seasonable and refreshing rain this morning and yᵉ night preceeding   this day spent in composing a sermon

— 22. Lords day I preached A. M. from 1 Sam. 2. 30 and P. M. from heb. 2. 6.

— 23. fair pleasant weather. get good habits   day spent with little reading, to little purpose

— 26. in studying, a rainy day   Mʳ Hall[5] of Sutton here.

— 27. Studying a sermon, a rainy day, perplexing thoughts.

---

[1] The officers this year were Joseph Talcott, Governor, Jonathan Law, Deputy-Governor, while the Assistants were Samuel Eells, Roger Walcott, James Wadsworth, Nathaniel Stanley, Joseph Whiting, Ozias Pitkin, Timothy Pierce, John Burr, Samuel Lynde, Edward Lewiss, William Pitkin, and Roger Newton.

[2] Rev. Benjamin Colton born in Longmeadow, Mass., probably in 1690; grad. Y. C. 1710; ordained pastor of the Fourth Church of Christ in Hartford (now West Hartford) Feb. 24, 1713-14; died March 1, 1759, aged about 69 years. His sermon on this election occasion was on "The Danger of Apostacie" and was published at New London, 1738. It would be inexcusable in the present editor of these Wadsworth memorials not to acknowledge his great indebtedness for facts concerning Mr. Wadsworth's ministrial cotemporaries to Professor F. B. Dexter's *Biographical Sketches of the Graduates of Yale College*, a book of quite indispensable importance in all similar enquiries.

[3] Rev. Isaac Burr, born in Hartford July 4, 1697, grad. Y. C. 1717, ordained at Worcester, Mass., Oct. 13, 1725; returned to Connecticut in 1745, preached at Northwest Society in Simsbury (now Granby) awhile, and died at Windsor in 1751.

[4] Rev. Stephen Hosmer, son of Dea. Stephen Hosmer of Hartford Second church; baptized Aug. 1, 1679; grad. H. C. 1699, pastor of the church in East Haddam, Conn., from 1704 till his death in 1749.

[5] Rev. David Hall, grad. H. C. 1724. Died at Sutton, Mass., May 8, 1789, aged 84, in the sixtieth year of his ministry.

— 29. Lords day in y⁶ forenoon I preached for Mʳ Whitman ¹ at y⁶ New Chh.² from rev. 3. 1. and P. M. in my own pulpit from 1 Joh. 3. 1. warm weather

— 30. This morning died John Pratt Junʳ very suddenly, being seized y⁶ morning before with an headache giddiness &ᶜ. warm day

— 31. This day y⁶ general assembly adjourned without day. John Pratt buried

June.

June 1. This day in reading &ᶜ a thunder storm in the afternoon, this day died Elijah Andrews

— 2. fair and cooler, this day Elijah Andrews was buried.

— 5. Lords day I preached A. M. from rom. 8. 28 P. M. 1 Joh. 2: 17 — under considerable difficulty and indisposition.

— 6. Warm weather, y⁶ querulous humour of some is unaccountable, O y⁶ times, y⁶ times, y⁶ badness of y⁶ times, is y⁶ burden of yʳ song, and even of such as are not very remarkable for yʳ good deeds neither

— 7. this day travelled to Kensington from thence to Farmington, Association held at Farmington this day

— 8. This day a lecture held at Farmington   Mʳ Marsh³ preached from psal. 139. 17. considerable rain this day, returned Home in safety thro' gods goodness.

— 12. Lords day. I am going to y⁶ Sacrament of y⁶ Lords supper. wᵗ are my preparations for it   am I anything grown in grace since y⁶ Last Sacrament, am I more holy, heavenly minded &ᶜ

— 15. This day in reading &ᶜ a hard thunder Storm in y⁶ afternoon, y⁶ lightning struck Thomas Burrs house.

— 17. this day in studying a Sermon, saw my uncle Thomˢ⁴

— 19. Lords day I preacht from Deut. 32. 46. 47, per totum diem.—

— 21. This day I went to Middletown to y⁶ general association.

— 20. This day died y⁶ widow (Mary if I mistake not) Sandford, in y⁶ 83 year of her age, and Nathaniel Potwin an Infant the son of Mʳ John Potwin.

---

¹ Rev. Elnathan Whitman, constantly hereafter referred to in the pages of this diary, was born at Farmington Jan. 12, 1709. He grad. Y. C. 1726, in the same class with Mr. Wadsworth, and was ordained pastor of the Second Church in Hartford, Nov. 29, 1732, two months after Mr. Wadsworth's ordination. He survived both Mr. Wadsworth, and Mr. Wadsworth's successor, Rev. Edward Dorr, and died March 4, 1777, in his 69th year.

² Although the Second Church of Hartford had now been in existence for sixty-seven years and its house of worship for about the same length of time, it seems to have been popularly known as the " New Church," the " New Meeting," as various entries in this diary will plainly indicate.

³ Rev. Jonathan Marsh of Windsor, grad. H. C. 1705, minister at Windsor from 1709 till his death Sept. 8, 1747; trustee Y. C. from 1732 to 1745. He preached the Election Sermon in 1721, and again in 1736.   ⁴ Born Jan. 6, 1679. Died 1771.

— 22. This day a lecture preacht at Middletown by ye Revd Mr Fisk¹ of Haddam

— 26. Lords day I preached per totum diem from 1 cor. 15. 34, under much indisposition

— 28. This day reading Fullers chh History, Visiting &^c this day Doct^r Morrison² set out for Boston in order to go to great Brittain

July begins.

July 3. This day I preached A. M. at ye New church from Hos. 2. 8. 9. and P. M. at my own from Heb. 12. 25. a thunder storm and great rain in ye time of ye afternoon exercise, two persons this day owned ye Covenant.

— 4. This day catechised children, went to Farmington &^c

— 10. Lords day I preached A. M. from heb. 13. 16. and P. M. from heb. 12. 25. Warm day East side people here at meeting.

— 12. . . . reading fuller &^c parish churches in England nine thousand, two hundred & eighty four, fuller. pag. 137. Lib. II. . . .

— 17. Lords day I preached p^r Totum diem from rev. 2. 21. 22. . . .

— 19. reading fuller . . . books to be purchased as soon as may be. M^r. Wadsworths³ explanation of ye assem^y. catechism, his Treatise on conscience, his guide to ye doubting

— 21. This day reading Fuller &^c. . . . a thunder storm very hard thunder I thank god y^t he saved me and my family and dwelling from harm by it.

— 23. This day in Studying &^c. warm moist weather,— at night heard y^t the Eastern Indians are come into hadley have sent to Mohegin to demand ye surrender of ye Indians that were Concerned in ye murder of two of y^r Indians in ye Last year; this a great part of it a mistake. ye story not told [*leaf torn*].

---

¹ Rev. Phineas Fiske, born at Milford, Mass., Dec. 2, 1682, grad. Y. C. 1704, ordained at Haddam Jan., 1714, died October 17, 1738.

² Dr. Norman Morrison, a native of Scotland, educated at Edinburgh, came to this country about 1733 or 34. A man of character and ability. He "owned the Covenant" at the First Church in Hartford, January 18, 1736. His house (Dr. Gurdon W. Russell says in his *Early Medicine and Early Medical Men in Connecticut*) used to stand on the site of the present Cheney Building, and now (1894) stands on Trumbull Street, and is the wooden building just north of the Charter Oak Bank. The Doctor's body was buried in his garden, and lies under a slab bearing a eulogistic inscription, surrounded by an iron fence, back of St. Paul's Church on Market Street. "He died much loved and lamented the 9th of April 1761, in the 55th year of his age."

³ Rev. Benjamin Wadsworth, b. at Milton, Mass., 1669, grad. H. C. 1690; ordained minister of the First Church in Boston, Sept. 8, 1696; elected president of Harvard College in June, 1725; died in office March 16, 1737.

— 24. Lords day I preached A.M. from Matt. 5. 25. 26. at yᵉ New church and P.M. at my own from luk. 18. 1. I am not without discouragements

— 25. This day to little profit, a poor account it seems as if I had to give of it, yet when I consider cant charge myself with criminal idleness in it

— 26. This day went to Newington to yᵉ arbitration between Wethersfield and Farmington

— 27. This day spent there upon yᵉ same business. Very uncomfortable & disagreeable to be concerned and perplext in such business

— 28. This day spent partly in yᵉ same business   came Home from thence. Mʳ. J. Ellery and Mʳˢ. Mary Austin this day married

— 30. . . . this day died yᵉ daughter of Samuel Howard.

— 31. Lords day I preached A.M. from Joh. 8. 47 and P.M. from luk. 18. 1.—forenoon more strength and easier delivery than at sometimes, afternoon faint and weak. This was yᵉ Last time I preached in yᵉ old meeting house[1]

August begins

Aug 1. This day went to Farmington. My friends well &ᶜ. returned from thence. this day was Interred yᵉ daughter of Samuel Howard.

— 2. This day partly in Study &ᶜ. rainy weather This day yᵉ people began to pull down yᵉ old meeting house, took down yʳ pulpit, seats and bell, and carried yᵉ pulpit into the State house

— 3. . . our people proceeded in taking down yᵉ old meeting house.

— 4. . . . yᵉ people made further progress in pulling down yᵉ old meeting house.

— 5. . . . this day our old meeting house was pulled down and Laied level with yᵉ ground

— 7. Lords day. I preached from Joh. 4. 23: this was yᵉ first day of our meeting in yᵉ State House for publick worship

— 8. This day yᵉ foundation of our new=meeting House was Laied at yᵉ Lower Corner of yᵉ burying yard[2]

---

[1] The old meeting house stood somewhere near the southeasterly side of Meeting-house Yard, or what is now called State House Square.

[2] The question of the location and building of a new meeting house had been now for several years the topic of active and sometimes acrimonious controversy in Mr. Wadsworth's Society. Mrs. Abigail Woodbridge, widow of the deceased pastor Timothy Woodbridge, had tendered successively two lots of ground for the purpose, on the east side of what is now Main Street, not far apart and not far from where St. John's Church now stands. Both these lots were successively accepted by the Society and successively declined; the latter under such circumstances of apparent

— 9. The workmen proceeded in ye foundation work of ye meeting house.

— 10. much disordered in body this day, little done, studying something — the workmen proceeded in ye foundation work of the meeting House

— 11. This day went to Farmington, my friends well. finished ye bargain with Samuel Peck.

— 12. . . . Very much indisposed, under bodily pain &^e ye mason goes on in Laying ye foundation of ye Meeting house

— 14. Lords day I preached from 1 Cor. 9. 24. per totum diem.

— 19. This day in Studying, took a resolution to read daily a chapter at least in my study, as well as in my family, not that I have neglected it till now, but not bin so constant in it as I design to be for time to come. . . .

— 21. Lords day I preached per Totum from 1 pet. 4. 7. . . . in the evening of this day about midnight died Goody Wicar a crazed woman in the work house

— 22. This day I went to Farmington, Saw my friends well, this day Goody Wicar was buried, and at evening about nine of ye clock died [blank] Adams a Lame man in ye work house.

— 23. This day was buried [blank] Adams who died yesterday

— 28. Lords day I preached A.M. from thes. 2. 12 and P.M. from Exod. 23. 2. This day John Pratt was taken into y^e church and Abigail y^e daughter of Thomas Hopkins Baptized

— 29. N. B. my Sermons from my first preaching in y^e State House are numbered beginning then. This day y^e mason finished the foundation of our New=Meeting house

— 30. upon y^e weather Cock that was taken off of our old meeting House was this Date. 1638. Whence I suppose our old meeting House stood ninety nine years, it being pulled down in y^e year 1737 as I have before entered.[1] . . .

— 31. This day my daughter Eunice is one year old. This day spent partly in reading, partly in visiting, but too much in idleness.

---

discourtesy to the generous donor that she withdrew some time from worship with the First Church and went to the Second. The unpleasantness was, however, smoothed over by an apologetic vote by the Society, and Mrs. Woodbridge returned. The lot finally fixed upon was a compromise between those who desired to accept Mrs. Woodbridge's offer, and those who did not want to go much further south than what is now the corner of Central Row and Main Street. It is substantially the ground now occupied by the First Church.

[1] Probably the date 1638 indicates the date of the reaching of that stage on the "old meeting house" implied in the setting up of this vane, for there are indications that it was not finished before 1640; the congregation meantime occupying, as they had for sometime before, a designedly temporary structure, which was afterward given to Pastor Hooker for a barn.

September

Sept. 1. . . . in y⁰ afternoon I went to Mʳ. Coltons Lecture
Mʳ. Colton preached from 2. Chron. 34. 3 his doct. yᵗ early piety
is a great and desirable Excellency

— 3. . . . not a little perplexed with one supposing himself
wronged by yᵉ testimony of another & seeking satisfaction.

— 4. Lords day I preached A.M. from psal. 104. 34 and P.M. at yʳ
New church from 1. Joh. 3. 8. . . .

— 6. . . . went to Weathersfield. bought 6000 2ᵈ nails for Mʳ.
Whitman. Supʳ. Court began

— 7. . . . The Superior court sat this day. Mʳ. White¹ Here.

— 8. under reflections and reproaches of enemies I would think
upon and be quieted by those words, 1. pet. 2. 15. for so is
yᵉ will of god, yᵗ with well doing yʳ may put to silence yᵉ
ignorance of foolish men.

— 11. Lords day Mʳ. Bostwick² preached for me in yᵉ forenoon
from luk. 16. 31. and P.M. I preached from gen. 39. 9. very
warm weather.

— 13. This day our people began to raise our new-meeting House.
Something rainy in the afternoon. a good beginning makes a
good end

— 14. This day yᵉ people proceeded in raising yᵉ meeting house.
cloudy weather

— 15. This day rainy in yᵉ forenoon, in the afternoon yᵉ people
proceeded in raising yᵉ meeting House. . . .

— 16. [Similar entry]

— 17. [Similar entry]

— 18. Lords day Mʳ Rockwell³ preached for me A.M. from 1
King. 12. 26. 27. 28. in the afternoon I preached from heb. 4.
11. warm day. yᵉ Gov. not well.

— 19. [Like the 16ᵗʰ]

— 20. [Ibid.]

— 21. This day I received a present of 20ˢ· from Mʳ Palmer,⁴ may
he and every other of my benefactors be bountifully rewarded
in spiritual gifts. This day our people proceeded in raising yᵉ
meeting House.

---

¹ Rev. Thomas White of Bolton, born at Hatfield, Mass., July 10, 1701 ; Y. C. 1720 ; ordained
at Bolton, Oct. 26, 1725 ; died in his pastorate there Feb. 22, 1763.

² Rev. Ephraim Bostwick, Y. C. 1729, ordained at Greenwich Oct. 8, 1735 ; dismissed 1745 ;
removed to Stamford where he died in February or March, 1755.

³ Matthew Rockwell, b. at East Windsor Jan. 30, 1707-8 ; Y. C. 1728 ; studied theology and
medicine ; employed by churches as an occasional preacher, but gave himself principally to medical practice. He died in East Windsor March 28, 1782.

⁴ Mr. Cotton Palmer of Warwick, R. I., the builder of the new meeting house.

— 22. This day cool weather. This day our people finished y[e] raising our New meeting House, without harm to any one. Thanks be to god that hath preserved them.

— 25. Lords day I preached per totum diem from 2 Cor. 6. 2. Sick persons prayed for   y[e] Govern[r]., Jerush. Talcot. Hannah y[e] daughter of Henry Nicholson baptized.

— 27. This day went to Farmington   Saw my friends well. Doct[r]. McLean[1] a son born this night

— 28. . . . the Gov. & his daughter sick   hopefully something better. this day five year since my ordination.

— 29. M[r]. Bolton (as quoted by M[r]. Baxter Vol. 1. pag. 194) was wont to say y[t] innocency and independency do steel y[e] face and help a minister to be bold and faithfull.

— 30. This day in Study. nothing remarkable.
         October.

Oct. 1. This day in Study &[c]. nothing remarkable.

— 2. Lords day I preached from Joh. 3. 3. per totum diem. this day Allan the Son of M[r]. Niel M[c].Lean was baptized

— 3. This day pleasant weather, visited y[e] Lame and wounded man

— 4. This day y[e] Association met at M[r]. Woodbridges[2] East Side, nothing very remarkable happened.

— 5. This day a lecture   M[r]. Whitman[3] of Farmington preached from prov. 19. 8 — he y[t] getteth wisdom Loveth his own soul. associations appointed. y[e] first Tuesday in June next at M[r]. Whites at Bolton, M[r]. Steel[4] to preach   the next the Second Tuesday of october at M[r]. Edwardss[5] at Windsor, M[r]. Colton to preach

---

[1] Doctor Niel McLean was born in Scotland. He came first to Wethersfield and then removed to Hartford where he was awhile associated in practice with Dr. Morrison. His wife (Hannah Caldwell) was received to full communion in the First Church Jan. 26, 1735, and died April 22, 1755.

[2] Rev. Samuel Woodbridge of East Hartford; grad. H. C. 1701; ordained in East Hartford March 30, 1705; Fellow of Y. C. from 1732 to 1743; died June 9, 1746. Mr. Woodbridge was now in ill health and Mr. Wadsworth's frequently recorded visits to him, made at a time when the crossing of the Great River was a more serious business than we now regard it, are interestingly indicative of his kindness of heart.

[3] Rev. Samuel Whitman of Farmington (father of Rev. Elnathan Whitman of Hartford) born at Hull, Mass., grad. H. C. 1696; ordained at Farmington, Dec. 10, 1706; a Fellow of Y. C. from 1724 to 1746; died in August, 1751. An "Old Light" in his views.

[4] Rev. Stephen Steel of Tolland, born in Hartford 1696 or 7; grad. Y. C. 1718; began to preach in Tolland early in 1719, but the church was not then organized, and his ordination did not take place till the latter part of 1723. He resigned his pastorate Dec. 21, 1758, and died Dec. 4, 1759. He preached the Election Sermon May 12, 1743, and the usual official request was made for its publication, but there is no evidence that it was ever printed. Inclined to the "New Light" side in the current controversies.

[5] Rev. Timothy Edwards of East Windsor, son of Richard Edwards of Hartford and father of Rev. Jonathan Edwards of Northampton. Mr. Edwards was born in Hartford, May 14, 1669; grad. H. C. 1691, receiving his degrees of A.B. and A.M. the same day on account of his eminent

— 9.   Lords day I preached A.M. at y⁰ new church from Exod. 23.
2. & P.M. at my own meeting from rev. 3. 16. pleasant weather

— 10.   This day in secular business, providing for my family &ᶜ.

— 11.   This day partly in visiting partly in assisting yᵉ Govern'. in some particular business

— 12.   . . . this day Ann Bunce yᵉ daughter of John Bunce was drowned in yᵉ great River. Coming up from Weathersfield in a boat yᵉ boat sunk ag' the South meadow. a barn burnt down with yᵉ Lightening this night at Windsor.

— 15.   . . . this day was found and Interred yᵉ body of Ann Bunce y' was drowned yᵉ 12. Instant

— 16.   Lords day I preached A.M. from Job 31. 14. & P.m. from rev. 3. 16. comfortable weather.

— 17.   . . . find in yᵉ Magazine¹ for June last y' Sir William Lee is appointed chief Justice of yᵉ Kings Bench.

— 18.   . . . necessary that a preacher have some constant design and y' his sermons be calculated all to promote y', and y' his preaching be not calculated merely for his ease or to avoid offence

— 21.   . . . yesterday I recᵈ a letter from yᵉ chh in Stafford desiring yᵉ pastor and a messenger from this chh. to sit in Councel upon the 4ᵗʰ Tuesday of Instant October at Stafford.²

— 23.   Lords day I preached p'. totum diem from psal. 73. 26. the Govern'. so far recovered of his illness y' he was this day at meeting.

— 24.   This day Training Daniel Goodwin chosen Ensign of yᵉ first Company, a day not very profitably spent by me

— 25.   This day Training in this Town . . . publick diversions often occasion much sin, I wish it may not be yᵉ case with this.

— 27.   . . . Sent a letter p'. James Bunce to my uncle James³ at New Haven.

proficiency; married Esther, daughter of Rev. Solomon Stoddard of Northampton, Nov. 6, 1694; began almost at once to preach to the new Society set off at East Windsor, but apparently not ordained as pastor till 1698 ; an eminently influential man, but a good deal involved in Church difficulties in his own parish ; preacher of the Election Sermon in 1732, in which he paid an extended tribute to his long time friend Rev. Timothy Woodbridge of the First Church of Hartford, who had died eleven days before. Mr. Edwards died Jan. 27, 1758, at eighty-nine years of age.

¹ "The Gentleman's Magazine," the publication of which began in 1731; the reference of Mr. Wadsworth is to be found in Vol. vii, p. 371. Johnson and other eminent writers of the eighteenth century contributed to the Gentleman's Magazine, the publication of which still continues, though now mainly as the vehicle of historical and antiquarian information.

² Stafford's difficulties will be noticed further on.

³ James Wadsworth, born at Farmington, July 6, 1677, Deputy, Assistant, Commissioner on Rhode Island boundary, etc., died 1756.

November begins

November 1.   This day came from Farmington, the County Court sat here.

— 2.   The news letter[1] from 20 to 27 of October Informs that Edmund Quincy Esq. is appointed agent for yᵉ Massachusetts province at yᵉ Court of Great Britain.

— 3.   . . .   Doctʳ. Morison returned from England.

— 4.   this day saw yᵉ commission to yᵉ Governoʳ of New York and his Counsel, Governʳ. of Rhoad Island and his assistants to Inquire into yᵉ Mohegin affair[2] &ᶜ.   it came last night by Doctʳ. Morison, who arrived last friday in Capt. Casy from Londⁿ

— 6.   Lords day I preached A.M. from Matt. 5. 12. & P.M. from Act. 2. 37. . . .

— 10.   This day a publick thanksgiving throughout Connecticut Colony   I preached from Deut 8. 10

— 13.   Lords day I preached A.M. from psal. 112. 7.   P.M. from prov. 1. 10. baptized Joseph yᵉ son of Mʳ. Joseph Talcot Jr. and Sarah yᵉ daughter of Samuel Marshall

— 15.   This day went to Windsor 3ᵈ Society to a Councel. Yᵉ Council convened and chose Mʳ. Timᵒ. Edwards Moderator Mʳ. Ben. Colton Scribe.   heard much talk but to little purpose

— 16.   This day yᵉ Councel at Windsor after much pains with people and M. Woodbridge to bring yᵐ to an accomodation, voted to dismiss Mʳ. Woodbridge.[3] . . .

— 20.   Lords day preached A.M. from Joh. 8. 28. P.M. from rom. 3. 17. · this day administred yᵉ Sacrament

— 21.   This day about nine of yᵉ clock at night died John Dod of yᵉ Cholick.

— 22.   This day was buried John Dod

---

[1] "The Boston News Letter;" the publication of which weekly journal began in 1704; its first number being "From Monday April 17, to Monday April 24, 1704."

[2] This was part of a long and involved controversy, reaching over seventy years, in which the claim of the Mohegan Indians to an extensive tract of territory comprising the larger portions of the townships of Colchester, Windham, Mansfield, Hebron and some other towns, were urged by themselves and by the descendants of John Mason, to whose ancestor it was alleged by the Masons that the lands had been conveyed in trusteeship in the Indians' behalf. The suit was prosecuted in successive trials here and in England but was ultimately determined (as Indian claims generally are) adversely to the Indians and in behalf of the Colony. In the process of the struggle, however, there was set out a tract of between four and five thousand acres which was to be secured in perpetuity to the Mohegans.

[3] Rev. John Woodbridge of "Windsor of 3d Society" (now Poquonock) was born in West Springfield, Mass., December 25, 1702; he grad. Y. C. 1726 in the same class with Mr. Wadsworth; was ordained at Poquonock probably in 1728; dismissed as above; removed to Suffield; installed at South Hadley, Mass., April 21, 1742; continued there till his death Sept. 10, 1783.

— 23. This day M'. Gorton[1] y' Baptist minister was at my house. Wee had a debate upon y' Controversy about baptism, many people were present; w' Influence and effect it may have I know not. I hope and trust in god y' my people will be preserved from the Infection of error.

— 27. Lords day I preached per totum from Matt. 28. 19. four children baptized this day

— 29. This day y' Councel met about the Mohegin affairs December.

December 4. Lords day I preached per totum from Matt. 28. 19. moderate weather.

— 7. . . . about three quarters of an hour after eleven at night was (as I'm told) a Considerable earthquake, but being in bed and asleep I heard it not.

— 11. Lords day M'. Woodbridge[2] of Suffield preached for me A.M. from Jer. 17. 17. and P.M. from gal. 6. 4.

— 14 This day . . a Journey to Weathersfield to view a negro boy[3]

— 15. . . . this night about twelve oclock Nathaniel y' Son of Capt. Nathaniel Hooker[4] was born and y' wife of Capt. Caleb Williamson died this night

— 17. This day was Interred [blank] y' wife of Capt. Caleb Williamson. . . .

— 18. Lords day I preached pr. totum diem from 2 cor. 5. 11.— this day M'. Jerusha Talcot was admitted to Communion with y' Church.

— 19. . . . delivered y' Contribution money for Elias Easton to John Easton his brother

— 20. . . . rec'd. 5 bushel Indian Corn & 2 bushel of wheat from Uncle Thomas by Josiah North. Sister Ruth here

— 25. Lords day I preached from Jer: 6. 8. per totum diem. Dorcas Dod and Hannah Catlin propounded to be admitted

---

[1] Elder Stephen Gorton, b. in Rhode Island March 21, 1703-4; ordained in New London March 28, 1726 ; an illiterate and unscrupulous man ; fell into disrepute ; turmoiled and broke up his church in New London about 1774 ; preached awhile afterwards in Southington, but died there in disesteem and obscurity.

[2] See note to Nov. 16.

[3] Apparently Mr. Wadsworth did not buy the lad. The inventory of his estate mentions only one piece of this kind of *personal* property, "an old Negro woman nam'd. Rose," valued at 40 pounds.

[4] Capt. Nathaniel Hooker, grandson of Rev. Samuel Hooker of Farmington, and great grandson of Rev. Thomas Hooker, was born Oct. 5, 1710; grad. Y. C. 1729. He married Eunice, daughter of Governor Talcott, and was consequently Mr. Wadsworth's brother-in-law. He lived almost directly opposite from Mr. Wadsworth, on land his mother, Mary, had inherited from her father, Nathaniel Stanley. Capt. Hooker died in Hartford Jan. 24, 1763, in his 53d year.

into y⁰ chh. and Rachel Goodwin, Sarah Spencer & Mary Farnsworth to own y⁰ Covenant

— 27. This night Eben'. Welles was found dead between Town · and y⁰ west division. died of an appo. fit.

January A. D. 1737/8.

Jany. 1. Lords day I preached pr totum diem from psal. 90. 12. . . . this day baptized Elizabeth y⁰ daughter of M'. Ben. Swett and Margaret y⁰ daughter of Ind. Wobbin¹

— 5. This day partly in study, partly in conversing with persons desiring spiritual direction and advice

— 8. Lords day I preached A.M. at y⁰ N chh. from Acts 2. 37 and p.m. at my own from heb. 13. 9. Laboured under great indisposition and difficulty in Speaking, very much overcome with a bashfull fear. O y' god would strengthen me ag' it, and help me in a better manner to discharge my duty.

— 12. . . . at night James Nichols and Mary Wadsworth were married

— 13. . . . This day died Thomas Ensign Sen' in y⁰ 70ᵗʰ year of his age

— 14. . . . Thomas Ensign Interred.

— 15. Lords day I preached A.M. from heb. 13. 9. and P.m. from psal. 16. 8.

— 16. What shall I do to encite my flock to a more serious and hearty concern for y⁰ wellfare of y' Souls

— 17. This day in study. M' Wards² advice concerning young people (Ward of Haverill) was, w'ever you do be sure to maintain shame in y'; for if y' become gone there is no hope y' they'll ever come to good.— Doct'. Preston³ was wont to say, y' w" wee wo'ld have any great thing to be accomplished, y⁰

¹ Apparently the engagement had been fulfilled made by Rev. Timothy Woodbridge (Mr. Wadsworth's predecessor in the pastorate) entered on the Church record Aug. 10, 1711, when he baptized "John Waubin my Indian servant. I publickly engaged that I would take care that he should be brought up in the Christian Religion." As nearly twenty-one years later Mr. Woodbridge, in his will dated April 1, 1732, bequeathed "the Improvement of John Waubin during the Time he is bound to serve me," Waubin must have been a very small Indian at his baptism, or the indentures must have been in some way renewed. Anyway it is satisfactory to know that service had not prevented the fulfilling of Mr. Woodbridge's promise, and that Waubin wanted his child baptized into the church of which his master had been the minister.

² Rev. Nathaniel Ward born at Haverhill in England between 1578 and 1580; educated at Emmanuel College, Cambridge, where he took his degree A.M. in 1603; rector of Standon Massey in Essex; came to New England in 1634; pastor some years at Ipswich, Mass.; returned to England late in 1646; became minister at Shenfield near his first charge, where he died, probably about 1653. He wrote several books, the most famous of which — "The Simple Cobler of Aggawam" — was published in 1647.

³ Rev. John Preston, 1587-1628, a celebrated Puritan divine. Master of Emmanuel College, Cambridge. The quotation is from Mather in his account of Rev. John Eliot, *Magnalia*, Book III.

best policy is to work by an engine which ye world sees nothing of. Mag^n.pag. 175. nil remarkable

— 18. Went to ye west division to examine Mr Coltons Son[1] in
order to preached [*Sic*] he was licensed to preach occasionally
as a candidate for ye ministry. . . . Difficult to please men.

— 22. Lords day administred ye Sacrament and preached p^r. totum
diem from John 17. 5. cloud cool rained at night

— 23. This day . . . spent partly in study and partly in
visiting. twas said of ye Fam's T: Hooker, that w^o doing his
Masters work he could put a King in his pocket, and by him
y^t ye Elders must have a church in a church if y^y would preserve ye peace of ye church. and y^t ye debating matters of
difference first before ye whole body of ye church will doubtless
break any chh in pieces, and deliver it up unto Loathsome
Contempt[2]

— 24. Spirit, Soul and body. 1 thes. 5. 23. when by spirit Some
understand ye natural temper or Humour. Magn^{lia} Am: Lib. 3
pag. 33. col. 1. . . . under considerable dejection and discouragement, in god is my help

— 26. This day . . . how indisposed and Confused. this
day heard y^t ye Rev^d. M^r. Andrews[3] of Milford died on Thursday Last.

— 29. Lords day . . . John ye son of John Shepherd baptized
I find great trouble and difficulty in my work from an intense
bashfullness and overaweing fear. I pray god to help me to
conq^r. it.

— 31. . . . a very cold day concludes ye month. This day
ye adj^d. County court sat here.

  February begins

Feby. 4. This day rec^d. a present from Doct^r. Colman[4] of some

---

[1] Eli, son of Rev. Benjamin Colton of West Hartford, hereafter to be noticed.

[2] These alleged sayings of and by Mr. Hooker are from Mather's *Magnalia*, Book III.

[3] Rev. Samuel Andrews, born at Cambridge, Mass., Jan. 29, 1656; grad. H. C. 1675; ordained
at Milford Nov. 18, 1685. Mr. Andrews was one of the original trustees of Yale College; rector
pro tempore awhile after the death of Rector Pierson, and died January 24, 1738, age 82.

[4] Rev. Benjamin Colman of Boston, b. in Boston Oct. 19, 1673; grad. H. C. 1692; ordained
in London, by Presbytery, Aug. 4, 1699; returned to Boston and assumed the care of the new Brattle
Street Church in November following. One of the leading New England ministers of his generation. He died Aug. 29, 1747. He is referred to several times in Mr. Wadsworth diary.

The reference to "proposals for subscriptions" for Dr. Guyse's and Dr. Doddridge's books
would seem to indicate that they were intended to be published if not jointly at least near together.
In point of fact the work of Dr. John Guyse (b. at Hertford, England, 1680, died 1761) entitled
Paraphrase on the New Testament, was published in three quarto volumes in 1739-42; while the
far more popular and useful work of Philip Doddridge (b. 1702; minister successively at Kibworth,
Market Harborough, and Northampton; died Oct., 1751) entitled, *The Family Expositor*, etc.,
six volumes quarto, was not published till 1760-62, after the author's death.

pamphlets, & printed proposals for subscriptions for printing Doct'. Guyse's and Doct' Doddridges paraphrases upon ye Evang.

— 5. Lords day I preached . . . My work difficult, speaking hard. I am much Concerned w^t. to do to revive a Concern about religion among my people. . . .

— 7. This day snow. This day I paied to Doct'. Morison 8 pound in money. £7. 17s. 6^d was for ye 10½ yards of black drugget I had of him.

— 8. This day . . . spent considerable time in searching records for Farmington affairs.

— 9. Books needed and to be bought as soon as conveniently I can are M^r. Boltons Instruction for ye right comforting afflicted Consciences, Dicksons Therapeutica Sacra, or method of healing ye diseases of ye Conscience, Dr Goodwins Child of Light walking in darkness, Mr Bridges Sermon on psa. 142. 11. M^r. Obad. Sedgwicks Doubting believer, M^r. Symonds Care & Cure of ye doubting soul. Doct'. Owen on ye 130 psalm. pleasant weather

— 10. This day understood p^r Uncle Willm y^t a book of chh records &^c. kept by Mr Hooker formerly minist^r. of Hartford is now in ye Hands of ye Rev^d. M^r. Whitman of Farmington.[1] a snowy day . . .

— 12. Lords day I preached per totum from psal. 73. 25. Benjamin Dod owned the Covenant. Deac^n. Thomas Richards and Deac^n. Nath^ll. Goodwin were chosen messengers by ye church to attend ye ordination at Wintonbury. M^r. Isaac Butler and Sarah his wife, Moses Cadwell and Penelope his wife and Agnes ye wife of Jn . Hubbard had a dismission from ye church

— 14. This day warm weather My people sledded wood for me, bro't about 43 Loads.

— 15. This day M^r. Hez. Bissel[2] was ordained at Wintonbury.

---

[1] It is tantalizing to think that the missing records of the First Church in Hartford, which in all probability contained its Covenant and its Newtown experiences, was still in existence in 1738, and its whereabouts known to Mr. Wadsworth. The story is not an improbable one. Pastoral records were formerly, much more than now, regarded as private memoranda of the pastor. Mr. Hooker's now invaluable notes of early events in the church's history naturally passed with his other papers into the hands of his son, Rev. Samuel Hooker, pastor at Farmington ; from him the transition was easy if not so natural to the hands of his successor, Rev. Samuel Whitman, in whose possession it appears they were in 1738. It has been conjectured that in default of any special concern about them on the part of the First Church pastor, they may have gone from Rev. Samuel Whitman of Farmington, to his son Elnathan of Hartford, and been burned in the fire which destroyed his house. But this is much of it conjecture, and the precious volume *may be* still in existence somewhere.

[2] Rev. Hezekiah Bissell, born at East Windsor Jan. 30, 1710-11 ; grad. Y. C. 1733 ; studied theology with his pastor, Rev. Timothy Edwards, ordained in a new parish called Wintonbury, (now Bloomfield), set off in southwestern part of Windsor, Feb. 15, 1738 ; continued pastor, though for the later years in a paralytic state, till his death Jan. 28, 1783.

M^r. Marsh preached from 2 cor. 3. 6.   Mr. S. Whitman gave
ye charge and M^r. Colton ye right hand of fellowship.

— 17.   . . .   observable y^t almost every newspaper of late gives
an ac^{ct}. of damage done by fires   houses burnt or in great danger of it, with difficulty prevented

— 19.   Lords day I preached   . . .   Mary Butler, Sarah Butler
and Sarah Hopkins owned ye Covenant

— 22.   .   M^r. Barber [1] of Mohegin came to my house at night

— 23.   . . .   now paied Capt. Hooker bushel & half wheat y^t I
had borrowed

— 26.   Lords day M^r. Cleveland [2] of Charlestown preached for me
A.M. from psal 23. 1. and P.M. from Haggai 1. 5.

— 28.   Came from Farmington in safety.   Laus Deo.   This day
four years since my Marriage, thanks be to him y^t has preserved me and those that he has graciously given me.

March begins 1737/8

March 1.   This day heard that Queen Caroline was dead, and y^t y^e
Spaniards have taken three East India ships.

— 2.   This day spent to little advantage, save some entertaining
conversation.   M^r. Hunn [3] here this day.

— 3.   This day rec^d. a letter from M Bull [4] of Westfield with a copy
of ye letter that ye K. sent to ye Prince of Wales forbidding
him ye palace.

— 11.   Last night it began to snow and continued snowing y^e
greater part of this day, a deeper snow than any wee have had
in ye winter past.

---

[1] Rev. Jonathan Barber, born at West Springfield, Jan. 31, 1712-13; grad. Y. C. 1730;
licensed to preach by Hampshire Co. Association in 1732; preached to the Indians in the Mohegan
country north of New London awhile; then gathered a congregation in a part of Southold, L. I.,
called Oyster Ponds. About 1740, inflamed with the reports of Whitefield's evangelistic labors,
and kindled by contact with Rev. James Davenport, he set out on a revivalistic tour of Long Island.
Meeting Whitefield on his first arrival in New England Mr. Whitefield was so much pleased with
him that he offered him the superintendency of his Orphan House in Georgia.   Mr. Barber
remained in Georgia about seven years, but returning to Oyster Ponds he was ordained Nov. 9,
1757.   His work there was short, however, for on Nov. 3, 1758, he was installed pastor of the church
in Groton, where he died October 8, 1783.

[2] Rev. Aaron Cleveland, b. at Cambridge, Mass., Oct. 29, 1715; grad. H. C. 1735; settled at
Haddam, Conn., July, 1739; dismissed 1746; took Orders in the Church of England at London in
1755; commissioned by the Society for Propagating the Gospel in Foreign Parts; died at the house
of Dr. Franklin in Philadelphia Aug. 11, 1757.

[3] Rev. Nathaniel Hunn, born at Wethersfield Sept. 10, 1708; grad. Y. C. 1731; ordained at
Reading, March 21, 1733; died on a visit to Boston in August or September, 1749.   He preached
the Election Sermon May 14, 1747.   His sermon referred to the success at Cape Breton and to the
disastrous effects of a paper currency.

[4] Rev. Nehemiah Bull, born in Farmington or Hartford in 1701; grad. Y. C. 1723; ordained
at Westfield, Oct. 26, 1726; died in his pastorate April 12, 1740.

— 12. Lords day I preached A.M. from 1 Joh. 3. 14. & P.M. from
luk 9. 59. Cool weather

— 15. Moist weather; Sundry Houses lately burnt as yᵉ News
letters tell us, a year very remarkable on y' accᵗ   this day yᵉ
Superʳ. Court adjourned

19. Lords day I preached . . . this night recᵈ. some further
confirmation of yᵉ Queens death. Said to be on yᵉ 20ᵗʰ of November Last. this night met with a news letter y' gives an accᵗ.
of several Houses burnt. in one of yᵐ yᵉ owner and four of
his children were consumed by yᵉ flames. Save me O Lord and
mine from such dessolation, I beseech thee for thy mercies sake.

— 20. This day recᵈ another news letter giving an accᵗ. of
houses burnt by fire. . . . in yᵉ afternoon I heard a noise
in yᵉ southeast, like the report of great Gunns, often repeated.
and continued till sometime in yᵉ night

— 23. This day finished reading Doctʳ. Hows lect. upon Consid-
eration, and his 2 vol. on Matt. 5. an excellent writer.[1] Inflamed with piety and devotion. At night I married Nathˡˡ.
Egglestone to Abigail Goodwin

26. Lords day I preached pr. totum . . . & baptized 2
children viz. Marion daughter to Mʳ. Normand Morison &
Abigail daughter to Mʳ. Samˡˡ. Flagg.

— 28. This day pleasant, business now done   uneasy tempers
difficultly Quelled or Satisfied.

— 30. This day Cosen James Wadsworth of Durham here. Joseph
Skinner Junʳ. married at night

— 31. This day . . . my Sister Betty rode from Farmington
hither, she has not bin able to ride so far for some years before
April begins

April 2. Lords day I preached . . . and administred yᵉ Sacramᵗ. and Mʳˢ. Helena Talcott was taken into the church.

— 5. Governʳ Clarks[2] letter this day came to yᵉ Governʳ.

— 6. Mʳ. Bull of Westfield at my house

— 7. Visited Jno. Bunce, very sick

— 9. Lords day I preached . . . how difficult my work, but
how good yᵉ Master I serve, yᵉ blessed Jesus.

— 10. Laboured under bodily indisposition. This day died John
Bunce.

— 11. Yᵉ County Court sits here to-day. a Vendue of one of yᵉ
western Townships. . . .

---

[1] Rev. John Howe, the celebrated Non-Conformist divine (1630-1705), minister in Great Tor-
rington and London, and some time domestic chaplain to Oliver Cromwell.

[2] Lt.-Governor George Clarke of New York.

— 15 This day heard y' Coln'. Edmund Quincy ag' for y' Province of the Mass: at y' Court of Great Britt: died in London, 3ᵈ day of March Last, and the news of the Queens death is now fully confirmed

— 16. Lords day I preached from Isai. 9. 6. p'. totum diem. Cool weath'.

— 18. This day heard y' on y' 18ᵗʰ Instant the house of John Barnett of Wintonbury and all his household goods, was burnt.

— 19. This day a day of publick fasting and prayer throughout Connecticutt: I preached A.M. from Isai. 58. 6. both congregations met in y' South meeting house P.M. M'. Whitman preached from Dan: 4. 27. . . .

— 21. . . . this day Tracy and Mason were in Town. left a Copy of y' Commission of Inquiry &c. with y' Govern'.

— 23. Lords day I preached pr totum from Isai. 9. 6. Ashbel y' son of Michael Burnham was baptized

— 25. This day M'. Hunn came hither and wee set out for boston and went as far as Lads.

— 26. this day in travelling, went as far as Worcester. thro' the good hand of god upon us no evil happened to us

— 27. this day wee arrived at boston safe, our friends well

— 28. This day spent in boston, little business

— 30. Lords day. A.M. I went to M'. Foxcrofts meeting.[1] M'. Foxcroft preached from 1 thes. 4. 14. & P.M. to M'. Hoopers meeting.[2] M'. Hooper preached from Act. 26. 9
         May begins

May 3. This day set out from boston home   came to Worcester

— 4. This day came to Springfield

— 5. This day came Home. and I thank god for his kind providence in preserving me, and returning me in safety and y' thro' his goodness 1 find so much health in my family

— 7. Lords day I preached A.M. at the new chh from luk 12. 15 and P.M. at my own from Isai. 9. 6. baptized Catherine y' daughter of Aaron Cadwell. at noon heard y' my uncle James was very sick

1 Rev. Thomas Foxcroft, b. 1696; grad. H. C. 1714; ordained pastor First Church, Boston, Nov. 20, 1717; a zealous promoter of the Great Awakening; author of many published pamphlets and discourses; died June 18, 1760.

2 Rev. William Hooper, pastor (from May 18, 1737) of the West Church in Boston, a new organization formed the year previous to Mr. Wadsworth's visit. After nine years' service Mr. Hooper went to England and was ordained an Episcopal minister and returning to Boston became (Aug. 28, 1747) rector of Trinity Church.

— 8. This day went to Durham to see my good uncle, found him sick. but not so bad as my fears.

— 10. This day (as I hear) ye Commission". Court is to be opened at Horse Neck

— 11. This day Election   Govern^r. & Dep. Govern^r. as in ye year past.

— 14. Lords day M^r. Burr preached for me   . . .

— 15 This day ye Govern^r. and Company cited to appear before ye Commissioners Court[1] on ye 24 Instant, at Norwich p^r. Jos: Tracy, ye citation read only in ye upper house

— 16. Capt. Bulkley & M^r. Raymond cited to ye Commissioners Court this day by Joseph Tracy Junr. . . . the Gen^{ll} assembly appointed Gentlemen to meet & wait upon ye Commissioners from N: York and Rhoad Island.— a post this day sent to Boston & another to Rhoad Island

— 18. Agents this day appointed by ye Gen. ass. for the Governm^t. Dep: Gov. Maj^r. Wolcot, Capt. Bulkley.

— 19. M^r. White of East Hampton here. Dan^{ll}. Goodwin ye post to Rhoad Island returned   agents added Fitch & Fowler.

— 20. This day credibly Informed concerning an extraordinary child (I had sometime before heard off) one Turner at New Haven, that at 18 months old w^c. was on ye 2^d day of Instant May, weighed 46½ pounds and as to bigness, speech, strength and behaviour equals a child of five or six years old.

— 21. Lords day I preached from prov. 11. 11. per totum, pleasant weather

— 22. M^r. Nott[2] of Saybrook here

— 24. This day ye Commissioners Court was to sit at Norwich, may Connecticutt be saved from destroyers

— 25. This day died my dear Mother Madam Eunice Talcot[3]

[1] This was a hearing in the long-drawn-out Mohegan case. See *ante*, p. 16 note. The Commissioners were the Lieut.-Governor and Council of New York, and the Governor and Assistants of Rhode Island. The Commissioners disagreed as to mode of procedure, and those of New York entered a protest and withdrew; those of Rhode Island, left alone, reversed a decision which had been made in the Mason's and the Indians' favor in 1705, and gave judgment in favor of the Connecticut Colony; a conclusion which, it will be observed, a few entries later in the diary, Mr. Wadsworth thought a salvation from " men of violence " ; an opinion the correctness of which it is quite possible to differ about.

[2] Rev. Abraham Nott, born at Wethersfield, Jan. 29, 1696-97; grad. Y. C. 1720; ordained pastor of the church in connection with the Second Ecclesiastical Society in Saybrook Nov. 16, 1725; continued in that relation till his death January 24, 1756.

[3] Mrs. Eunice Talcott was Governor Talcott's second wife, the daughter of Matthew Howell of Southampton, L. I., and the widow of Rev. Jabez Wakeman of Newark, New Jersey. Her death occurred while the General Assembly was in session and public business was pressing. The Lieutenant-Governor was absent at the Commissioners' Court in Norwich; so not to delay concerns of wider interest the Governor returned to the State House and presided in the session of the Upper

Consort to yᵉ Honbˡᵉ Joseph Talcot Esqʳ. about 12 o'clock in yᵉ forenoon.   She was seized about 11 o'clock with (as supposed an Epileptick) fit, sitting in her chair in usual health: Teach me O God to number my days aright

— 27.   This day in yᵉ afternoon Madᵐ Eunice Talcot was Interred. Bearers were Majʳ. Elles, Capt. Standly, Capt. Whiting, Capt. Oz. Pitkin, Majʳ. Pierce & Majʳ. Burr, the coffin covered with black cloath, and four escutcheons fixed upon it ; there was a vast Concourse of people, it was yᵉ Largest funeral that ever I saw in Connecticut.

— 28.   Lords day Mʳ. Whitman preached for me pʳ. totum.   Mʳ. Hunn preached for Mʳ. Whitman

— 29.   This day I went to Farmington.   my friends well, returned safe thro' yᵉ good hand of my god upon me.—this day Mˢ. Palmer began to work upon yᵉ Steeple of our meeting house

      June begins.

June 2.   This day in study . . .   Sister Jerusha returned from Boston

— 4.   Lords day.   I preached pʳ. totum from Eccles. 12. 5.   East side people here.

— 6.   This day heard that yᵉ Commissioners Court at Norwich did yesterday after Long hearing &ᶜ reverse Dudleys Judgement in yᵉ whole of it, and after that dissolved the Court.   Thanks be to god that has protected us from men of Violence.

— 7.   This day went to Bolton to the assocⁿ.   Mʳ Steel preached from 1 cor. 4. 15.[1]

— 8.   This day Mʳ Russel[2] of Middletown and Mʳ. Woodbridge[3] of Glastonbury here

---

House in the afternoon. "A joint committee was appointed by both Houses to confer on what might be proper to offer to his Honor on the sudden and sorrowful event, and the Lower House also appointed Mr. Speaker, the Clerk, and Capt. Samuel Willard, to draw an address of condolence," which with the Governor's reply is printed in the *Massachusetts Historical Society's Collections*, 3d series, i, 246, and also in Palfrey's *History of New England*, Vol. iv, 583, 584.

[1] At the Association it was voted that Rev. Mr. Whitman of Farmington and the Rev. Jonathan Marsh of Windsor and all the ministers of Hartford be a standing committee to examine all candidates for the ministry "within our Circuit."

[2] Rev. William Russell born at Middletown Nov. 20, 1690; grad. Y. C. 1709; ordained successor to his father, Rev. Noadiah Russell, in the pastorate at Middletown, June 1, 1715; Fellow of Y. C. 1745 till his death, June 1, 1761, on the anniversary of his ordination, after a ministry of forty-six years. He preached the Election Sermon in May 14, 1730.

[3] Rev. Ashbel Woodbridge, son of Rev. Timothy Woodbridge of the First Church of Hartford, born June, 1704; grad. Y. C. 1724; ordained at Glastonbury, Oct. 23, 1728; Fellow of Y. C. 1755 till his death in the Glastonbury pastorate Aug. 6, 1758. He preached the Election Sermon in May, 1752.

— 9. This day in Study, drew Madam T's ch. & a copy of the H. of R's. address to send to y⁰ Printer.[1]

— 11. Lords day I preached p'. totum . . . this night John Shepherd came to discourse me about being admitted to communion with y⁰ chh.

— 12. This day catechised children, made some visits among y⁰ sick, cloudy weather

— 16. This day Brother Matthew Talcott returned from Sea, well in health, thanks be to God who hath preserved him

— 17. This day died M͏ͣ. Susanna Hosmer alias Bunce, wife to M͏ͬ. Stephen Hosmer.

— 18. Lords day I preached . . . this day was Interred M͏ͫ Susanna Hosmore

— 19. This day about day light my wife was delivered of a daughter   Thanks be to god that there is a living mother and child. this day I catechised children at Lieut. Jon. Cooks

— 20. The County Court began here. M͏ͬ Bull of Westfield here at night.

— 21. This day went to Windsor, returned &⁰. found M͏ͬ. Jos. Moody[2] of York here, a man of piety and edifying conversation tho' too talkative. This day fast at Weathersfield in order to seek one to help in y⁰ ministry

— 24. This day in Study, very warm, y⁰ Sabbath approaches O y͏ͭ god would assist me in preparing for it. ——— This day bought me a horse

— 25. Lords day I preached pr. totum . . . M͏ͬ. Whitman being absent his people were at our meeting. . . . Laboured under great indisposition and difficulty in speaking.

— 27. John Shepherd here at night. appointed y⁰ 2͏ͩ Sabbath in July for his admission to y⁰ chh. I pray God to direct and assist him in preparing for it.

---

[1] A draught of the "character" (or as we should say the biographic notice) of Mrs. Talcott, prepared by Mr. Wadsworth for "the Printer," remains among Mr. Wadsworth's papers; a kind but formal tribute; lacking the really touching feeling which belonged to the House of Representatives address, which he copied to accompany it. Mr. Wadsworth was essentially a kind though formal man ; and he may have felt that the relationship involved laid him under special necessity of restraint.

[2] Rev. Joseph Moody the more eccentric son of an eccentric father, Rev. Samuel Moody of York, Me. Joseph, the son, was born in 1700 ; grad. at H. C. 1718 ; at first a Town Clerk, Register of Deeds, and Judge of Probate, in which functions he did well, but was overpersuaded by his father to become a minister. He was a considerable part of his life a hypochondriac, and in extended periods wore a handkerchief over his face, at which time he would turn his back toward his congregation, and lift the handkerchief so far as to read his sermon with his face to the wall. He was widely known from this habit as "Handkerchief Moody." He was a good man ; is said to have been marvelously gifted in prayer ; he spent the latter years of his life in the seclusion of a voluntary retirement from society, and died in 1753.

— 30. . . . heard Dan⁰ Colliers vessel sprung a leak at sea, put in at Boston in distress

July begins.

July 1. Lords day I preached p'. totum from Matt. 9. 2. . . . pleasant weather. Laboured under considerable indisposition and weakness

— 5. Visited a sick man, prayed with him. I pray god to heal and savingly to convert him

— 9. Lords day I preached per totum diem from Deut. 6. 11. . . . Moses Cook sick prayed for. I Laboured under great difficulty . . .

— 10. This day Catechised children at Jon: Butlers, Visited &ᶜ. took care of secular affairs &ᶜ.

— 15. . . . visited yᶜ sick children of Jos: Shepherd

— 16. Lords day I preached . . . John Shepherd and Daniel Catlin were recᵈ into the church. Laboured under great difficulty in speaking.

— 19. This day wrot a letter to Doctʳ. Doddridge at Northampton in England and another to go to Long Buckby.

— 23. Lords day I preached A.M. at yᵉ N chh from heb. 13. 9. & P.M. at my own meeting from rom. 6. 12. . . .

— 25. This day about 7 oclock in afternoon died Moses Cook in yᵉ [blank] year of his age.

— 26. This day was Interred Moses Cook.

— 27. Went to Windsor on a visit to Mʳ. Marsh &ᶜ.

— 28. This day in Study. little remarkable   a prospect of a war between England and Spain.

— 30. Lords day I preached p'. totum diem . . .   Laboured . . . Elisha Pratt and wife, Abijah Catlin and Hannah yᵉ wife of Eleazer Goodwin propᵈ. for admission to Com: with yᵉ chh.

— 31. Went over yᵉ River in yᵉ afternoon to Visit Mʳ. Woodbridge

August 1738.

Aug. 1. Hannah yᵉ wife of Lieuⁿᵗ. Aaron Cook came to desire Admission to communion with yᵉ church. . . .

— 2. This day went to Durham with yᵉ Governʳ. & Sister Hooker &ᶜ. Saw Mʳ. Noyes¹ at Middletown. my friends all well

---

¹ Probably Rev. Joseph Noyes, pastor of the First Church of New Haven, whose wife, Abigail Pierpont, was half-sister to Mary Pierpont, the wife of Rev. William Russell, the Middletown pastor. Mr. Noyes was born in Stonington Oct. 16, 1688; grad. H. C. 1709; tutor Y. C. 1710-15; ordained at New Haven July 4, 1716; had a long controversy in his church growing out of the agitation of the Great Awakening period and following discussions, respecting both which he belonged to the Old Light party; died June 14, 1761.

— 4. This day some rain, yᵉ Governʳ. not well, wee returned from
Durham, got Home a little after nine o'clock

— 6. Lords day I preached . . . yᵉ Governʳ. sick and prayed
for. and Jno. Haynes Lord. Hannah yᵉ daughter of Nehemiah
Cadwell baptized. A sacrament notified for yᵉ next Sabbath.

— 8. . . . This day our people gat yᵉ spire pole into yᵉ Tower.

— 11. This day in Study, warm weather, yᵉ Governʳ. very ill.

— 13. Lords day I preached . . . and administred yᵉ Sacrament . . . Governʳ yet sick. Elisha Pratt & his wife,
Abijah Catlin and Hannah yᵉ wife of Eleazer Goodwin admitted
to communion with yᵉ church.

— 15. Yᵉ Governʳ Hopefully better. this day at night Capt.
Hooker took my horse to keep.—and kept him till yᵉ Wednesday following—

— 16. This day went to Farmington to Examine Mʳ. Bartholomew[1]
in order to ordination and Mʳ. Marsh[2] in order to preaching.
warm weather.

— 17. This day our people raised yᵉ spire of our Steeple without
hurt to any. thanks be to god who has preserved yʳ Lives and
limbs. at night died Mʳ. Robert Bartlett aged 35

— 19. This day was Interred Mʳ. Robert Bartlett. at night heard
yᵗ brother Nathan Talcot died sometime this week.

— 20. Lords day I preached per totum from 1. pet. 1. 17. . .
Sundry persons sick and prayed for.

— 22. This day visited Jnᵒ. Cook, sick, went to Glastonbury returning went to visit Mʳ. Mix.[3]

— 23. This day little study. Mʳ. White[4] of South=Hampton here.
I went with him to the West=Division.

— 26. This day is six year since I came to live in Hartford.

— 27. Lords day I preached A.M. . . . P.M. Mʳ. White of
South Hampton preached for me from rom. 5. 12.—a very
warm day

— 28. . . . This day about 6 o'clock in yᵉ afternoon died yᵉ
Revᵈ. Mʳ. Stephen Mix of Weathersfield.

----

[1] Andrew Bartholomew, born at Branford, Nov. 7, 1714; grad. Y. C. 1731; ordained pastor at
Harwinton, Oct. 4, 1738, the church having been formed the 27th of September previous. Mr. B.
was dismissed Jan. 26, 1774, but continued to live in Harwinton till his death, March 6, 1776. A
defender of the Half-Way Covenant in opposition to Bellamy.

[2] Jonathan Marsh, Jr., son of Rev. Jonathan of Windsor, born Jan. 1, 1713-14; grad. Y. C.
1735; ordained pastor at New Hartford Oct. 10, 1739; remained in office till his death, July 5, 1794.
An "Old Light," like Mr. Bartholomew, in theology.

[3] Rev. Stephen Mix of Wethersfield, born at New Haven; grad. H. C. 1690; ordained pastor
at Wethersfield 1694; died in office, Aug. 28, 1738.

[4] Rev. Silvanus White born 1704; grad. H. C. 1722; ordained at Southampton Nov. 17, 1727;
died Oct. 22, 1782.

— 30.   This day was Interred yᵉ Revᵈ. Stephen Mix   Mʳ Marsh
preached a sermon from 2 cor. 4. 13.   a great number of people were at yᵉ funeral and this day died yᵉ widow Hinsdel of
this Town.

> September begins

Sept. 3.   Lords day I preached A.M. from Isai. 57. 15. at yʳ n chh
and P.M. at my own meeting from Act. 26. 28.   Hannah Cook
yᵉ wife of Lieutˡ. Aaron Cook was taken into yᵉ church.

— 5.   This day visited yᵉ sick   read some of Berry Street
Sermons.   Superior Court opened in this Town to day.

— 6.   This day went to Middletown ordinatⁿ.   The Revᵈ. Mʳ. Edward Elles¹ was ordained Pastor of yᵉ North chh or Society.
The Revᵈ. Mʳ. Eells of Scituate preached from Act. 20. 28. and
then prayed and gave yᵉ charge, Mʳ. Hosmore made yᵉ next
prayer, Mʳ. Burnham² gave yᵉ Right Hand of fellowship.   Mʳ.
Russel made yᵉ prayer previous to yᵉ Sermon, psal. 118 from
yᵉ 25: v. to yᵉ end was sung.

— 7.   This day yᵉ news of yᵉ death of Brother Nathan Talcott of
New Milford comes confirmed.

— 10.   Lords day Mʳ. Goss preached pr totum A.M. from Jer. 17.
9. 10.   P.M. from matt. 7. 12.   a cold day

— 13.   This day Commencement at N. Haven, yᵉ affairs of yᵉ day
managed in tolerable order.   took yᵉ first degree 15, yᵉ 2ᵈ
[blank] Chauncy Whittlesey³ made yʳ Salutatory oration and
Sam: Williams⁴ yᵉ Valedictory.

— 15.   This day returned from N: Haven in safety and found my
family well God be praised for it.

---

¹ Rev. Edward Eells born at Scituate (where his father, Rev. Nathaniel Eells, who preached,
made the ordaining prayer and gave the charge on this occasion, was pastor), grad. H. C. 1733, and
continued in the pastorate of this North Society (now Cromwell) till his death, Oct. 12, 1776, aged
sixty-four.   He preached the Election Sermon in 1767, and published some pamphlets in the Wallingford Controversy.

² Rev. William Burnham of the Second Society in Farmington (now Kensington), born in
Wethersfield; grad. H. C. 1702; settled as pastor Dec., 1712; died Sept., 1750.   Under Mr. Burnham's ministry a prayer and conference meeting existed, at which the brethren presided in rota-
tion, each one naming the next to preside and designating the Scripture passage to be considered.
The explanation of this (at this date) unusual practice is probably to be found that Mr. Burnham
had lived an unordained person among the people of his charge for five years previous to his becom-
ing their official pastor.

³ Afterward Rev. Chauncey Whittlesey,of the First Church in New Haven.   He was born at
Wallingford, Oct. 8, 1717; grad. Y. C. 1738; tutor in Y. C. six years though preaching occasionally; ordained pastor of the First Church, as colleague with
Rev. Mr. Noyes, March 1, 1758; continued after Mr. Noyes' death, in the sole pastorate till he
died July 24, 1787.   He preached the Election Sermon May 14. 1778.

⁴ Samuel Williams, son of Rector Williams.   He had graduated three years before, in 1735,
and was now probably giving his Master's oration.   He was born in the Newington parish of
Wethersfield, Aug. 16, 1720; and died, two years later than this event mentioned by Mr. Wadsworth, Nov. 15, 1740, at Wethersfield.

— 17. Lords day I preached . . . and baptized 3 children, viz. Amos Shepherd, Ezekiel Sandford, and Hannah Catlin

— 21. This day some study, pleasant weather. the Govern^r. first came hither after his sickness. this day died Orange Webb

— 23. This day . . . Orange Webb was Interred.

— 24. Lords day I preached per totum . . . Daniel Messenger dismissed from my chh. in order to Joyn with ye people at Herwinton in forming into Church State

— 25. This day ye son of Jos: Holtum was buried.

— 27. This day . . . visited ye sick, this day died Joseph Collier.

— 28. This day Joseph Collier was buried. this day is six years since I was ordained to ye work of ye ministry.

     October begins

Oct. 1 Lords day I preached. . . . a very rainy stormy day. this day Ben: Catlin and Margaret his wife & Anna the wife of Jon: Hopkins dismissed to Harwinton church.

— 3. This day I went to Harwinton to the ordination of M^r. Bartholomew, gat there safely

— 4. This day ye Rev^d. M^r. Andrew Bartholomew was ordained pastor of ye Church and people at ye Town of Harwinton according to ye direction of ye ordination Councel. I began with prayer, ye Rev^d. M^r. Whitman of Farmington preached from Jer. 3. 15. and made ye prayer previous to ye charge, and gave ye charge, ye Rev^d. M^r. Marsh made ye next prayer, ye Rev^d. M^r. Whitman of Hartford gave ye right Hand of fellowship and ye part of ye 118. psalm was sung and ye Rev^d. M^r. Bartholomew pronounced the blessing.

— 5. This day I heard that M^r. Rosewell Saltonstall[1] of Branford died at New London the first day of this month.

— 8. Lords day I preached per totum from psal. 22. 27. Laboured under weakness and difficulty

— 9. . . . this day our people set fire to their Kiln of oyster Shells, containing about 1200 bushel.

— 10. This day went to Scantick to ye Association. nothing remarkable happened. ye govern^r set out for New-Haven.

— 11. This day a lecture at Scantick by M^r. Elmer.[2] . .

---

[1] Capt. Rosewell Saltonstall, H. C. 1720, died Oct. 1, 1738.

[2] Rev. Daniel Elmer, born in East Windsor about 1690; grad. Y. C. 1713; preached awhile in different places in Massachusetts, removing in 1727 to New Jersey; ordained in 1728 pastor of the Church in Fairfield, Cumberland Co., in that State, where he died Jan. 14, 1755. An "Old Side" man in the troubles attending the Whitefieldian movement.

— 15. Lords day I preached per totum from phil: 2. 5. John Spencer Sen'. was admitted into communion with y' chh

— 17. . . . M'. Hobart[1] of fairfield here upon a Journey to Boston. M'. Bissel here.

— 19. . . . Great expectation of a war with Spain. rec'd. a letter from y' gov. at N: Haven

— 20. this day received twenty pounds in money of Sam[l]. Peck

— 21. . . . this day was buried a child of Sam[l]. Halladays who died yesterday of y' throat distemper as was supposed, and this day died a child of Daniel Seymours of y' throat distemper.

— 22. Lords day I preached per totum . . . between services the child of Daniel Seymour y[t] died yesterday was buried. Jemima y' daughter of Ben: Richards was baptized.

— 26. . . . this day heard that Will[m] Thall died yesterday

— 27. At night M'. Curtiss[2] here, came from y' Councel at Stafford   at night my horse was put into C. Hookers past

— 29. Lords day I preached per totum . . . and baptized John Jones upon his Masters acc[tt]. John Spencer, he ingaging to bring him up in y' christian faith.

— 31. This day very little study. . . . this day our people got y' bell up into y' Steeple in order to hang it
    Novemb'. Begins

Nov. 1. . . . Doct'. Hull[3] came to Capt. Hooker, who continues very sick of y' Cholick

— 2. . . . This day our meeting house bell[4] was hung and first Rang in our Steeple   this day a child, Charter by name was buried. this day y' gen[ll]. assembly adjourned without day.

— 3. . . . this day y' Govern' got home well from y' general assembly

— 5. Lords day I preached A.M. . . . at y' n chh. and P.M.

[1] Rev. Noah Hobart, born at Hingham, Mass., Jan. 12, 1706; grad. H. C. 1724; ordained pastor First Congregational Church, Faisfield. Feb. 7, 1733. A leading minister of the day, an active Controversialist in behalf of the principles of Congregationalism as against the claims of Episcopacy. He published many sermons and pamphlets, among which is the Election Sermon of 1750. He died Dec. 6, 1773.

[2] Rev. Jeremiah Curtis, born in Stratfield (now Bridgeport), Connecticut, in May, 1706; grad. Y. C. 1724; ordained at Southington, Nov. 13, 1728. In the Whitefieldian troubles he was an "Old Light," and in Nov., 1755, he was dismissed from his charge. He continued to live in Southington for forty years longer, where he died March 21, 1795.

[3] Doctor Benjamin Hull of Wallingford; licensed to practice physic, Oct., 1717. Dr. Gurdon W. Russell in his *Early Medicine and Early Medical Men in Connecticut* says that Dr. Hull's petition to be admitted to practice, "shows that *orthography* was not among the 'arts and mysteries' he had cultivated with success."

[4] See as to the history of the bell, Mr. Rowland Swift's paper in the *Two Hundred and Fiftieth Anniversary* volume of the First Church.

. . . at my own meeting. Sarah yᵉ daughter of Jonathan
Alcot was baptized. in yᵉ evening I preached a lecture at
Decⁿ. Merrills from Jos. 24. 15.

— 6. . . . this day I bo't Benjamin Catlins House, barn, Home
Lot ¹ &ᶜ. for £500. to be paid £200. February next, £200.
Augᵗ 20ᵗʰ next coming, £100. Febʸ 20 1740. yᵉ lot contains 8
acres. This day my horse was taken from Capt. Hookers pasture. last friday week he was put in

— 9. thanksgiving I preached from psal. 103. 1 to yᵉ 5.

— 12. Lords day I preached . . . baptized Mehitable Marvin
and Ann Brace. Dorcas Brace and Rebecca Brace owned yᵉ
Covenant yᵉ wife of Seth Young & Abigail Ashley propounded to own yᵉ Covenant

— 14. This day went to Farmington. Saw my friends well. This
day I suppose is my birth day

— 15. This day Came From Farmington, thanks be to god yᵗ
hath preserved me. . . .

— 16. . . . this day Mʳ. Wᵐ. Keith and Mⁿ. Marrianne Lawrence were joined in Marriage.

— 19. Lords day I preached per totum from phil: 3. 8. and administred yᵉ Sacrament: in yᶜ afternoon yᵉ South Side people
were at our meeting. Mʳ. Whitman not being well.

— 21. This day I first perceived something like a tooth cutt in yᵉ
roof of my mouth under my right foretooth. May not yᵉ
effects thereof be hurtfull

— 22. Cold weather. this day my uncle Thomas here. yᵉ County
Court adjᵈ. to yᵉ last Tuesday in January. 2 persons whipt
for stealing

— 23. partly in study. observed something in one of my
parishioners gives me fears what he may come to. I pray god
to restrain him from sin, and keep him from the iniquity wᶜ.
I fear may be his ruin.

— 26. Lords day I preached pr totum from I. pet. 4. 17. Abigail
Ashley owned yᵉ Covenant

— 28. I find by looking over my register of baptisms yᵗ I have
baptized since my ordination, in my own parish, 66 males and
69 females snowy day, snow fell shoe deep.

---

¹ Mr. Wadsworth had bought of Mrs. Abigail Woodbridge "about one acre more or less" for
a home in 1733. This ground on which he proceeded speedily to build was that on which he lived,
and on part of which the Athenæum building now stands. Some fragmentary accounts of pay-
ments made on the cellar and the well and other items of construction are still extant. This pur-
chase from Benjamin Catlin was an additional one.

— 29. . . . at night rec^d a present of 40^s. from M^r. Palmer
  December begins

Dec. 3. Lords day M^r. Burr of Worcester preached for me A:M.
  from Col. 3. 17. & P.M. from heb. 4. 3.

— 7. This day sold my Lot by Ephraim Smiths at £13 p^r. acre.
  returned from Farmington.

— 8. this day partly in Study, reading the Turkish Spy,[1] nothing
  remarkable occurs.

— 10. Lords day I preached pr totum from 2 Epist. Joh. 4. v. . . .

— 12. Some Study. a snowy day. M^r. Serjeant[2] of ousatannack
  here at night

— 13. This day more moderate .   M^r. Serjeant went from
  hence

— 14. this day ye weather Something moderated, my Self under
  difficulties and perplexities

— 17. Lords day I preached pr. totum from rom. 6. 21. baptized
  James son of Ozias Pitkin Esq.

— 18. this day went to Wintonbury, borrowed Stackhouses body
  of Divinity

— 21. this day without Study. this day my people sledded wood
  for me. this day died ye wife of W^m. Day

— 22. . . . this day was buried ye wife of William Day

— 23. Visited ye sick Capt. Williamson & widow Day.

— 24. Lords day I preached pr totum from psal. 77. 6. this day
  died Capt. Caleb Williamson

— 26. This day died ye widow Day

— 27. This day cold. ye widow Day Interred

— 29. . . . this day ye Society voted me £200. salary

— 31. Lords day I preached from psal. 94. 12. and baptized Joseph
  ye son of Seth Youngs

  January a new year begins. 1738/9

Jany. 3. little Study very cold. visited M^r. Woodbridge

— 4. This day some Study. Capt. Ozias Pitkin very ill with y^e
  Cholick

---

[1] *The Turkish Spy. Letters writ by a Turkish Spy, who lived five and forty years un-
discovered at Paris*, a book written by John Paul Marana, a Genoese, first published in 1611 and
which went through twenty-six editions by 1770.

[2] Rev. John Sergeant, born in 1710 in Newark, New Jersey; grad. Y. C. 1729; tutor some
time in Y. C.; ordained Aug. 31, 1735, as a religious teacher among the Housatonic Indians residing
in what are now the towns of Stockbridge and Great Barrington in Massachusetts. In this work he
attained a most honorable success and continued in it till his early death in his thirty-ninth year July
27, 1749.

— 7. Lords day I preached pr totum from heb. 3. 12 and baptized
Samuel the son of Capt. George Wyllys

— 8. This day Study and visiting &ᶜ. this day writt a will for yᵉ
wid: Hannah Hopkins

— 10. This day I went to Farmington saw my friends well, saving uncle Hez. who is Lame, returned safe. Misty
weather. called up in yᵉ night to visit a sick child

— 11 providence is yᵗ care wᶜ god has over all things in yᵉ world,
to preserve yᵉ being he has given yᵐ, and to direct their
motions and actions to yᵉ ends he has purposed. Snowy
weather this day

— 13. . . . this day died yᵉ widow Kelsey

— 14. Lords day I preached A.M. at yᵉ new chh. 1. cor. 1. 30. and
P.M. at my own from heb. 3. 13.

— 15. This day visiting yᵉ sick, writing &ᶜ. this day yᵉ widow
Kelsey was buried

— 16. . . . this day yᵉ son of moses Seymour was buried

— 17. This day . . . a child of Henry Nicholson was buried

— 19. . . . This day died Abigail yᵉ daughter of Ben: Richards
in yᵉ 7ᵗʰ year of her age

— 20. This day . . . Abigail Richards was buried

— 21. Lords day I preached from heb. 3. 13. pʳ. totum. Barzillai Clark & Deb: Cook were admitted to full communion
with yᵉ chh

— 26. This day . . died Nathˡˡ Marsh Junʳ.

— 27. This day . . . Natt: Marsh was buried

— 28. Lords day I preached and administred yᵉ Lords Supper
. . . Nabby 4 year old this day

— 30. The adjourned County court sits here today. very cold
weather. at night died Benjamin Richards aged 6 years, yᵉ
son of Benj: Richards.

— 31. This day yᵉ son of Ben. Richards, Interred. a warm day.
little study. Mʳ. Bissel here.
February begins.

Feby. 1. This day little study. Cumbred with visits to little
profit. raining in yᵉ afternoon

— 4. Lords day I preached pʳ. totum from Eccles. 7. 14 yᵉ new
church people at our meeting, Mʳ. Whitman being sick. Ros-
well yᵉ son of Daniel Steel was baptized.

— 5. William Nichols and Mary Farnsworth were Joined in
marriage

— 6. This day . . . died Jonath[n] y[e] son of Benjamin Richards.

— 7. This day went to Glastonbury, a lecture there. M[r]. Lockwood[1] preached from Matt. 25. 46. Jonathan y[e] son of Ben. Richards was buried this day.

— 10. This day in Study   Cool weather: close application to business, y[e] way to have it easy and pleasant

— 11. Lords day I preached pr. totum from Exod. 20. 16. a snowy day

— 13. This day . . . went to Farmington   Many sick there

— 14. This day finished a bargain with Elisha Lewis about my pasture by Lieut. Harts and took his bond for £90. returned from Farmington.

— 16. . . . Eben: Belding paied me £27. on account of Samuel Peck.

— 18. Lords day I preached from Exod. 20. 17 and finished my discourses upon the Commandments. Aaron y[e] son of John Shepherd was baptized

— 19. This day little study. a case of weight and importance proposed to me. may I be directed in resolving it

— 20. . . . this day paied £10. at M[r]. Sloans shop of what I owed him, and £5. 17 more for our maid

— 22. . . . at night married Capt. Josiah Hart & Lois Goodwin

— 25. Lords day I preached pr totum from psal. 96. 4. . . . a thunder storm at night. the thunder now rattles in y[e] sky, and y[e] heavens are as it were on fire.

— 27. . . . this day paied to Thomas Abbe £50. on y[e] acc[t] of Dan[ll]. Brown, being part of y[e] £200. I was to pay Ben. Catling. & Dan[ll]. Catling gave me credit £50. on his fathers Bond.

— 28. This day M[r]. James Lockwood was ordained pastor of y[e] first church in Weathersfield. M[r]. Ashbel Woodbridge began with prayer. M[r]. W[m]. Russel preached from Col. 4. 17. M[r]. Steph[n]. Hosmore made y[e] next pray[r]. and M[r]. Dan[ll]. Russel[2] gave y[e] Right Hand of fellowship.

March begins

— Mch. 1. In y[e] afternoon a number of M[r]. Whitmans parish met

---

[1] Rev. James Lockwood, born at Norwalk, Dec. 20, 1714; grad. Y. C. 1735; ordained at Wethersfield, successor of Rev. Stephen Mix, Feb. 28, 1738 39; a Fellow of Y. C. from 1760 to his death; a favorer of Whitefield and new measures; preacher of the Election Sermon May 9, 1754, and again May 10, 1759; published several Occasional Sermons; died July 20, 1772.

[2] Rev. Daniel Russell, born in Middletown, June 3, 1702; grad. Y. C. 1724; ordained at Stepney (now Rocky Hill) June 7, 1727; died in the pastorate Sept. 16, 1764. He was brother of Rev. William Russell of Middletown, and son of Rev. Noadiah of the same place.

to pray for y[r] ministers, life and health, he being sick. M[r].
Hosmer, Bissel and my self there.

— 4. Lords day M[r]. Levinsworth[1] preached for me . . .
Hannah Youngs owned y[e] Covenant. John y[e] son of Cornelius
Knowles was baptized.

— 8. M[r]. Backus[2] & Bartlett[3] here at night

— 11. Lords day I preached pr totum from heb. 2. 3. rainy,
snowy weather

— 13. This day . . . my uncle Thomas here. Some ill news
of one of my friends afflicts me greatly

— 18. Lords day I preached . . y[e] new church people met
at our meeting house.

— 20. Paied Ben: Catling £20 money.

— 24. This day in Study. this day took up my bonds given to
Ben. Catling, and in lieu of y[m] gave new bonds to Daniel
Brown one £130 another £200 to be paied next August,
another 100 to be paied next February.

— 25. Lords day I preached per totum from heb. 12. 14. Laboured
under great difficulty by reason of faintness & weakness at my
breast.

— 26. This day   reading Pierce his vindication[4] &[c].
April.

April 1. Lords day I preached from 1 King 11. 9. baptized Mary y[e]
daughter of John Knowles.

— 5. This day . . .   paied M[r]. Sloane £3. in money. Training day

— 8. Lords day I preached per totum from psal. 50. 1. and baptized Mary y[e] daughter of Ichabod Wadsworth and Sarah y[e]
daughter of Barzaillai Clark.

— 11. This day a publick fast, I preached per totum at y[e] new
chh from Isai. 48. 8. warm weather. after meeting Elisha
Diar was Interred.

— 14. I hear y[t] two men were y[e] killed with y[e] lighning at Middletown last night. blessed be god y[t] has preserved me
and mine from destruction by it

[1] Rev. Mark Leavenworth, born in Stratford in 1712; grad. Y. C. 1737; invited in
October of this year (1739) to the ministry of the First Society in Waterbury: ordained there in
March, 1740; continued pastor till his death, Aug. 20, 1797. He was an enthusiastic " New Light ";
and preached the Election Sermon May 14, 1772.

[2] Rev. Simon Backus of Newington, born at Norwich, Feb, 11, 1701 ; grad. Y. C. 1724 ; ordained at the Newington parish in Wethersfield Jan. 25, 1727. Died at Louisburg while Chaplain
to the Connecticut troops at that port, February 2, 1745-6.

[3] Rev. Moses Bartlett, born in Madison, Feb, 8, 1707-8 ; grad. Y. C. 1730; ordained at Port-
land parish in Chatham, June 6, 1733; died Dec. 27, 1766.

[4] A Vindication of Dissenters, by Rev. James Pierce of Exeter, England, 1718.

— 15. Lords day I preached per totum from Joh. 1. 29 and administred yᵉ Sacrament.

— 17. This day . . . heard yᵉ Mʳ. Judah Lewis¹ of Colchester died last Lords day night

— 18. This day went to Windsor to a Councel²: a case of no small difficulty laied before yᵉ Councel

— 19. This day spent at Windsor in yᵉ business aforesᵈ. Came home at night.

— 22. Lords day I preached per totum from 1 tim. 6. 8. . O yᵗ I could with more facility and comfort discharge yᵉ duties of yᵉ Sabbath

— 24. This day freemans meeting Capt. Marsh & Mʳ. Buckingham Chosen Deputies. went to Farmington . . .

— 26. This day received a letter from Doctʳ. Doddridge at Northampton in England another from Jno. Wadsworth of yᵉ same place. another from Thomas and Ann Wadsworth at Long buckby in old England. as cold water to a thirsty soul. so is good news from a far country.³

— 28. this day . . . yᵉ wife of Joseph Barnard (who died yesterday) was buried.

— 29. Lords day I preached pʳ. totum from luk. 3. 8. . . at night Governʳ. Talcott recᵈ. a letter from agent Wilks⁴

May begins

May 3. Mʳ. Samuel Talcott and Mⁿ. Mehetable Wyllys were Joined in marriage

— 5. This day . . . recᵈ. from yᵉ Revᵈ. Doctʳ. Colman a

¹ Rev. Judah Lewis, born in Colchester June 6, 1703; grad. Y. C. 1726; ordained at what was called the Westchester Society, set off from Colchester and East Haddam, Dec. 17, 1729. He died April 15, 1739, in his 36th year.

² This Council was called on one special phase of a controversy which in various forms had a good while continued between Rev. Timothy Edwards and his Church at East Windsor. The *fons et origo* of the difficulty was an opposition between pastor and people about church-government; the pastor being a strong advocate of the Ecclesiastical System established at Saybrook in 1708; the church claiming to be Congregational according to the system of the Westminster Platform adopted at Cambridge in 1649.

The particular point round which the antagonism just now centered was the case of one Joseph Diggins, whom Mr. Edwards refused to allow the church privilege of Owning the Covenant and having his child baptized; alleging against him the "scandalous offence of having married Mr. William Stoughton's daughter contrary to her father's wish." The church sustained Mr. Diggins' claim; Mr. Edwards refused to hear the church, affirming a right of *negative* on the church, and that until his opinion changed it was useless for the church to meddle in the matter. The matter will be referred to again.

³ Mr. Wadsworth maintained correspondence with his English relatives with considerable activity considering the time, and an interesting letter to him from Dr. Doddridge dated Northampton, March 6, 1741, acknowledging one received from Mr. Wadsworth written Sept. 15, 1740, is still extant in the possession of Dr. J. H. Trumbull.

⁴ Francis Wilks, Esq., agent of the Colony at the English Court. He died in 1742.

present of 3 Sermons & about a dozen of Watts Songs, and
a dozen of Henrys Catechism, I pray god bless and preserve
yᵉ life of yᵗ useful man

— 6. Lords day I preached from luk. 3. 8. A.M. and P.M. from
Jam. 1. 21. a pleasant day . . .

— 10. This day election. Governᵣ. Dept-Governᵣ. and assistants
all as in yᵉ year past excepting that Mᵣ. Stillman was chosen
an assistant and Mᵣ. Lewis was left out. this day heard by
Mᵣ. Clap¹ that some people have lately discovred spots in yᵉ
sun

— 13. Lords day Mᵣ. Burr preached for me . . .

— 16. This day . . began to pull down my old barn, workmen. Jos. Talcot & Wᵐ. Goodwin

— 20. Lords day I preached per totum . . . may yᵉ divine
blessing attend my Labours. May I be successfull in yᵉ
ministry

— 22. . . this day Mᵣ. Douse came to board at our house

— 23. . . . . this day paied to Daniel Brown of Infield 76
pound, being part of the first bond yᵗ he has agᵗ. me

— 27. This day preached . . . Laboured under great indisposition especially in yᵉ forenoon. . . .

— 27. This day in secular business. raised a barn &ᶜ.

— 31. nil remarkable. Save yᵗ Epaphras Lord Junᵣ. died in yᵉ
7ᵗʰ year of his age.
June begins

June 2. Epaphras Lord Interred in yᵉ afternoon.

— 3. Lords day I preached . Laboured under much weakness and indisposition

— 4. This day writing letters &ᶜ. for England . . . at night
heard yᵗ brother Matthew Talcot is come from sea.

— 5. This day went to yᵉ association at Toland

— 6. This day a lecture Mᵣ. Marsh preached from act. 9. 6. returned home, I thank god that has bro't me to see my family
in safety

— 10. Lords day I preached A.M. for Mᵣ. Whitman yᵉ sermon
composed on 1 tim. 6. 8. tho' the text I took for it was heb.

---

¹ Rev. Thomas Clap, now of Windham, but next year to be inducted Rector of Yale College.
Mr. Clap was born at Scituate, Mass., June 26, 1703; grad. H. C. 1722; ordained pastor at Windham Aug. 3, 1726; transferred to the Presidency of Yale College April 2, 1740; resigned the office in
September, 1765; died at New Haven Jan. 7, 1767. He was an "Old Light" in the religious controversies of his day; an opposer of the Whitefieldian methods, and author of several important
historical and controversial publications.

13. 5. . . . Laboured under great indisposition by reason of a cold

— **12.** This day went to a Councel at Windsor rainy weather

— **13.** This day spent at Windsor in ye affair between M^r. Edwards and ye chh came to a Conclusion Late at night[1]

— **15.** . . . brother Matthew came home from sea.

— **17.** Lords day I preached . . and administred ye Sacram^t. . . .

— **19.** This day ye gen^{ll}. assoc^n. meets at Wallingford I was appointed a Delegate but could not with convenience go.

— **20.** paied to M^r. Sam^{ll}. Dwight of Somers £55. 11. 0. on acc^{tt} of Daniel Brown, and took up my bond

— **21.** . . . perplexed with variety of affairs   M^r. Hobart of Fairfield here at night

— **24.** Lords day I preached . . . and had a Contribution for ye presbyterians at Southington.[2] 14 pound contributed

— **28.** . . . writ a letter to send to M^r. Sylvester Wadsworth in England

    July begins

July 1. Lords day I preached   baptized William ye son of Ben. Swett

— **5.** . . . advised to take care of my health which seems to be very much broken

— **6.** This day in Study M^r. Eliot[3] of Kellingsworth here, advises

---

[1] A further stage of the Edwards-Diggins affair (see *ante*, p. 37, note). Mr. Edwards since the last Council had charged Mr. Diggins with having broken the Fifth and Eighth Commandments, and called a church meeting for his trial. The church sustained Mr. Diggins and pronounced him not guilty. From this verdict Mr. Edwards and two of the church members dissented, and called a Council to judge in the matter. The Council met as above and decided in favor of the Church. The Council, however, commended Mr. Edwards for his "tenderness, prudence, faithfulness and caution" in the matter; suggested if the pastor had scruples not to be overcome that Mr. Diggins' friends cease to press for his admission to the Covenant; and that Diggins better apply to some other minister and church for the privileges which Mr. Edwards did not see his way to accord. With this two-sided "Conclusion Late at night," the Council broke up. But the trouble, as we shall see, was not over.

[2] The vigorous administration of the Consociation System established by law in Connecticut had led to a conception of Congregationalism little different from Presbyterianism. Ministers and churches alike forgot the principles of the first founders of Congregationalism on the soil, and even forgot the name except to contemn it. They called themselves Presbyterians, in contrast with the few churches here and there (East Windsor whose troubles we have had occasion to notice among them) which were disposed to adhere to what was called the Strict Congregational Way, *i. e.*, such churches clung to the Cambridge Platform of 1649, and denied the binding authority of the Saybrook System. So Mr. Wadsworth called the Southington church, now struggling into existence, a Presbyterian church; just as Dr. Strong, seventy-five years later, used to print on the title-page of the sermons preached by him in the First Church in Hartford, " By Nathan Strong, Pastor of the North Presbyterian Church."

[3] Rev. Jared Eliot, born in Guilford, Nov. 7, 1685; grad. Y. C. 1706; ordained at Killingworth (now Clinton) Oct. 26, 1709; trustee of Y. C. from 1730 till his death; an "Old Light" in

me to take a vomit once in awhile of Ipacacuania, and also bitters, as gentian, camamile &c in powder or steeped in wine, and also ye yolk of an egg in cyder sweetened with honey, once twice or 3 times a day, according as ye Catarrhous humour affects me

— 8. Lords day I preached pr. totum from Mark 6. 20. Laboured under some difficulty . .

— 15. Lords day I preached . . . this day John Ripenear was buried

— 18. . . . recd visits &c. Mr. Russell of Stepney, Mr. Lockwood & Mr. Brainard.

— 19. this day sent a letter to Boston by Mr. Whitman to go to England to Doctr. Doddridge

— 20. An awfull spectacle I saw this day of a man reduced to misery, deprived of sense, speech and afflicted with constant convulsive motions, all occasioned by ye excessive use of strong drink as I supposed.

— 22. Lords day I preached A.M. at ye new chh . . . and P.M. at my own meeting . . . went thro' my work with less difficulty than at some other times, thanks be unto god for it.

— 23. This day went to Farmington saw my friends well &c. this day Jonathan Wadsworth died in a very sudden manner in ye woods

— " . . . Henry Nicholson died, Jonathan Wadsworth was Interred.

— 28. This day heard yt Samuel only son of Mr. Daniel Edwards of New=Haven died on thursday last of ye throat distemper.

— 29. Lords day I preached . . . Says Mr. Chillingworth I wo'd in ye pulpit use none as enemies but ye devil & sin August begins.

August 1. Went to Weathersfield &c. Wee had much talk about Conversion, and how far and what an unconverted man can and wt he cannot do, but with what darkness and confusion do wee talk of these things

4. nothing very remarkable occurs. Saving that Jery Allen [1]

theological sympathies; practiced physic; reputed an eminent botanist; member of the Royal Society; four times Moderator of the General Association; published several addresses and sermons among which was the Election Sermon of May 11, 1738; died April 22, 1763, in the 78th year of his age. See Dr. Gurdon W. Russell's *Early Medicine*, etc.

[1] Probably Jeremiah Allen of Boston, son of Rev. James Allen of the First Church in that place, and at one time Treasurer of the Massachusetts Colony. Apparently his "push" for the employment he sought was not successful.

came to Town to push for to be employed in ye affairs of this
Governm^t. at ye Court of great Brittain

— 5. Lords day I preached . felt but little if anything of
weakness at my breast.

— 7. This day went to Farmington to visit my friends. bro't
with me from thence sixty eight pounds ten shillings in Money
rec^d. of Elisha Lewis, and deliv^d. up his bond

— 10. This day took Physick, viz. Ipacacuana &^{c}. Study, rainy
toward night . . .

— 11. this day I think John Burkitt first came to live with me

— 12. Lords day ye Rev^d. M^r. Morison[1] preached for me A.M. . . .

— 13. This day . . . preparing for my Intended Journey &^{c}.
This day by an Express from Boston ye Governm^t is Informed
y^t Commissions of Marq and Reprisal are granted upon y^e
Spaniards.

— 14. This day set out on a Journey for my health in Company
with M^r. Colton, travelled as far as New-Haven, the throat
distemper prevails there.

— 15. proceeded on my Journey as far as Fairfield.

— 16. proceeded on my Journey as far as Norwalk.

— 17. Proceeded as far as Rye, and understanding y^t ye Small pox
was in our Rhoad, viz. at East Chester, N. Y. thot it not safe
to proceed and so returned ye same day as far as Horsneck.

— 18. This day came to Norwalk.

— 19. Lords day tarried at Norwalk. M^r. Dickinson[2] preached
A.M. from Matt. 5. 6. and P.M. I preached from John 1. 29.

— 20. This day went to Reading. Sent a letter to ye Gov. and
another to my wife p^r. M^r. Colton.

— 22. This day came to Fairfield. Lodged at M^r. Hobarts.

— 23. This day came to New Haven lodged at M^r. Pundersons.[3]

[1] Rev. Evander Morrison, a brother of Doctor Norman Morrison the physician (ante p. 10
note); born, educated, and ordained in Scotland. He apparently, from the frequency of his preaching for Mr. Wadsworth, lived in Hartford without stated charge, saving that in 1750 he was installed pastor of the newly organized church in West Simsbury (now Canton) a relationship which
continued, however, only about eleven months. During this pastoral experience he was a member
of the Hartford North Association, and his name appears several times in its records. During a
part of 1748 he supplied Mr. Woodbridge's troublesome pulpit at East Hartford for which he was paid
twenty-six pounds. In 1752 he was in New Jersey preaching at the Forks of Delaware. He minis-
tered in several churches under care of the Newcastle and Abington Presbyteries as late as 1756,
but returned to Connecticut and died in Hartford, Jan. 18, 1760.

[2] Rev. Moses Dickinson, born in Springfield, Mass., Dec. 12, 1695; grad. Y. C. 1717; preached
several years in New Jersey; installed at Norwalk Nov. 1, 1727; Fellow of Y. C. from 1738 to 1777;
a Controversial writer and publisher of several tracts on current discussions; a moderate "New
Light" in sentiment. He died May 1, 1778, aged 82 years.

[3] Probably Mr. Thomas Punderson, the father of Rev. Ebenezer Punderson (Y. C. 1726) who
just before this date, after a ministry of some years in Groton, had taken orders in the Episcopal
Church.

6

— 24. This day Came Home, found my family well and under Comfortable circumstances: I desire with my whole heart to give god thanks for it.

— 26. Lords day M[r]. Campbell[1] preached for me . . . This day 7 years since I came to live in Hartford.

— 29. This day paied to Billy Keith £7. 12[s]. 6[d]. money. Nothing remarkable occurs

September begins

Sept. 1. . . . its reported y[t] a frenchman is seized at Albany on suspicion of being a spy

— 2. Lords day I preached A.M: from Joh. 16. 22. and administred y[e] Sacrament and Sir Webster[2] preached for me in y[e] afternoon from rev. 3. 30.

— 8. M[r]. Sergeant and wife came here at night.

— 9. Lords day I preached A.M: . . and P.M. M[r]. Sergeant preached for me from psal. 139. 7.

— 11. This day went to New Haven, a prosperous Journey by the will of god

— 12. Commencement at New=Haven. Rector Williams[3] resigned his post

— 13. This day spent at New=Haven.

— 15. This day went to Long Island. arrived at Southold about midnight

— 16. Lords day kept Sabbath at Southold M[r]. Az. Horton[4] preached

---

[1] Probably Rev. James Campbell who, there is reason to believe, was a friend of Rev. Evander Morrison, and like him a Scotsman. He was, not far from this time of his preaching for Mr. Wadsworth, under great mental depression thinking he had never been converted; but under the persuasions of Whitefield and Tennent came out from his gloom, and preached at various places in New Jersey and in South Carolina. He seems to be last mentioned in the records of Orange Presbytery in 1780.

[2] Rev. Elisha Webster, b. at West Hartford, Nov. 12, 1713; grad. at Y. C. 1738; ordained Oct. 1, 1740, at Canaan. He was an "Old Light" in the divisions attending the Great Awakening period and consequently obnoxious to Bellamy and the other New Light leaders in his vicinity, who, there is some evidence to suppose, fomented disturbances in his parish resulting in his dismission in 1746 or 47. He died at Southington Jan. 29, 1788. The title "Sir" applied to him by Mr. Wadsworth was a customary designation of a man who had taken his bachelors degree at college; perhaps oftenest applied to those, however, looking to the clerical profession, between their graduation and their ordination.

[3] Rev. Elisha Williams, born at Hatfield, Mass., Aug., 1694; grad. H. C. 1711; engaged several years in civil affairs at Wethersfield; ordained at Newington, Oct. 17, 1722; transferred to the Rectorship of Y. C. 1726; resigned office Sept., 1739; resumed duties of civil life; was judge of the Superior Court, colonel of a regiment, etc.

[4] Rev. Azariah Horton, born at Southold, L. I., March 20, 1715; grad. Y. C. 1735; preached occasionally till 1741, when he was ordained by the Presbytery of New York to labor as a missionary among the Indians on the South Shore of L. I. Subsequently he was settled pastor at Madison, New Jersey, and died March 27, 1777.

— 17. This day went to the Marishes,[1] saw my wifes grandmother and other relations

— 18. This day spent at Marishes

— 19. This day went to Southampton

— 21. This day went to Southold.

— 22. This day came to guilford & from thence to Durham

— 23. Lords day at Durham M[r]. Chauncy[2] preached A.M. . . and P.M. I preached from heb. 11. 16.

— 24. This day I returned home thro' the good hand of my god upon me & found my family well   Laus Deo.

— 25. This day paied to Dan[ll]. Brown 31 pound which with 9 pounds paied by my wife a few daies ago makes 40 pound.   6 pound I borrowed of Sister Hooker.[3]

— 28. This day is Seven year since my ordination.   alas how little good I have done.   may I be encouraged and strengthened to do more for y[e] future.

— 30. Lords day I preached . . . found some difficulty in speaking in y[e] afternoon tho' not any thing of y[e] weakness at my breast y[t] I have sometimes bin troubled with
October Begins.

Oct. 5. M[r]. Bull of Westfield here.

— 6. Jno. Burkitt went from hence—

— 7. Lords day I preached per totum . . .   Wid: Abigail Wadsworth admitted to Communion with y[e] chh.   Tho. Welles Jun[r]. made Confession . . and owned y[e] Coven[t]. and Tim: his son was baptized.

— 11. This day rec[d]. a letter from M[r]. Prout giving an acc[tt] y[t] y[e] Govern[r] is sick at his house, I pray god to Look upon and heal him

— 14. Lords day M[r]. Morison preached for me from psal. 4. 3. p[r]. totum   cloudy cool weather

— 19. M[r]. Welstead and Lady here

— 21. Lords Day I preached . . . felt nothing of y[e] weakness about my breast y[t] I have bin in sometime past troubled with.

— 24. This day some study.   Mainly spent in Secular business, its a burden to me.   This day received a letter from y[e] Govern[r].

---

[1] Moriches, a parish in the township of Brookhaven.   Mrs. Wadsworth's mother, Madam Talcott, was a Howell from Long Island.

[2] Rev. Nathaniel Chauncey, born in Hatfield, Mass., Sept. 21, 1681; grad. Y. C. 1702; preached some years at Durham before his ordination Feb. 7, 1711; Fellow of Y. C. from 1746 to 1752; preached the Election Sermon, May 14, 1719, and again May 9, 1734; an "Old Light" in the controversies of his time; died Feb. 1, 1756.

[3] Eunice Talcott wife of Capt. Nathaniel Hooker.

— 26. paied Daniel Brown nine pounds in money.

— 28. Lords day I preached A.M. at y⁰ new chh . . . Laboured under considerable difficulty with weakness at my breast.

— 30. . . . in conversation at Mʳ. Coltons he mentioned yᵗ Mʳ. Woodbridge[1] my predecessor observed yᵗ ministers sons (of a liberal education I suppose) seldom prospered in merchandize Novembʳ. begins.

Nov. 1. Mʳ. Hun from Boston. nil remarkable

— 2. This day Mʳ. Hun set out for Home

— 4. Lords day I preached A.M. from Col. 3. 11. and administred yᵉ Sacrament and P.M. from psal. 197. 19. 20

- 8. Day of publick thanksgiving throughout Connecticutt. I preached from psal. 48. 1. a cool day nil remarkable

— 11. Lords day I preached A.M. . . . P.M. Mʳ. Burr preached for me . . .

— 13. This day went to Windsor to yᵉ Examination of Mʳ. Jonᵗʰ. Marsh in order to his ordination.

— 14. This day not very profitably spent &ᶜ. this day I suppose is my birth day

— 15. . . . This day died suddenly Mary Richards

— 16. This day Study &ᶜ. Mary Richard Interred, very cold

— 18. Lords day I preached . . . laboured under great difficulty in speaking by reason of a defluxion, as I suppose, of Rheum out of my head upon or into my windpipe

— 19. This day little study. Mʳ. White of Bolton here.

— 22. This day . . . at night James Shepherd and Sarah Hopkins were Joined in marriage

— 25. Lords day preached pʳ. totum from 1 pet. 4. 3. Laboured under some difficulty in yᵉ afternoon with a tickling in my throat. pleasant weather

December begins.

Dec. 2. Lords day I preached pʳ. totum from Zech. 8. 28.

— 4. Went to Farmington.

— 5. This day went to New Hartford where Mʳ. Jonathan Marsh Junʳ² was ordained Pastor of yᵗ Town. Revᵈ. Mʳ. Whitman of Hartford began with prayer, the Revᵈ Mʳ. Colton preached

---

[1] Rev. Timothy Woodbridge, born in the parish of Barford St. Martins in Wiltshire, England; baptized Jan. 13, 1656; grad. H. C. 1675; began to preach in Hartford as early as 1682; ordained Nov. 18, 1685; continued pastor till his death, April 30, 1732, aged seventy-six years and three months; having served the church in a ministerial capacity forty-eight years and eight months. He was a Fellow of Y. C. from its original foundation till his death, and a prominent member of the Saybrook Synod; preached the Election Sermon, May 12, 1698.

[2] *Ante*, p. 28, note.

from 1 cor. 4. 1. 2. ye Revd Mr. Whitman of Farmington prayed and gave ye charge, ye Revd Mr. Marsh of Windsor made ye next prayer, and I gave ye right hand of fellowship.

— 8. . . . this day heard yt brother Matt. Talcot arrived at New London ye 5 Instant thanks be to god for it

— 9. Lords day I preached A.M. at ye N chh . . . I'm informed yt Mr. Jno. Austin Joined to Mr. Whitmans chh this day

— 11. . . . heard of ye sudden death of Mr. Welsted who died abt. 5 o'clock last night this night ye Comtee. of ye Society reckoned with me. due to me .40. 0. 6.

— 12. This day went to Middletown to Mr. Welsteds funeral.

— 16. Lords day I preached A:M. from heb. 12. 9. and P.M. from rom. 8. 16. . . .

— 18. Society meeting at night. Mr Rector Clap here at night, but went to Weathersfield

— 20. This day died ye wife of John Knowles

— 21. this day paied Daniel Brown £10. 10s money this day Mr. Wm. Reed here

— 22. this day was decently Interred ye wife of John Knowles

— 23. Lords day I preached . . . baptized Hannah ye daughter of Danll Butler. This was ye Last Sabbath I preached in ye State House.

— 24. This day ye Joiners finished our meeting house.

— 30. Lords Day. Haggai 2. 9. I preached on this text all day. this was the first Sabbath wee met in ye New Meeting House.[1] Thanks be to god for ye favour, may we there have much of ye presence of Christ to render it truely glorious: from this time I began again to number my sermons.

January begins. 1739/40

Jany. 1. This day went to Symsbury to ye Association

— 2. This day a lecture at Symsbury I preacht from Jam. 1. 21. very cold weather

— 3. Rector Clap here at night.

— 6. Lords day I preached per totum from 1. Kings 18. 21. Mr. Whitman being sick his people were at our meeting

— 8. This day study &c. Mr Russell of Stepney here &c.

---

[1] This was the only discourse of Mr. Wadsworth's ever printed. It is entitled: "*Christs Presence the Glory of an House of Publick Worship. a Sermon from Haggai ii. 9. Preached at Hartford, December 30. 1739. At the Opening of a New Meeting-House.*" N. Lond., 1740, p. 28.

— 13. Lords day I preached per totum . . . and administred ye Sacrament and baptized Susannah ye daughter of M^r. W^m. Keith.

— 14. This day . . . at night at ye House of M^r. George Wyllys I set my hand as a witness to ye last will of Capt. Cyprian Nickols.

— 16. This day study. M^r. Colton here. at night wounded my knee

— 20. Lords day I preached per totum from gen. 6. 3. and baptized Mary ye daughter of John Turner Junr.

— 22. nil remarkable save y^t I was very lame and at night in extreme pain.

— 23. This day paied Dan^{ll}. Brown of Infield 60 pounds in money on acc^{tt} of my 2 bond

— 24. This day study &^c. M^r. Marsh of Windsor here.

— 26. This day study &^c. nil remarkable occurs save y^t I saw ye proc: of war with Spain published Oct. 23. 1739.

— 27. Lords day, being Lame I tarried at home. fair weather

— 29. This day my people sledded wood for me.
February. Month begins

Feby. 2. This day in study. fair weather and severe cold. Candlemas

— 3. Lords day I preached A.M. from Nch. 9. 30 at ye new chh. and P.M. at my own meeting from luk. 12. 21. felt dull and indisposition, ye Lord forgive ye imperfection of my services.

— 5. This day went to ye East Side to M^r. Woodbridge, saw M^r. Whitefields Sermons [1]

— 7. This day study &^c. uncle James here. ye Councel sat to hear N: London &^c.

— 8. This day . . . a person comes to object ag^t. S: N: owning the Coven^t. charges her with slander &^c. god direct me to a prudent and faithfull discharge of my duty in this affair

— 9. Y^e difficulty ab^t. S. N. owning ye Coven^t. seems to increase. I pray god to direct & assist me to discharge my duty faithfully. quiet ye minds of those fierce and wrathful people

— 10. Lords day I preached A.M. . . . P.M. M^r. Morison preached for me from Josh. 24. 15.

— 11. This day in ye forenoon had ye hearing of a troublesome affair ; may I be directed in ye discharge of my duty in it

---

[1] The first mention in this Diary of the name of a man whose appearance in Connecticut soon after was to be the occasion of consequences seriously affecting not only Mr. Wadsworth's but all his ministerial associates' subsequent history.

— 15. This day in Study, but troubled with the afore mentioned controversy. I pray god to help me to see clearly y^e way of my duty. help me to direct y^e parties controverting in y$_r$ way of y^r duty, and help y^m to hearken to counsel & submit to my direction.

— 16. This day in Study. more moderate weather, under some trouble ag^n ab^t y^e unhappy Controversy &^{c}. I thank god y^t he has given me a strength to bear it, I pray y^t god would help me to give y^m good advice, and y^m grace to hearken to it.

— 17. Lords day M^r. Morison preached for me A.M. and M^r. Pratt[1] P.M. . . . ye Lord make y^m useful men. I pray god y^t ye affair y^t has cost me so much trouble in ye week past may be comfortably issued. quiet and compose ye minds of y^r persons in Controversy persuade y^m I pray to submit to Councel and advice.

— 18. . . . Col^{nl}. Morris here with a Commission of Admiralty &^{c}.

— 20. . . . went to Farmington.

— 21. This day went into ye woods to view land &^{c}

— 22. This day returned from Farmington. Again troubled with ye former difficult affair. I pray god to direct and assist me in it

— 23. . . . troubled with ye old quarrel. o y^t god wo'd grant y^t it might be comfortably Issued

— 24. Lords day I preached . . . S[. . .] N[. . .] made publick confession of ye sin of fornication and owned ye covenant

— 27. This day Stafford Com^{tee} here for advice. P.M. visited &^{c}. I pray God preserve, protect and bless me

— 28. . . . O y^t god in his providence would quiet ye minds and inspire peace into ye hearts of such of my people as are at variance

March begins

Mch. 2. Lords day I preached pr. totum from gen. 2. 3. M^r. Sam^{ll} Talcot[2] owned ye Covenant and Samuel his son was baptized

[1] Rev. Peter Pratt, born at New London July 19, 1716 ; grad. Y. C. 1736 ; ordained at Sharon April 30, 1740 ; dismissed and silenced on account of intemperance, Oct. 13, 1747 ; died at New London in 1780.

[2] Samuel Talcott was Mr. Wadsworth's brother-in-law. He grad. Y. C. 1733 ; a man of public spirit ; in 1746 Lt. Col. of a regiment raised for the Canada expedition, and in 1755 Col. of a regiment raised to go against Crown Point. He died March 6, 1797.

— Superior Court opened here.   M[r]. Woodbridge [1] M[r]. Marsh & M[r]. Williams here.

— 5.   little remarkable.   Cool weather.   Courts &[c] are troublesome

— 6.   Study &[c].   M[r]. Clap, Steel & Woodbridge here.   Snow in y[e] night

— 7.   Study.   much interrupted by visitors, visiting &[c].   cold at night

— 8.   . . .   heard y[t] Admiral Vernon had taken Porto Bello

— 9.   Lords day I preached A.M. at M[r]. Whitmans meeting . . . and P.M. at my own   .   baptized Joseph Flagg and Sarah Nickols

    10.   This day visiting y[e] sick   . . .   M[r]. White here at night

— 12.   The storm of hail or snow continues all this day also.   M[r]. White went from hence in y[e] morning, M[r]. Woodbridge here at night

— 13.   . . .   Stafford advised to Lay y[r] Case before y[e] Asso[n]. &[c].

— 16.   Lords day I preached A:M: from Eccles. 5. 1. and P.M: from gen: 2: 15.   more moderate weather

— 17.   This day visiting y[e] Sick &[c].   warm weather, broth[r]. John here

— 18.   . . .   rec[d]. letter fm M[r]. Woodbridge, wrote letters to Mess[rs]. W. C. M. & B. to attend the Assoc[n]. next week at W.[2] Broth[r] lewis [3] and sister here at night

— 19.   B[r]. L. went home & Sist[r].   this day paied M[r]. Sloan 14. 16. o.   10 pound in money, & 4. 16. by his rate

— 23.   Lords day I preached   . . .   and administred y[e] Sacrament   . . .   baptized Benjamin y[e] son of Benjamin Richards

— 24.   . . .   at night had a severe fit of y[e] cholick, thanks be to god y[t] has relieved me

— 25.   This day went to y[e] Assoc[n]. at Windsor   . . .   M[r]. Pain [4] and Stafford Com[tee]. agreeing, y[e] Assoc[n]. advised to a Councel

---

[1] Rev. Timothy Woodbridge of Simsbury, oldest child of Rev. Timothy Woodbridge of the First Church of Hartford, baptized Oct. 3, 1686; grad. H. C. 1706; ordained at Simsbury, Nov. 13, 1712; continued in office, with some parish disturbances owing to quarrels about meeting-house location and division of the Society, till his death Aug. 28, 1742.   He preached the Election Sermon May 10, 1739, which does not, however, appear ever to have been printed.   He was accounted an "Old Light."

[2] Mr. Wadsworth was at this time Scribe of the Association.   But the probability is that the meeting was a meeting of the Standing Committee spoken of ante, p. 25, note, rather than of the Association itself, as its records bear no evidence of a meeting at the time specified.   The persons to whom Mr. Wadsworth wrote were Revs. Timothy Woodbridge, Benj. Colton, Jonathan Marsh, and Hezekiah Bissell.

[3] Elisha Lewis of Farmington, who married Ruth, Mr. Wadsworth's sister.   Ruth was born April 14, 1711; married April 18, 1739; died Oct. 15, 1776.

[4] See post under date of June 12.

w⁰ is to be Con⁴. at Stafford on yᵉ 2ᵈ. Tuesday in May. returned home

— 27. . . paied 20 pound to Geo. Pynchon on acc" of Dan". Brown

— 28. . . . this day yᵉ wife of Richard Burnham who died yesterday was Interred

— 30. Lords day I preached . . . Sarah Bidwell made confession of &ᶜ. and her child Sarah was baptized.

April 1. April begins with a great shower of snow. it snowed yᵉ greater part of the day freemans meeting this day Mʳ. Colton preached from 1 Sam. 12. 23. Deputies Capt. Marsh and Mʳ. Buckingham.

— 4. Study &ᶜ. . . . heard uncomfortable news from Long Island with respect to enthusiasm prevailing there among some ministers may it be stopt.

— 6. Lords day I preached per totum from gen. 4. 3. 4. 5.— baptized Samuel yᵉ son of Moses Ensign. Cool weather.

— 8. Uncle Wᵐ.¹ & brothʳ Lewis here: County Court began

— 9. a publick fast. I preached A:M: from Ezk. 16: 49. and Mʳ. Whitman P:M: from Isai. 3: 22: pleasant weather, will god accept our fasting.

— 12. This day . . . Mʳ. Burr of Worcester here, this day heard yᵗ Aaron Cadwell died yᵉ 25ᵗʰ of feb. last in Barbadoes

— 13. Lords day I preached: A:M: from rom. 13. 14. at Mʳ. Whitmans meeting and P:M: at my own from gen. 5. 24. o my leanness. yᵉ Lord of his infinite mercy direct and keep me

— 14. This day went to Farmington . . heard yᵗ Mʳ. Bull of Westfield died last Saturday.

— 15. This day returned from Farmington The Governʳ. has orders from home to Inlist volunteers &ᶜ. for yᵉ west Indies and to proclaim war with Spain

— 18. This day . . . yᵉ Kings declaration of war against Spain was published²

— 20. Lords day I preached . . Stayed yᵉ chh and chose Capt. Cook a messenger &ᶜ.

---

¹ William Wadsworth, born at Farmington, June 22, 1671; Deputy for Farmington, Justice, etc.; died 1751.

² The king's proclamation of war against Spain having been made, the Assembly at its following sessions in May, June, and July made provision for raising troops for an expedition against the West Indies. The troops were to be under the general command of Col. Spotswood, till joined by the regular troops from Great Britain, the whole then to be under the command of Lord Cathcart. They were to be paid by the king; to share in the booty; sent back home unless they desired to settle elsewhere; their local officers were to be appointed by the governor and commissioned by the king, and five pounds premium was offered for enlistment up to five hundred men.

— 22. This day went to Windsor to ye Councel there, came to no conclusion ¹ &^c.

— 23. This day ye parties declining to come into such a method as ye Councel tho't w'd issue ye controversy, nothing done &^c. y^t by advice &^c. ye matter hopefully accomodated. returned home

— 27. Lords day I preached A: M: & P.M: from gen. 6. 11. 12. 13. warm weather. nil remarkable occurs.

— 30. This day reading, visiting &^c. went to Weathersfield &^c. heard y^t M^r. Whitefield is arrived at New York.

   May begins

May 1. This day study &^c. Cool windy weather

— 4. Lords day I preached pr totum from Hosea 10. 12.— warm pleasant weather tho' something cloudy

— 8. This day election, Gov. & Dep: Govern^r. as in y_e year past. 3 new assistants viz. M^r. Fitch, Trumble and Huntington remarkably cold weather

— 11. Lords day M^r. Webster preached for me A: M: from Eccles. 8. 8. and M^r. Morison P.M: from luk. 12. 5.

— 14. Some Study. visiting, visited &^c. the trustees here

— 15. Study &^c. little remarkable

— 16. This day study &^c. nil remarkable occurreth

— 17. This day study &^c. nil remarkable

— 22. This day study &^c. nil remarkable rec^d 7 pounds money of uncle James for books &^c.

— 25. Lords day I preached A: M. at ye new chh. from heb. 11.

---

¹ A further stage of the East Windsor difficulty. Mr. Edwards had refused to abide by the acquittal of Mr. Diggins by the church (*ante*, p. 37, note), and declined to accord to him the privilege of seeking church fellowship elsewhere as recommended by the last Council. Mr. Diggins, therefore, made formal charges of maladministration against the pastor. The pastor called a Council. To this council the church propounded four questions for advice :

  1. Concerning the pastor's power to appoint the messengers of the church.
  2. Concerning the pastor's power to negative the action of the church.
  3. Concerning the pastor's power to determine what complaints should come before the church.   4. The case of Joseph Diggins.

  The first three of these questions went to the root of the Windsor difficulties, but the Council declined to consider them at all, though professing willingness to give advice on the Diggins' case only. Meantime the strained relations of the church and pastor had been such that for nearly three years no Lord's Supper had been administered. The advice of the present Council, thus limited, was apparently of little consequence.

  As to the future progress of the controversy, it appears that Mr. Diggins, at the importunity of his brethren, withdrew his complaint against Mr. Edwards ; and on Aug. 11, 1741, eighteen of the leading men of the church addressed Mr. Edwards a letter, regretting that the Council had not given them the advice they asked ; deploring the opposition of opinion between pastor and people on questions of church order, but asking, nevertheless, that the Lord's Supper might be administered. The pastor acceded to the request and "propounded the Sacrament" ; the disturbed condition of things manifested itself in various ways, however, for several years to come.

16. and P.M. from Tit. 2. 14 at my own   Laboured under
weakness & difficulty of speaking.

— 26.   This day study, visiting &c.   a child of Joseph Barnards
buried.

— 28.   .   .   .   paied to Mr. Sloan £16. 1s. 7d due to ballance.

-- 29.   This day received a letter from the Revd. Mr. Field Sylvester Wadsworth[1] at Burton in England dated Feby. 11.
1739/40.

    June Begins

June 1.   Lords day I preached A.M: from tit. 2. 14. and P.M: from
heb: 13. 6.   ye general assembly and South Society present

— 3.   This day Assocn. met at Mr. Coltons nil remarkable occurs.

— 4.   This day a lecture at West Hartford Mr. White preached
from Joh. 4. 19.

— 5.   This day ye general Assembly adjourned without day.
Gideon Merrills and Mary Biggelow married at night

— 8.   Lords day I preached per totum from prov. 22. 6.   Laboured
under great difficulty in speaking

— 9.   This day went to Toland.

— 10.   This day to Stafford to a Councel Mr. Edwards chose
moderator

— 11.   This day in Councel at Stafford, uncomfortable

— 12.   This day in ye same, ye articles of Complaint agt. Mr. Pain
not found ye Councel advised Mr. Pain to resign his office, he
consents.[2]

— 15.   Lords day I preached A:M: from heb. 9. 14. at my own
meeting and administred ye Sacrament and P.M: at Mr. Whitmans meeting from Jam. 1. 21.

— 18.   Lecture this day at Mr. Woodbridges meeting &c.   Mr. Ed-

---

[1] Rev. Field Sylvester Wadsworth was a dissenting minister who about this time became an
assistant to his father, Rev. John Wadsworth, in care of a "chapel" in Sheffield, Yorkshire. A Mr.
Field Sylvester had in 1700 laid the "first stone" in the foundation of the Chapel, and Mr. John
Wadsworth, who married Mr. Sylvester's daughter Rebecca, became its minister in 1714 (succeeding Rev. Timothy Jollie) and continued in its charge till 1744. Rev. Field Sylvester Wadsworth,
who obviously got his name from his maternal grandfather, became associated with his father in
1740, and remained after him till 1758. The Chapel is now Unitarian.

[2] The Stafford Church and Society had been some time in discord with their minister, Rev.
Seth Payne. Mr. Payne was born in Braintree, Massachusetts, Jan. 16, 1712. He grad. Y. C.
1726, and was ordained at Stafford Aug. 7, 1734. Difficulties soon arose and grave charges were
brought against him. The Council which met as above did not find the charges sustained, but, as
is seen, advised his resignation. He took the advice and resigned July 24th, but continued to reside
in Stafford. He tried to collect arrearages of salary by legislative aid, but failed. In 1745 he
became Episcopalian and offered to go to England for Orders if the Society for Propagating the
Gospel would send him. The encouragement appears not to have been afforded. He is supposed
to have died in Stafford early in 1753.

wards preached from psal. 119. 59. heard y⁺ Broth⁺. Matt is arrived at N. London & y⁺ Col^ℓ. Spotswood¹ is dead at Amboy

— 19. . . . Mʳ. Nott, parsons² and gaylord³ here. Bettys birth day

— 22. Lords day I preached . . . Laboured under considerable difficulty in yᵉ afternoon thro' faintness and weakness

— 23. . . . nil remarkable. Uncle James here this day.

— 26. . . . an Express with fuller news relating to yᵉ Expedition &ᶜ. Moses Griswold & Mary Nickols married.

— 29. Lords day I preached . . . baptized Dick a negro boy of Capt. Nickols, had a Contribution &ᶜ.

     July begins

July 4. This day in study. nil remarkable occurs.

— 5. This day in study. nil remarkable

— 6. Lords day I preached . . . and baptized Simeon yᵉ Son of Sam^ℓℓ. Graham and Susannah yᵉ daughter of Mercy Gilbert

— 8. This day catechising &ᶜ. yᵉ General assembly of yᵉ Colony met here this day.

— 11. This day Study &ᶜ. nil remarkable. the general assembly broke up.

— 12. . . . yᵉ British lieutenants arrived in yᵉ forenoon⁴

— 13. Lords day I preached A:M: for Mʳ. Whitman and Mʳ. Morison for me. & P:M: at my own meeting

— 20. Lords day I preached A:M: . . . and Mʳ. Morison from rom. 2. 4. 5. & baptized his brothers child.⁵

— 24. . . . Mʳ. Eastabrook⁶ here

— 27. Lords day I preached A:M from phil. 3. 13. 14 and P.M: from Col. 1. 13. Laboured under . . .

---

¹ See *ante*, p. 49, note.

² Rev. Jonathan Parsons of Lyme; born at West Springfield, Mass., Nov. 30, 1705; grad. Y. C. 1729; ordained at Lyme, March 17, 1730-31. At his settlement he was an ardent Arminian, but became, as he thought, converted under Mr. Whitefield's preaching in 1740, and followed in a like itinerating course of evangelizing effort. Difficulties arose in his congregation and he was dismissed in October, 1745. In March, 1746, he was installed pastor of a Presbyterian church in Newburyport, Mass. He published many sermons, among which was one on the death of Rev. George Whitefield, an event which took place at Mr. Parsons' house in Newburyport in September, 1770. He was a devout and earnest man, though somewhat hasty in temper. He was one of the most active laborers in the Great Awakening period. His death was on July 19, 1776.

³ Rev. William Gaylord of Wilton; born at West Hartford, Nov. 29, 1709; grad. Y. C. 1730; ordained at Wilton, Feb. 14, 1732-3. He was an earnest " New Light "; a man of kindly spirit, and died in office Jan. 2, 1767.

⁴ Assisting in raising and drilling troops for the Spanish expedition.

⁵ Jennet, daughter of Dr. Norman Morrison.

⁶ Rev. Hobart Estabrook then preaching as a candidate in Salisbury, Mansfield, and elsewhere. He was born at Canterbury, Dec. 17, 1716; grad. Y. C. 1736; licensed to preach May 16, 1738; ordained at Millington Nov. 20, 1745; died there in office Jan. 28, 1766, æ. 49.

— 29. This day nil remarkable. Jno. ye son of Hez. Collier died. M^r. White and Lockwood here.

- 30. . . . our child Eunice sick and hath bin for some daies with ye measles.

— 31. This day Study but little, visits rec^d. &^{c}. M^r. T. Wood- bridge of Hatfield, and M^r. Jno. Woodbridge of Sutt. a pleas- ant and refreshing shower at night.

    August

Aug. 1 . . . part of the afternoon spent in prayer with Capt. Seymour

— 3. Lords day I preached . . . P.M. from 2 cor: 13. 5. at M^r. Whitmans meeting. Rebecca y^e daughter of Elisha Pratt was baptized p^r. M^r. Whitman

— 4. This day no study. Visiting &^{c}. uncle Thomas here

— 8. this day the soldyers y are going upon the expedition into y^e Spanish West Indies went from this Town in order to go to New=Haven where y are to embark

-- 10. Lords day I preached from rom. 12. 12. pr totum. Edward Cadwell Junr. owned y Coven^t.

— 13. . . . 2 of our children sick with y measles, I pray god heal'm

— 17. Lords day I preached . . . and administred y^e Sacra- ment. baptized Ruth y^e daughter of Edward Cadwell Junr.

— 18. Capt. Newberry [1] set out for New=Haven in order to em- bark for y^e west Indies

— 19. This day went to Farmington, my uncle Hez.[2] very ill.

— 23. This day y^e muster master Pitcher came to Town. at night died y^e aged M^n.Hamlin

— 24. Lords day I preached A.M: from gen. 3. 19. at y^e new meeting and P.M. at my own from luk. 24. 34 and baptized Timothy ye son of Caleb Spencer

— 25. . . . M^n. Hamlin Interred

— 27. This day went to Farmington. My uncle Hez. something better &^{c}.

— 28. This day went over ye River, about an affair not very comfortable

---

[1] Capt. Roger Newbury of Windsor, born June 4, 1706; grad. Y. C. 1726; Deputy in General Assembly eleven sessions; commanded one of the Connecticut companies in the West Indian ex- pedition; present at the repulse of Admiral Vernon at Carthagena in April, 1741; died on the return voyage May 6th of the same year.

[2] Hezekiah Wadsworth of Farmington, born Dec. 18, 1682, died unmarried Oct. 20, 1740. The dates of the birth of Mr. Wadsworth's brothers mentioned in these notes are from a memorandum i i Mr. Wadsworth's handwriting; they differ to some extent from those found in the "Wadsworth Genealogy."

— 30. this day died Capt. Thomas Seymour 72,   died
also a child of Edward Cadwell Jun'.

— 31. Lords day I preached . . . and baptized Peter and
Bilhah servants of Capt. Jos: Cook. Capt. Seymour Interred
September begins

Sept. 3. Study &ᶜ. Mʳ. Hobart & wife here to-day nil remarkable

— 4. Study. Went to Court to give an Evidence &ᶜ. nil remarkable, save yᵗ this day heard yᵗ Lord Cathcart Sailed &ᶜ. on the
26. of July last

— 7. Lords day I preached from 2 Cor. 6. 18. pʳ. totum rainy
weather

— 8. this day went to New-Haven. a comfortable Journey. Laus
Deo.

— 10. Commencement at New-Haven 21 Batchellors commenced.
about 13 or 14 masters the first commencement yᵗ Rector Clap
presided.

— 11. This day returned home found my family well, Laus Deo.

— 14. Lords day I preached A:M: at yᵉ new meeting . . . &
P.M: . . . at my own. Laboured under . . .

— 16. This day went to Farmington. My uncle Hez: not well.

— 18. This day . . yᵉ widow ——— Steel Interred.

— 19. This day . . . went to Farmington to see my uncle Hez.

— 21. Lords day I preached . . . baptized Jerusha yᵉ daughter
of Daniel Spencer

— 24. This day went to Farmington, my uncle Hez. something
better

— 28. Lords day I preached A:M. from tit. 2. 14. at yᵉ new meeting and P.M: at my own from 2 cor. 4 18. nil remarkable

— 30. Visiting &ᶜ. reading. Mʳ. Flaggs House raised.
October begins

Oct. 1. Mʳ. Hobart &ᶜ here from Boston. Burr also. Joseph
Barnard died aged 86 or 89 as they inform me

— 2. This day . . . Mʳ. Whitman married[1]

— 3. Some pious and refreshing conversation this day with B.
and L.

— 5. Lords day I preached   cool weather and something
rainy

---

[1] Rev. Mr. Whitman married Abigail Stanley, daughter of Col. Nathaniel Stanley, Jr., son
of Nathaniel Stanley, a man of distinction in Hartford affairs. Her grandmother was Anna Whiting, daughter of Rev. John Whiting, fourth pastor of the First Church and first pastor of the
Second in Hartford.

-- 6. Saw a copy of letter from Roland to Noble, giving an account of wonders wro't by his preaching &c. but alas w' are y'.

- 7. This day y* association met at my House, discussed various matters &c

8. association Lecture here M'. Whitman of F: preached from gen. 3. 8. 9. a good sermon.

— 9. This day in business &c. Conversation writt &c. how lamentable it is that y* ministry is grown into such Contempt. What are y* reasons of it ? W'. are y* meanes by w*. y*. honour of it may be recovered [1]

- 11. This day in study. at night received a letter from D. Colman concerning M'. Whitefield, and M'. Smiths' sermon on his character, preaching &c.

-- 12. Lords day I preached and administred y* Sacrament . . . and P.M: at M'. Whitmans meeting from act. 3. 22

— 13. Writt a letter to send to Doctor Doddridge.

— 15. This day went to Farmington, my uncle Hez: much worse.

-- 16. Came from Farmington left my uncle Hez: in a weak low state may god Look upon and save him

— 18. This day in Study, o that I might be more inflamed with y* love of god and a more ardent desire after y* Salvation of Souls

— 19. Lords day I preached p'. totum . . . at Evening Comes the Sorrowfull news y' uncle Hez. is not likely to Live till morning. he died between 12 and one in y* 58th year of his age, may this providence be sanctified to me

— 21. This day went to Farmington, my uncle Hez: Interred. a sorrowfull day: at night y* famous M'. Whitefield came to Town.[3]

---

[1] Apparently the "decay of the pulpit" was a theme which troubled people in 1740 as much as in 1890 and probably with about as much reason.

[2] Rev. Josiah Smith, born in Charleston, South Carolina, in 1704; grad. H. C. 1725; ordained at Boston July 11, 1726, but performed his ministerial service mainly in Bermuda and Charleston. When Mr. Whitefield was denied admission to the Episcopal pulpits in Charleston Mr. Smith published the sermon above referred to on the "Character, Preaching, etc., of the Rev. George Whitefield impartially represented and supported," 1740. Mr. Smith died in Philadelphia in October, 1781.

[3] Rev. George Whitefield, having completed a preaching tour through the Middle and Southern Colonies, arrived at Newport on Sept. 4th. He preached at Boston with triumphant success. He held meetings on the Common, and in the adjacent region about Boston as far as Marblehead ; sometimes as many as twelve or sixteen a week. No such prostration of a community before one man, and he a gospel preacher of twenty-five years of age, has ever beside been known in New England. Leaving Boston Monday, October 13th, "kisse'l" by Governor Belcher, whom he left bathed in tears, he preached his way from point to point in Massachusetts, till, on Friday, October 17th, he reached Northampton. Sunday evening he left Northampton accompanied by Jonathan Edwards who attended him as far as East Windsor to the house of Jonathan's father, Rev.

— 22. This day M^r. Whitefield preached in ye forenoon to a vast Concourse of people here from rom. 14. 17 verse. and in ye afternoon at Weathersfield from 2 Cor. 5. lat: part of ye 14. verse. old things are past away &^{c}. w^t to think of ye man and his Itinerant preachings I scarcely know: ye things w^e I know not I pray god to teach me, wherein I am in error I pray god to discover it to me, wherein I have embraced ye truth I pray god y^t I might hold it fast to ye end.

— 23. This day thoughtfull[1] &^{c}. I would pray y^t I might be saved from mistakes and be directed in ye way of truth.

— 24. This day . . . rec^d. a letter from my uncle James at New Haven.

— 26. Lords day I preached A:M: from 1 pet. 1. 6: and P.M: from Eph. 5. 14. I pray god to bless ye word y^t I have spoken o y^t some one at least might be awakened and some edified by it.

— 27. Writt a letter to &^{c}. visited sick. had some edifying Conversation with two ministers at my house. . . . O Lord show unto me ye way of truth

— 30. Study &^{c}. great are my perplexities and troubles o y^t god would appear for my help and fulfill his good word unto me on w^e he has caused me to hope

Nov. 1740

Timothy. On the way Mr. Edwards cautioned Mr. Whitefield about his habit of declaiming against the ministers who did not at once fall into line with his methods as unconverted men ; a caution which Mr. Edwards thought was rather unfavorably received. He preached on the way from Northampton on Monday at Westfield and Springfield, Mass.; on Tuesday at Suffield and at East Windsor. On Wednesday, Oct. 22d, he was at Hartford and Wethersfield. From Wethersfield he went *via* Middletown and Wallingford to New Haven, preaching at each place by the way. Thence after holding several services at New Haven, he departed, preaching as he went, through Milford, Stratford, Fairfield, and Norwalk to Rye and New York.

[1] It is not strange (quite aside from any questions of ecclesiastical order or of religious methods) that Mr. Wadsworth and all the other ministers should have been made "thoughtfull" by such an apparition among them as George Whitefield. The ministers of New England at the period, with very few exceptions, preached from closely written manuscripts, which must generally have been held in the hand, and often close to the eyes, and with few or no graces of manner or elocution. Here suddenly appeared among them a man whom nature had endowed with some of the greatest gifts of an orator ; a splendid physique, a marvelous voice, a vivid dramatic power, and one who seemed to pour forth his torrent of seemingly unpremeditated speech without fatigue or study. It was a novel experience to listen to such a man. New England congregations had never heard the like; New England ministers were startled by the phenomenon. Most of the accounts present the picture of a man who at any time and anywhere would have commanded applauding crowds. Yet it is but fair to say there was, certainly, another side to the picture. Aside from his censoriousness, his uncharitableness in judging men as good as himself as "unconverted", his overweening confidence in his own ability to know the mind of the Lord and the Lord's judgment respecting men, there were, sometimes at least, drawbacks to the worthiness of his style of speech, even as a Christian orator, which have been often too entirely forgotten in the general acclaim which accompanied and has followed him. Rev. Jonathan Mayhew of Boston (a certainly competent though doubtless not a sympathetic critic) said " I heard him [Whitefield] once, and it was as low, confused, puerile, conceited, ill-natured, enthusiastic a performance as I ever heard."

Nov. 1.   .   .   .   yᵉ Gov: returned from New-Haven.   recᵈ. a letter
from my uncle James.   Another from Thomas Wadsworth of
Long buckby.   blessed be yᵉ Lord for all Instances of his
favour to me

— 2.   Lords day I preached per totum from Ezek. 38: 11.
Laboured under considerable difficulty in speaking.

— 3.   This day not well   this day died Richard Lord of
Weathersfield

— 5.   This day a publick Thanksgiving throughout Connecticutt.
preached from phil. 3. 1.   at night married James Bicknel of
Ashford and Deborah Cook of Hartford

— 9.   Lords day I preached A:M. at the N:M: from 2 thes. 2. 14.
and P.M. Mʳ. Morison preached for me from numb. 22. 6.

— 12.   This day returned from Farmington found my family well
Laus Deo.   how Good art thou o God and how gracious.   yᵉ
Councel sat in this Town

13.   .   .   .   Mʳ. Beauchamp died this day

— 14.   This day Study.   .   .   .   this I suppose is my birth.   o
monument of mercies   has god spared me thus long   wᵗ
little fruit have I borne

— 15.   This day study &ᶜ.   Mʳ. John Beauchamp, who died yᵉ 13ᵗʰ
Instant was this day interred

16.   Lords day I preached pr. totum from Luk 15. 3. 4. 5. 6. 7.
cold weather nil remarkable

— 23.   Lords day I preached A: M: from luk. 15. 3. 4. 5. 6. 7. and
P.M. from luk. 14. 11. 18   .   .   .   o yᵗ God would bless his
word tho' sown in much weakness

-- 24.   rainy weather.   this day interred a daughter of Daniel
Bunce wᵉ died on Saturday Last

— 25.   This day in visiting yᵉ sick &ᶜ.   John Shepherd had a son
born.   her safe delivery apprehended an immediate answer to
prayer.   may my faith be strengthened

26.   .   .   yᵉ general assembly met here, little done

-- 28.   .   .   .   nil remarkable occurs.   Saving yᵗ there is a very
great flood of yᵉ great river.   rarely one so big in yᵉ Spring

— 30.   Lords day I preached A:M: .   .   .   and P.M. Mʳ. Morison preached for me   .   .   .   I spake with more ease and feel
better in health to day than I have done upon yᵉ Sabbath for
some time

December 1740

Dec. 3.   Study &ᶜ.   Mʳ. Whitefields Journal & Sermons read to day.

a great flood, bigger than has bin for 30 years past　yᵉ General assembly adjourned.

— 7.　Lords day I preached　　　　a very rainy tempestuous day

— 8.　This day reading &ᶜ.　Whitefields Sermons, Laws Christian perfection.

— 9.　This day went to paquannack to yᵉ ordination there

— 10.　Mʳ. Tudor¹ ordained.　yᵉ Revᵈ. Mʳ. Marsh of Windsor preached from Eccles. 12: 4　The Revᵈ. Mʳ. Edwards prayed & gave yᵉ Charge yᵉ Revᵈ. Mʳ. Colton made yᵉ next prayer and yᵉ Revᵈ. Mʳ. Whitman of Hartford gave yᵉ Right hand of fellowship.

— 11.　This day returned home, cold weather, found my family well Laus Deo　Dealt with a friend for his fault, o yᵗ god would convince & reform him

— 12.　Uncle James here to-day.

— 14.　Lords day I preached pr totum from 1 Joh 2. 15.　a very cold day.

— 16.　Uncle Thomas here at night.　Snowy at night.

— 18.　Uncle Thomas went from hence in yᵉ afternoon: 2:45.　may he have a prosperous Journey home.

— 21.　Lords day preached and administred yᵉ Sacrament. . . . Laboured under great difficulty in speaking, o yᵗ god would appear for my help and give me health

— 23.　. . . finished a letter to Thomas Wadsworth at Long-buckby

— 24.　This day visiting yᵉ sick &ᶜ. a refreshing Conversation in yᵉ evening with one of my people

— 25.　Went to Weathersfield &ᶜ. nil remarkable, save yᵗ Isabel Spencer departed this life

— 26.　Isabel Spencer Interred in yᵉ evening.　Study.

— 28.　Lords day I preached A.M: at the new meeting from 1 Joh. 3. 9. & P.M. from heb. 9. 27. at my own meeting

— 29.　This day visiting yᵉ sick &ᶜ.　Conversation with a zealous &ᶜ.

— 31.　Met with the famous Mʳ. Whitefields life and read it.　but what is it.

---

¹ Rev. Samuel Tudor, born in Windsor March 8, 1704-5; grad. Y. C. 1728; preached awhile in Goshen, N. Y., then in Guilford, and was ordained as above Dec. 10, 1740, at Poquonock Society in the northwestern part of Windsor from which Rev. John Woodbridge had lately gone. He died Sept. 21, 1757.

January begins. [1741]

Jany. 1. . . . a new year begins   may I be more invigorated with the principles of a new life

— 4. Lords day preached per totum from rom. 10. 3. y⁰ wife of Nathˡˡ. Goodwin Interred

– 6. This day my people sledded wood for me, very cold weather

– 11. Lords day I preached A.M: & P.M. from rom. 10. 21. felt dull and heavy and indisposed in y⁰ forenoon, better afternoon, pray god to bless what was spoken agreeable to his will

– 14. Returned from Farmington, found my family safe Laus Deo. visited y⁰ aged Wid. Phelps

– 18. Lords day preached per totum from Ezek. 18. 31. Laboured under . . .

— 21. This day reading, visiting &⁰. at night went to a religious meeting where I found myself greatly refreshed[1]

— 22. Study &⁰. a lecture in y⁰ afternoon at Mʳ. Whitmans meeting, he preached from 2. pet. 3. 18.

24. This day in Study. finished my preparations before night. a great Comfort to be seasonably prepared for the Sabbath, I pray god I may always be so.

— 25. Lords day I preached per totum from rom. 13:11. Laboured under . . .

– 26. This day reading Evans on y⁰ christian temper &⁰. &⁰. Snowy stormy day

— 28. . . . Nabbys birth day. Laus Deo.

— 31. Certain news of y⁰ arrival of Lord Cathcart with English fleet at the West Indies

February begins

Feby. 1. Lords day I preached   went thro' my work with great difficulty

— 3. This day Stormy. no association met according to appointment . . .

— 4. Lecture Mʳ. Whitman preached from heb. 4. 13. very cold, I was forced to leave the meeting house by reason of great pain &⁰.

— 7. This day indisposed, heard y⁰ Lord Cathcart is dead[2]

---

[1] See Mr. Wadsworth's statement about the origin of these meetings later under date of May 11. They appear to have been neighborhood gatherings for conference and prayer. See 18th of February following, et seq.

[2] Lord Cathcart died Dec. 20, 1740. His death was probably a turning point in the fortunes of what proved to be a most disastrous and humiliating expedition from which scarce one in ten came home alive.

— 8. Lords day not able to go out M'. Whitman preached for me
A: M. and M'. Morison P.M.

— 9. The Emperor of Germany and Zarina of Muscovy both died
in Octob'. Last

— 10. This day writing &ᶜ. M'. Russel here, yesterday yᵉ Governour recᵈ. a letter from Admiral Vernon.

— 12. This day cold. better as to my indisposition. o yᵗ god
would direct me in yᵉ difficulties in my work, and especially in
directing dark and wandering Souls

— 13. o Lord have mercy upon me in how much darkness and
difficulty have I spent this day, Send forth yᵉ light and help of
thy holy Spirit into my heart

— 14. This day in study, better in health of body and I hope
something better in mind. . . . this or yᵉ night following
'dreamt yᵗ I saw Capt. N-b-r-y unhappy

— 15. Lords day M' Newel[1] preached A.M. . . . and P.M. I
preached myself from Eph. 4. 1. and thank god that enabled
me to preach with so much ease and freedom.

— 17. This day visited and discoursed a poor mulatto who seemed
to be Concerned

— 18. This day not well; some edifying Conversation, present in
yᵉ evening at John Shepherds at yᵉ religious meeting there.

— 19. Nil remarkable occurs. yᵉ Govern'. recᵈ. Letters from yᵉ
D. of New Castle and from yᵉ Adm'ʸ. board

— 22. Lords day preached A:M: at M'. Whitmans meeting . . .
and P.M. from Isai. 55. 3. at my own. . . .

— 23. This day . . . nil remarkable occurs. Saving yᵉ lamentable story of El: Sh: being delivered of a child, lays it to M'.
M. o times. o manners

— 26. This day Consulting &ᶜ. about yᵉ lamentable case of M'. M:
in yᵉ afternoon a lecture M'. Whitman of Farmington preached
. . . at night I married Richard Seymour and Elizabeth
Wadsworth

March begins.

Mch. 1. Lords day I preached per totum from Jam. 48. and ad-

---

[1] Rev. Samuel Newell, born in Farmington (Southington district) March 1, 1714; grad. Y. C.
1739; just at this date studying theology and probably licensed. His preaching at this time and
point of experience at Mr. Wadsworth's church is one instance among many discoverable in these
notes of Mr. Wadsworth's habit of availing himself of the services of very young ministers; perhaps
for their encouragement as well as for his own need. Mr. Newell was preaching in East Hartford
a few months later than this, but was not ordained till Aug. 12, 1747, at New Cambridge (now
Bristol) where he continued in the pastorate till his death Feb. 10, 1789. He was a "New Light"
in his period.

ministred yᵉ Sacrament   went thro' my work with great difficulty . . .

— 2. This day . . . dreamt at night I saw S. O. from yᵉ West Indies, runaway &ᶜ.

— 4. This day . . . in yᵉ afternoon went to visit Mʳ. Woodbridge, found him hopefully mending

— 5. This day . . . went to Weathersfield to a lecture, Mʳ. Backus preached from Col. 1. 19.

— 8. Lords day I preached from rom. 13. 12. per totum, baptized Elizabeth daughter of Mʳ. Samᵘ. Talcot

— 9. This day drew a proclamation for a fast,[1] visited &ᶜ.

— 11. This day kept a fast I preached A:M. from Joel 1. 18. 19 . . . and Mʳ. Whitman P.M.   . . o y God would hear our cry and relieve us

— 12. . . . Mʳ. Pomroy[2] preached from luk. 11 at Mʳ. Whitmans meeting. this day I paied Danᵘ. Brown 56 pounds in money on accᵗ. of my bond and Jos: Skinner £5 for wheat

— 15. Lords day I preached A:M: . . . at Mʳ. Whitmans meeting and P.M: . at my own.   Laboured under . . .

— 19. This day Study &ᶜ. cool weather   what is to come I know not

— 20. Study. under great perplexity. o yᵗ god would direct me to a text for tomorrow

— 22. Lords day I preached A:M. from John 6. 44 and P.M: from Eph. 5. 6. Abig: Graham made Confession . .   & owned yᵉ Covenant

— 24. This day study &ᶜ. preached at night at a young mens meeting at Madam Woodbridges.[3]

— 25. This day . . . some young people here to discourse about yᵉ great affairs of yʳ Souls

— 26. paied £8. 10ˢ. o to Daniell Brown indorsed it on yᵉ bond.

---

[1] Doubtless the proclamation for the Public Fast issued by his father-in-law, the Governor, and observed on the 8th of April following. The fast spoken of on March 9th (the day after this entry) was plainly a local one, observed by the churches uniting in it of their own motion, as was a not unfrequent custom at the period.

[2] Rev. Benjamin Pomroy, born in Suffield, Nov. 19, 1704; grad. Y. C. 1733; ordained at Hebron, Dec. 16, 1735. An active sympathizer with Whitefield and the new measures; according to Rev. Absalom Peters "a most thundering preacher of the new light order"; one of the trustees of Dartmouth College, from which institution he received the degree of D. D. in 1774. He died at Hebron Dec. 22, 1784, aged 80 years. There will be occasion to refer to him hereafter.

[3] This meeting of "you·g men" at the house of the widow of the old pastor indicates a form of religious effort not as modern as some have supposed; as will also a "boys" meeting to be noticed a little later.

Parmenas King received it. at night preached at M'. Churches
from 1. King: 18: 21. ye great river continues froze. Yesterday horses passed over on ye Ice and this day men passed over
on foot.

— 27. . . . John Andrews died.

— 28. This day Study &^c. M'. Lamb¹ here in ye afternoon. John
Andrews Interred at night

— 29. Lords day M'. Lamb preached A.M. from Joh. 7. 37 and
P.M. from act. 10. 43. pleasant weather

— 31. This day little done. how heavily do I drive, o y^t god
would give me health. strength &^c.

        April begins

Apl. 1. This day little study. M'. Brainard² here, preached at
night at a meeting at ye State House

— 2. . . . . a lecture ye afternoon at M'. Whitmans Meeting
house. M'. Lockwood preached from psal. 119. 60.

— 3. This day indisposed &^c. at night privately discoursed and
reproved T. T. for his Intemperance, hope and pray y^t it may
be to good effect.

— 5. Lords day M'. Burr of Worcester preached for me. . . .
P.M. I preached for M'. Whitman. . . . This day admin-
istred ye Sacrament and Richard Goodman, Diostheus
Humphrys, Samuel Andrews, Mary Butler, Dorothy Skinner,
Hannah Skinner, Hannah Shepherd and Sarah Shepherd were
admitted to full Communion with ye chh.

— 6. Little Study. at night spent some time at a meeting of
little boys, prayed with y^m, and read a discourse to y^m from
those words in 2 Epist. Joh. 4. they behaved with reverence
and decency

— 8. a day of publick fasting & prayer, A: M: I preached from
Jer. 5. 25. and M'. Whitman P: M: from Joel 2. 12. 13

— 9. . . . . . nil remarkable save a Story y^t Admiral Vernon
has destroyed 16 frenchmen of war. . . .

— 12. Lords day I preached p'. totum from Joh: 6. 44. Laboured
under . . . Susanna Gross & Abigail Benton owned y^e
Covenant

¹ Rev. Joseph Lamb, born in Stonington, Conn., about 1790; grad. Y. C. 1717; ordained
Dec. 6, 1717, at Mattituck, L. I.; began to preach in the Fourth Church in Guilford in 1735; went
thence to New Jersey; died at Barking Ridge in that State July 28, 1749. A trustee of the College
of New Jersey and Moderator of the Synod of New York in 1748.

² Rev. Nehemiah Brainard of Eastbury in Glastonbury; an older brother of Rev. David
Brainard the missionary; born at Haddam Feb. 20, 1712; grad. Y. C. 1732; ordained at Eastbury
Jan. 23, 1740; died Nov. 9, 1742. An earnest "New Light."

— 13. This day freemans meeting. M'. Whitman preached from
rom. 13. 3. and Capt. Marsh and Capt. Jos: Pitkin were
Chosen Deputies.

— 15. This day under great concern for a poor friend, at night
M'. Edwards' of Northampton preached a lecture at M'. Whitmans meeting from Matt. 11: 12

16. . . . M'. Whitman preached a lecture at night at my
meeting from Isai.

— 18. This day Study. light on M'. Whitefields Journal of his
progress in New–England &'. Scarcely yet know w'. to think
of y' man I pray God to direct me in y' way of my duty

19. Lords day preached A.M. for M'. Whitman . . . and
P.M. from rom. 10. 3. Laboured under great difficulty in
speaking by reason of a Cough . . .

— 21. . . . M'. Meacham' of Coventry here, high water a
flood.

— 22. This day went to Wintonbury &' at night a lecture M'.
Meacham preached from psal. 110. 3

— 23. This day visited a sick person &'. met with some trouble
from over hot [illegible] o god Direct me. . .   M'. Wheelock' preached at night from act. 7. 51

¹ Rev. Jonathan Edwards, son of Rev. Timothy of East Windsor, and grandson of Richard
Edwards of the First Church of Hartford. Born at East Windsor Oct. 5, 1703; grad. Y. C. 1720;
declined calls to North Haven and Bolton; ordained at Northampton Feb. 15, 1726-7; dismissed in
June, 1750; removed to Stockbridge in 1751; chosen President of the College of New Jersey in
1757; inaugurated to that office Feb. 16, 1758; died of inoculation for small-pox March 22, 1758.
"The most eminent graduate of Yale College, the greatest theologian of his century, the ablest
metaphysician of the period between Leibnitz and Kant." Dexter's *Yale Graduates*, p. 218. His
text at this lecture, " From the days of John the Baptist until now the kingdom of heaven suffereth
violence and the violent take it by force," obviously indicates that his discourse was keyed to the
religious interest now prevailing.

² Rev. Joseph Meacham, born at Enfield; grad. H. C. 1710; settled at Coventry Oct., 1714;
died Dec. 16, 1752.

³ Rev. Eleazer Wheelock, born at Windham, April 29, 1711; grad. Y. C. 1733; ordained at
the North Parish in Lebanon, June 4, 1735. An active participator in the Great Awakening movement, coöperating with Pomroy and James Davenport, which last named minister was his wife's
half-brother. He took boys into his house for instruction (among others the Indian boy who became
the celebrated Rev. Samson Occom) and thus gradually established an institution which came to be
known about 1755 as "Moor's Indian Charity School." This enterprise developing and finding
European patrons, especially by the aid of Occom who went to England for the purpose, it was
deemed best to expand the institution to collegiate proportions, and, as Governor Benning Wentworth offered a tract of land in aid, the College was planted in New Hampshire and named Dartmouth College from the young Earl of that title who had been one of its benefactors. Dr. Wheelock, who had received his degree from Edinburgh University, was dismissed from Lebanon, April
15, 1770, and removed to Hanover, N. H., continuing in the arduous duties of his new calling as
President, Professor of Divinity, and Pastor of the College Church till his death, April 24, 1779.
He was of course a strenuous "New Light." He published successive "Narratives" of the state
of his school, and other pamphlets and discourses, and left many manuscripts, some of which have
been published since his death.

— 26. Lords day preached per totum from gal. 6. 15. Laboured under . . .

— 29. This day Laboured under indisposition &ᶜ. o yᵗ god would direct and assist me in yᵉ way of my duty with respect to Anne Williamson

— 30. This day indisposed. Mʳ. Colton preached a Lecture for me from rom. 9. 23. I pray god to bless him.

      May begins

May 1. . . . Mʳ. Woodbridge here at night.

— 3. Lords day I preached . . . and administred yᵉ Sacrament. Laboured under indisposition but not so much as on yᵉ last Sabbath . . . Ozias Goodwin, Stephen Hopkins and Anne Humphrys admitted to Communion. Nath: Brace, Abig: Farnsworth & Susannah Butler owned yᵉ Covenant. Jerusha Farnsworth and Reb: Barnard propounded to own • yᵉ Covt.

— 4. . . . yᵉ wife of John Brace who died Last night buried this day

— 7. . . . at night preached a lecture &ᶜ from 2 Cor. 6. 2

— 10. Lords day I preached from psal. 68. 21 per totum. Laboured under difficulties by reason of my Cough and weakness, yet was enabled to speak with some life and power . . . Sus: Gross and patience Marshall propounded for adm: to Com: &ᶜ.

— 11. This day visiting &ᶜ. . . . at night felt better more clear in my mind enjoyed Comfort, o yᵗ god would . . . save this Town my congregⁿ. in particular from envying strife and Confusion.¹

— 13. This day a letter from my good friend Mʳ. Sergeant by his Lieut. Aaron ² &ᶜ. This day comes news yᵗ yᵉ English have

---

¹ This is the first distinct expression in this diary of apprehension respecting the now rapidly increasing signs of strife and division which followed the first stages of the Great Awakening, and which turmoiled to a greater or less extent almost every town in Massachusetts and Connecticut. The churches and ministers were divided about the wisdom of the new measures ; about the signs of conversion, about the expediency of the itineracy which assumed sudden popularity and sometimes pretentiousness. Old landmarks seemed adrift ; and in almost every congregation (even of congregations disposed to cling to old ways and to hold to their old ministers) there were found individuals, and often in considerable numbers, who denounced established methods as antiquated, settled ministers as idle lords over God's heritage, and who clamored for the presence and the excitement of peripatetic revivalists and the scenes which often accompanied their fervent and sometimes tumultuous meetings.

² Lieutenant Aaron was an Indian of the Housatonic tribe by the name of Umpacheene. In furtherance of the mission enterprise among these Indians Governor Belcher, who was much interested in the success of the endeavor, conferred commissions sometime in 1734 upon two of them, who were known respectively as Captain Konkapot and Lieutenant Umpacheene. When, later, in 1735, a church came to be formed, and Mr. Sergeant was ordained pastor, these two Indians among others were received as members, and baptized with more familiar names. Capt. Konkapot on

taken ye forts at Carthagena and are bombarding ye Town [1]

— 14. This day Election. Gov, Dep: Gov: and assistants as in ye year past. M^r. Sol: Williams [2] preached from Joshua 1: 7. under some difficulty this day by reason of ye Itinerant preachers.

— 15. M^r. Mills [3] preached two sermons.

- 17. Lords day I preached A.M: from Matt. 22. 39, and P.M: M^r. Rector Clap preached for me from John 3. 3. a good sermon I pray god to bless it to me and all y^t heard it.

— 20. This day went to Farmington with Rector Clap . . . much Talk and running after new preachers in this Town to-day. o lord direct me I pray and ye other ministers of this Town in ye way of y^r duty.

-- 22. M^r. Mills preached P: M: from Zech. 14. 6. 7.

— 23. This day Study &^{c}. examined Jno. Sherwin for admission &^{c}. found him to reserved but I hope a good bias in his heart towards god

— 24. Lords day I preached . . . found assistance and Courage more than usual, hope god is restoring my health blessed be his name

-- 25. This day pray^d. at court. god gave me presence of mind and utterance thanks to him, . . . some refreshing Conversation with M^r. Kent, [4] may our hearts be more and more united, visited at night by ye Ingenious M^r. Brown may god

Nov. 2, 1735, was baptized "John," and his wife "Mary"; and on Nov. 16th, Lieutenant Umpacheene and his wife were baptized "Aaron" and "Hannah." Lieut. Aaron was a useful man in his tribe and in the mission; and though at sometimes overtaken with the Indians' easily besetting sin, a love for the strong drink which unscrupulous white men put in his way, lived on the whole a creditable Christian life. Of his wife Mr. Sergeant often spoke warmly as a virtuous and valuable woman.

[1] Carthagena is the capital and chief town of Colombia, South America. The fleet under Admiral Vernon gained a victory over the harbor defences; but the land attack which followed, under General Wentworth, suffered disastrous repulse, resulting in the abandonment of the siege, as Mr. Wadsworth afterward has occasion to note.

[2] Rev. Solomon Williams of Lebanon, who preached the Election Sermon on this occasion, was born at Hatfield, Mass., Jan., 1701; grad. H. C. 1719; ordained at Lebanon, Dec. 5, 1722. He was one of the most eminent men of his period; a cousin of Jonathan Edwards with whom he was brought into controversy in the Half-Way Covenant discussion. He was inclined to the "Old Light" position in the Whitefieldian troubles. He died Feb. 29, 1776, in the fifty-fourth year of his honorable ministry.

[3] Rev. Jedidiah Mills of Ripton (now Huntington); born at Windsor March 12, 1697; grad. Y. C. 1722; ordained at Ripton, Feb. 12, 1723-4. An ardent supporter of Whitefield, and the "New Light" party, and himself an itinerating evangelist. He continued in his pastoral relation nearly fifty-two years, dying "greatly lamented," Jan. 10, 1776.

[4] Probably Rev. Elisha Kent of Newtown. Born at Suffield, Mass., July 9, 1704; grad. Y. C. 1729; ordained at Newtown, Sept. 27, 1732. He was dismissed from this parish, after a period of considerable disquietude, Feb. 25, 1742-3, and installed over a church at Philippi, New York, where he continued in office till his death in July, 1776.

bless him, greater serenity of mind this day than usual, courage and boldness . . .

— 26. . . . Visited by a woman Concerned about ye times, by
another under great Concern, o god be mercifull to her

— 28. This day prayed at Court, went to ye West Division,
preached from 2 Cor. 6. 2. at night married George Alcot and
Dorothy Skinner. returned home Laus Deo

— 29. This day was Interred ye wife of Caleb Bull

— 30. This day study Laboured under bodily indisposition,
visited by M^r. Pratt. nil remarkable occurs. . . .

— 31. Lords day I preached A:M: . . . and P.M: M^r. Morison preached for me . . . Jerusha Farnsworth and Ben:
Barnard owned ye Covenant Ed: Cadwell and wife propounded
for admis: to Communion with ye chh.

Sometime in ye winter past our people began to set up weekly
meetings for religious exercises. A concern for y^r souls prevailed among many, and y^t continues, they have run into some
irregularities and disorders and still continue to do. I pray
God to overrule all for his own glory and ye Good of Souls,
and to direct me in ye way of my duty and to assist me to a
faithfull discharge of it

  June 1741

June 1. . . . ye news comes y^t Carthagena is taken

— 2. This day went to Farmington to ye association.[1] Saw my
friends in usual health

— 3. Lecture at Farmington M^r. Bissell preached from heb. 7.
25. returned home found my family well Laus Deo.

— 4. This day a lecture in ye afternoon M^r. Bissel preached from
1 Joh. 3. 2.

— 6. . . . discoursed with one y^t has bin a great Sinner, who
I hope is returning to god, god grant he may be a true penitent, and y^t I may be guided so as to guide him aright.

— 7. Lords day I preached . . . and administred ye Sacra-

---

[1] The Association at this session (Mr. Wadsworth being Scribe) passed and put on record the
following Resolve:

"Whereas there appears a general awakening and Religious Concern among many of our
people and a disposition to hear the gospel preached more frequently than it has usually been;
which awakening and religious Concern if duly cultivated and directed may have a very happy Influence to promote Religion and the Saving Conversion of Souls: Wee therefore Judge it expedient
that the ministers of this association, in such Convenient Vicinities or neighborhoods as they think
proper, set up frequent Lectures and preach alternately for each other, and that they Labour to
open, explain and Inculcate the great and important doctrines of Christianity."

ment. this day Edward Cadwell and his wife, John Skinner,
Susan: Gross, Pat: Marshal, Matthew Bidwell and Mary Butler
were admitted to Communion with yᵉ Church, this day went
thro' my work with greater boldness ease and courage than
usual, tho' Laboured under much bodily weakness.

— 8. Visited M. Woodbridge. I pray God to heal him restore
him to health and usefulness again

— 10. This day went to a lecture at the west division Mʳ. Marsh
preached from psal. 34. 8.

— 14. Lords day I preached per totum from 2 Cor. 5. 20. went
thro' my work with less difficulty than at many other times
. . . this day 96 year was Naseby fight

— 15. This day wrote a letter to go to Doctʳ. Doddridge, another
to Boston.

— 16. This day catechised children at Jonathan Butlers.

— 17. This day went to Wintonbury, preached a lecture from luk.
3. 7. . . . Spake with freedom blessed be god . . .

— 18. This day some refreshing Conversation with Mʳ. K. and H:
. . . at night came news that yᵉ Spaniards had landed a
1000 men on Long Island had burnt yᵉ town of Rockway, 30
sail of vessels said to be there

— 19. This day 2 troops of horse went to New-London &ᶜ. . . .
Lord guard our Coasts, Save us from our Enemies hands.

— 21. Lords day I preached pʳ. totum from James 3. 17. Baptized
Daniel yᵉ Son of Daniel Badger Junʳ. in yᵉ afternoon while I
was at meeting my wife was safely delivered of a Son[1] Thanks
be to god for it. o Lord I give him up unto thee bless him, o
Lord, I pray and make him a blessing. . . .

— 22. paied Billy Keith £4. 4s. o. remains due 4. 11. 8.

— 23. . . . Mʳ. Whitman returned from his Journey, blessed
be God yᵗ has returned him. Bellamy[2] yᵉ preacher here, made

---

[1] Daniel. The boy lived to be only about nine years old, dying Nov. 3, 1750.

[2] Rev. Joseph Bellamy of Bethlem; born in Cheshire Feb. 20, 1718-19; grad. Y. C. 1735; ordained at Bethlem April 2, 1740. He entered earnestly into the Whitefieldian movement and became one of the most powerful if not sensational of the itinerating preachers. There is reason to believe he subsequently took a more conservative view of the proprieties of that episode of his history. He was a man of domineering temper and did not always use kind or Christian methods in his opposition to those who at this period differed from him in opinion as to what the cause of religion asked for. He was unquestionably the ablest preacher in Connecticut in his day; and somewhat later than this Great Awakening era was one of the most prolific and able of controversial pamphleteers. His True Religion Delineated, published in 1750, rises to the hight of an important treatise, which was republished in Edinburgh in 1788, and had, both in England and America, a wide circulation. He became teacher of theology to many young men; was invited to a pastorate in New York in 1753 and 54; received the degree of D.D. from the University of Aberdeen in 1768; preached the Election Sermon May 13, 1762; died March 6, 1790.

a disturbance here.   I pray God direct me in yᵉ way of my
duty in this difficult day.   .   .   .

— 24. Lord teach me how to bear up under reproach.   Sanctify
all my troubles unto me.

— 25. This day . . .   Mʳ. Gould¹ of Stratford here . . .
I thank God for his goodness to my wife, in giving her so
much comfort and ease   .

— 26. This day study &ᶜ.   o Lord direct me to a text for
tomorrow Instant

— 28. Lords day I preached A:M: from Jam. 3: 17. and P.M:
from heb. 10. 31.   .   .   .   Laboured under weakness . . .

— 30.   .   .   .   read Walters sermon, entitled yᵉ thots of yᵉ heart
best evidence of a spiritual state, a good sermon.
          July begins.

July 1.   .   .   .   at night conversed with one very zealous, I pray
God to save him from enthusiasm and wickedness

— 2. a lecture at Mʳ. Whitmans meeting   Mʳ. Whitman of Farmington preached from 2. Cor. 5. 15. discoursed with a delin-
quent I pray God humble him and bring him to repentence.

— 5. Lords day I preached pʳ. totum from Eph. 2. 13, administred
yᵉ Sacrament. admitted Amy Richards into yᵉ chh. . . .

— 6. This day writing, visiting, Conversation &ᶜ. I pray God
direct me in yᵉ important affair I have discoursed of this night.
Lord give us Love, peace & purity

— 7. This day . . .   Mʳ. White here. Long discourse abᵗ yᵉ
religious affairs of yᵉ present times, o God direct me I pray
thee, give me to understand my duty and Courage intrepidly
to discharge it.

— 8. This day went to Farmington Mʳ. E. Whitman preached a
lecture from Mark 8: 36, much concern among some people
there.

— 9. . . .   returned home found my family in safety Laus Deo,
     .   .   .

— 10. Yᵉ melancholly news of our forces drawing of from Carthagena with great Loss is Confirmed. . . .

— 12. This day preached A:M: at Mʳ. Whitmans meeting . . .
and P.M: . . .   at my own. . . .   Laboured under great
weakness. o Lord help me

<hr />

¹ Probably Rev. Ebenezer Gould, H. C. 1723; ordained at Greenwich, New Jersey, 1728;
and a few weeks later than Mr. Wadsworth's entry (viz. Sept., 1740,) to be installed over a parish
in Southold, L. I. Dismissed from there in 1747, he was installed at Middlefield, Oct. 10th of the
same year, from whence again he was dismissed in 1756. He died at East Granville, Mass., in
1778 or 9.

— 13. This day reading Shepherds Sincere Convert [1] &ᶜ. at night married John Tilly and Martha Burnham.

— 14. . . . Some pleasant Conversation with Mʳ. A. Woodbridge.

— 15. Lecture. Mʳ. Whitman of Farmington preached from Matt. 11. 28. a good sermon

16. This day . . . visited Mʳ. Woodbridge I pray God Look in Mercy upon him. . . .

— 19. Lords day I preached A:M: from heb. 4. 7. lat. pᵗ. and P.M. from Gal. 4: 18 on religious zeal I pray god I might be possessed of it, influenced & acted by it and my people also, and yᵗ wᵗ I have preached might be recᵈ. by & blessed to yᵐ so far as is agreeable to thy will.

— 20. Uncle Thomas here, and at night Mʳ. Hunn

— 21. This day in Conversation with good Mʳ. Hunn, I pray god bless him and me

— 23. This day went to yᵉ West Division preached a Lecture from 1. Joh. 3. 9. o God bless thy word . . .

— 24. Went to Wintonbury to see brother Bissel, but he was not at home returned safely Laus Deo.

— 26. Lords day I preached   laboured under some difficulty in speaking

— 27. This day Reading Bailys History of Brownists, independents &ᵉ. afternoon visited Mʳ. Woodbridge.

— 29. . . . the sorrowful news of yᵉ death of Capt. Newberry arrives [2] . . .

— 30. a lecture at Mʳ. Whitmans meeting Mʳ. Colton preached from Eph. 2. 13. a private meeting at night at yᵉ governours August begins

Aug. 1. This day Study &ᶜ. Mʳ. Colton here. Theodore Woodbridge returned from yᵉ West Indies. this week arrived yᵉ news of yᵉ death of my good friend Capt. Newberry. When mine acquaintances are hid in darkness may I prepare for my own great change.

— 2. Lord day I preached . . . and administred yᵉ Sacrament, and recᵈ. Jemima Brace into yᵉ chh.

— 4. This day visited Mʳ. Woodbridge &ᶜ. Mʳ. Eliot here.

— 5. This day went to Farmington preached a lecture from luk. 3. 7 & returned Home Laus Leo

---

[1] Shepherd's *Sincere Convert* was one of several books belonging to the previous century which the newly awakened religious interest in New England caused to be republished and extensively read. Among these books to which Mr. Wadsworth refers, besides this of Shepherd's, was Hooker's *Poor Doubting Christian Drawn to Christ*, and Giles Firmin's *Real Christian*.

[2] *Ante*, p. 53.

— 6. . . . at night preached at yᵉ Govern, something Strait-
ened, I pray God deliver me from a blameable fear of man

— 7. recᵈ. a letter from Mʳ. Clap. . .

— 9. Lords day I preached A:M: . . . at Mʳ. Whitmans
meeting and P.M: Mʳ. Morison preached for me . . . Sarah
Jones owned yᵉ Covenant and was baptized . . .

— 10. at night saw Lieutⁿᵗ. Ward returned from the Spanish
Expedition.

— 11. Association met at Mʳ. Woodbridges entered into Consider-
ation of our religious affairs &ᶜ. Came into various resolves [1]

— 12. a lecture yᵉ East Side Mʳ. Whitman of F. preached from
Isai. 32. 15 yᵉ assoⁿ. broke up

— 15. This day little study. Laboured under considerable indisposition. yesterday yᵉ post brought us an accᵗ of Davenports [2]
boisterous management at Stonington.

---

[1] These "resolves" so distinctly indicate the difficulties which really right-hearted men like
Mr. Wadsworth were encompassed by, that they must be quoted.

"The following questions were considered and Resolved.

1. Whether it be not at this time in an Especial manner needful for the ministers studi-
ously to endeavour to maintain peace and unity among themselves and in the churches. Agreed
upon by the Association to be needful.

2. Whether it be not contrary to the mind of Christ and destructive to the peace of the
Churches for a minister or ministers to preach in a parish or parishes where there is a settled minister or ministers, without the desire, liberty or consent of such settled minister or ministers. Agreed
in the affirmative. Act. 20. 28. 1 pet. 4. 15. 1 Cor. 14. 40.

3. Whether any weight is to be Laied upon those screachings, cryings out, faintings and
convulsions, which sometimes attend the terrifying Language of some preachers and others as evi-
dences of or necessary to a genuine Conviction of sin, humiliation and preparation for Christ.
Agreed in the Negative, as also that there is no weight to be Laied upon those Visions or visional
discoveries by some of Late pretended to, of Heaven or Hell, or the body or blood of Christ, viz. as
represented to the eye of the body.

4. Whether the assertion of some Itinerant preachers that the pure gospel and especially
the doctrines of Regeneration and Justification by faith are not preached in these Churches: their
Rash censuring the body of our Clergy as Carnal and unconverted men and notoriously unfit for
their office is not such a sinfull and Scandalous violation of the fifth and ninth Commandments of
the Moral Law as ought to be testified against, and such preachers not be admitted to preach in our
pulpits and parishes until they have as publickly manifested their repentence as they have given
out their false and scandalous assertions. Agreed in the affirmative.

5. Whether the pronouncing persons Converted so hastily and upon so slender grounds as
some do, be not exceeding dangerous. Agreed in the affirmative.

6. What is to be tho't of the religious Concern that is at this day so general in the Land?

Wee trust and believe that the holy Spirit is moving upon the hearts of many, that many
have received of Late a Saving Change in many of our Towns, and hope and desire that thro'
grace many may yet be Savingly wrought upon. But there are sundry things attending this work
which are unscriptural and of a dangerous Tendency ; and therefore advise both ministers and people in their Respective Stations cautiously to guard against everything of that nature. And wee
for ourselves seriously profess our willingness to encourage the good work of God's Spirit agreeably
to his word to the utmost of our power."

These resolutions were passed at an unusually full meeting of the Association, sixteen members being present.

[2] Rev. James Davenport, the most extravagant of the itinerating evangelists of the period.
Born in Stamford in 1716 or 1717 ; grad. Y. C. 1732 ; preached awhile in New Jersey ; ordained at
Southold, L. I., Oct. 26, 1738. With Rev. Jonathan Barber, before mentioned in this Diary, he

— 16. Lords day Laboured under indisposition I went not forth : in yᵉ forenoon yᵉ Congᵐ. both met at Mʳ. Whitmans meeting in yᵉ afternoon Mʳ. Whitman preached for me. rainy weather

— 18. This day recᵈ. a letter from Mʳ. Worthington . . .

— 19. This day a lecture Mʳ. Bissel preached from Isai. 55. 7. at night visited Obad: Spencer, sick prayed with him &ᶜ.

— 21. . . . Uncle Thomas here under infirmity. Obadiah Spencer Senʳ. died

— 22. Ob: Spencer Interred as my earthly friends fail I pray God to take me up.

— 23. Lords day I preached pr totum from act. 16. 31 relieve me I pray under my difficulties . . .

— 25. This day at Farmington with my friends Mʳ. Whitman preached from prov. 8. 32. returned home found my family well, praised be god. O Lord I pray appear for yᵉ help of thy ministers & chhs. guide me in yᵉ way of my duty under yᵉ present difficult situation of affairs, & give me strength and courage faithfully to perform it.

— 26. This day went to yᵉ West division to Lecture Mʳ. Whitman preached from heb. 2. 3. . . .

— 27. This day in Conversation &ᶜ. at night preached a lecture to yᵉ youth

— 30. Lords day I preached per totum from 2. tim. 1: 13.

— 31. Last night died and this day was Interred John yᵉ Son of Timothy Biggelow. Visited Mʳ. Woodbridge. found him not worse.

    Sept begins

Sept. 1. This day yᵉ Court Super. sat here. great divisions and Contentions seems to be arising in some Towns.

— 2. This day visiting, discourse &ᶜ. prospect of our religious affairs Looks melancholly. yᵉ great awakening &ᶜ. seems to be degenerating into Strife and faction.

— 4. This day prayed at Court. discoursed with Capt. Oz. P. abᵗ. our religious affairs a Long time, ye Lord bless him and direct me.

— 6. Lords day I preached . . . and administred yᵉ Sacrament. Laboured under great dullness, difficulty of speaking, inward weakness &ᶜ· o Lord bless my weak endeavours.

traversed a chief part of Long Island, and in July, 1741, he started on another and more notorious journey, characterized by denunciation of the ministers of almost every place as unconverted men, indulgence in the most violent language and bodily behavior, and encouragement of the wildest outcries and ecstacies of terror or delight in his hearers. There will be occasion to refer to him hereafter.

— 9. Commencement at New-Haven. Davenport and Bellamy preached and Mills at night, great Confusion.

— 10. Much Confusion this day at New-Haven, and at night yᵉ most strange management and a pretence of religion yᵗ ever I saw.

— 11. Went to Stratford in yᵉ afternoon.

— 12. Went to Reading. weary &ᶜ.

— 13. preached pr. totum from gal. 6. 15.

— 14. Went to fairfield, nil remarkable

— 15. Came to New-Haven

— 16. returned home found my family well, Laus Deo

— 20. Lords day I preached A:M: for Mʳ. Whitman . . . and P.M: . . . at my own meeting. Mary Pratt owned yᵉ covenant

— 21. Visiting yᵉ sick &ᶜ. a time of great distress. 3 persons buried this day

— 22. . . . Rector Clap here at night

— 24. A day of fasting and prayer on accᵗ. of yᵉ distressing sickness among us. A.M. I preached from Job. 14. 10. & P.M. Mʳ. Whitman preached from mic. 6. 9.

— 27. Lords day I preached per totum from rom. 14. 17. . . .

— 30. This day went to yᵉ west division preached A:M: from Job 14: 10 & P.M. Mʳ. Whitman preached Mic. 6. 9. returned home found my family well Laus Deo. I pray God to direct me in my duty to my poor B. H. O Lord save him from ruin —

The religious stir yᵗ has bin amongst us seems to have had different effects, some I hope are reformed and Converted. others I fear are only turned from one sort of wickedness to another. divisions and Contentions seem to be arising among us I pray yᵗ god would mercifully Interpose and prevent them if it may consist with his holy will and pleasure, but if not to prepare me for his will and help me to do and suffer wᵗ he has appointed for me.

Itinerant preaching which some have gone into yᵉ practice of, is liked by some and greatly disliked by others; I know not but yᵗ they may have done good in some places, but I think in many places and Especially in this Town they have done a great deal of mischief. I think they have bin very influential of weaning of yᵉ religious impressions yᵗ were on yᵉ minds of our people, and Turning yᵐ to disputes, debates and quarrels, and wᵗ will be yᵉ event God only knows. The principle Itinerant preachers among us are Jed: Mills, Pomroy & Wheelock, some others young ministers are getting into y' way. Steady christians & y* most Judicious among ministers and people so far as I can Learn generally dislike these new things set afoot by these Itinerant preachers.

October 1741

Oct. 1. This day lecture M'. Colton preached . . .

— 2. . . . received a Letter from Doct' Doddridge Dated March 6. 1740/41. very kind and obliging. this day died Mary Farnsworth

— 3. This day . . . Mary Farnsworth Interred, y* Gov. sick

- 4. Lords day I preached per totum from heb 5. 9. adminis-tred y* Sacrament, had a Contribution for wid: Esther Mer-rel . . .

— 6. . . . Sickness prevails among us .   in y* night died Jos: Gilbert Jun'.

— 7. This day went to Windsor to y* Assoc".' M'. Colton preached from act. 16. 31. . . .

— 8. . . . y* Govern'. still very sick I pray God to spare his life in mercy to thy people if it may be. Jos: Gilbert Jun' In-terred. Gen". Court Sits at New-Haven.

— 9. This day Joseph Farnsworth died, a sickly time . . .

— 10. This day study, visiting y* sick &*. a time of great dis-tress. y* Govern'. exceeding sick, I pray God to heal him. not heard

— 11. Lords day. 15 minutes after 6 oclock in y* morning died my dear' father· Talcott, a pattern of piety, a good man and did good in our Israel, served his Country with faithfulness and to great acceptance in y* stations of a Justice, an assistant, a deputy Govern'. and then of Govern' successively, he was also a Judge of y* County Court, a Judge in y* Super' Court, and major of y* Regiment in y* County of II: for many years. he was made a Justice of peace in May 1705, of y* quorum in may 1706, and in may 1710 appointed major of y* regiment in y* County of Hartford. in may 1711 he was Chosen into y* Council, in may 1714 appointed Judge of y* County Court and

---

¹ This Association, obviously exercised about the flocking of the people after the Itinerating preachers, debated this question : —

"Whether it be not sinfull and scandalous for a person to forsake the preaching and admin-stration of his own Lawful Pastor and travel upon the Sabbath much further to another place of worship in order to hear some other minister ? "

To which question the Association put on record th's reply : "That for a person to do this under a pretense of going from an unconverted minister to hear a Converted minister, or pretend-ing that they get more good by the minister whom they go to hear, is altogether unwarrantable."

of yᵉ Court of probates. in Octobʳ 1723 was chosen Dep:
Governʳ. and in Oct. 1724 he was Chosen Governʳ.   while
an assistant he was one year a Judge in yᵉ Superior Court   he
continued Governʳ from yᵉ time of his being first Chosen to yᵉ
day of his death, was accepted by the multitude of his people.
O Lord sanctify this Loss to me and them.   He was in yᵉ 72ᵈ
year of his age [1]

— 12. This day visiting &ᶜ. nil remarkable   recᵈ a letter from
uncle James at night pʳ. Mʳ. Bicknel

— 13. This day was Interred my very honᵈ. father and dear friend
Governʳ. Talcott, a pattern of piety an eminently useful man
in his generation what a breach is made in yᵉ Government,
in yᵉ Town, and in our chh. its main pillar is fallen   o Lord
help me, sanctify this affliction I pray unto me, give me the
grace to bear it patiently,   now my father and mother has
forsaken me o Lord take me up, I pray

— 14. This day . . . Mʳ. Whitman of F. preached a Lecture
from Matt. 25. 21. gave Governʳ Talcott a good Character

— 16.   . . . news from boston a french war expected.

— 17. This day . . . died Susannah Spencer

— 18. Lords day I preached pʳ Totum from Act. 13. 36.
Laboured under . . . this day was Interred Susannah
Spencer and Jemima Brace.

— 20.   . . . reading in Doctʳ. Mathers direction to Candidates
for yᵉ ministry

— 21. This day went to Farmington lecture there. •Mʳ. E. Whitman preached from Isai. 42. . . . great talk &ᶜ. about religion. I wish there was much of it to be seen.

— 22. This day returned from Farmington found my family
alive Laus Deo. . . .

— 23. This day died James Lee.

— 24.   . . . James Lee interred

— 25. Lords day I preached pʳ. totum from Job. 5: 6. 7. . . .
o Lord help me   Save my people I pray from Contentions and
divisions

— 27. yᵉ mother of yᵉ familistical and antinomian opinions yᵗ distracted new England (about 1636, 1637 &ᶜ.) was yᵗ a christian
should not fetch any Evidence of his good state before god
from yᵉ sight of any inherent qualification in him, or from any
conditional promise made unto such qualification. hence

[1] Gov. Talcott was born Nov. 16, 1669.

sprung their revelations & monstrous opinions &ᶜ. Doctʳ. M.
Magn: Lib: 3ʳ pag. 87. visiting yᵉ sick &ᶜ.

— 28. . . . At night married Mʳ. Allan Mᶜ.Lean and Mᵐ
Susanna Beauchamp.

-- 29. Lecture in yᵉ afternoon Mʳ. Colton preached from Matt.
5. 26. at night Joseph Farnsworth and Mary Blin were
married

Novembʳ. Begins happy may it be

Nov. 1. Lords day I preached pr totum from Job: 12. 15. and administred yᵉ Sacrament. Laboured under great weakness, o
Lord help me.

— 2. Went to Windsor about the affairs of yᵉ General Consociation,[1] I pray God yᵗ it may be directed and Issue well. returned in Safety, Laus Deo

— 5. Publick Thanksgiving, preached from act. 26. 22. Cool
blustering weather . . I bless God yᵗ has preserved me
thro' another year.

— 8. Lords day I preached A:M: from Job. 5. 6. 7. at Mʳ. Whitmans meeting, and P.M at my own from rom. 8: 13. . . .

— 10. This day yᵉ Consociation met here to choose delegates to
attend yᵉ Genˡˡ Consociation to be convened at Guilford on yᵉ
24 Instant, & choose yᵉ Revᵈ. Mʳ. Samˡˡ Whitman, The Revᵈ.
Mʳ. Benjamᵉ Colton and yᵉ Revᵈ. Mʳ. Stephen Steel, and of yᵉ
messengers Capt: John Marsh Deacᵉ John Edwards & Capt:
Thomas Pitkin. I pray God to Direct & bless yᵐ

— 13. Uncle Thomas went from hence toward night

— 15. Lords day I preached from Col. 3: 16 per totum, Laboured
under great indisposition in yᵉ forenoon

— 16. . . . Save yᵉ people of my parish from Contention and
Confusion, reduce those yᵗ are wandering

— 18. Went to yᵉ West Division, preached a lecture from heb. 6.
4. 5. 6. returned home in Safety, Laus Deo . . .

— 20. . . . conversed at night with a zealous man I pray
God prevent his going astray, reduce him to yᵉ rules of sobriety
and truth.

---

[1] At the session of the General Assembly of October previous to this date a call for a General
Consociation of the churches in the Colony, to take into view the "unhappy misunderstandings
and divisions subsisting in this Colony, whereby the peace of our churches is much threatened,"
was legalized by the Assembly and its expenses assumed by the Colonial treasury. It was to meet
at Guilford, and "to consist of three ministers and three messengers from each particular consociation." This is historically (aside from any other significant features) a very interesting gathering;
as being, under whatsoever variation of name, Consociation or Convention, precisely the old-fash-
ioned and familiar Synod of New England history, and the last one to be called by civil authority.

— 22. Lords day I preached per totum from gal. 5. 22. 23. went thro' my work with less difficulty than at some times

— 23. Tim. yᵉ son of Caleb Spencer interred. pulled down yᵉ old house

— 24. This day rainy &ᶜ. our Delegates set out upon yʳ Journey to Guilford I pray God to prosper yʳ Journey, and preside in yᵉ Convention, & bring their Debates & Consultations to a happy Issue and Conclusion.

— 25. A lecture in yᵉ afternoon at Mʳ. Whitmans meeting. Mʳ. Marsh of Windsor preached from Matt. 3. 10.

— 26. Mʳ. Marsh preached a lecture A:M: from Hos: 13. 13. as I'm informed at Mʳ. Whitmans meeting

— 28. This day in Study . . . recᵈ a letter from Mʳ. Woodbridge, I pray God to direct him in yᵉ important affair before him and me wᵗ advice to give him.

— 29. Lords day I preached . . . I pray god to bless wᵗ was agreeable to his will to those that heard it.
        Decembʳ.

Dec. 3. . . . in yᵉ afternoon Mʳ. Whitman of Farmington preached a lecture here from Isai. 55. 6.

— 6. Lords day I preached per totum from luk 2. 10. 11. administred yᵉ Sacrament, admitted Tim: Phelps Junʳ. into yᵉ Church. baptized Lucy yᵉ daughter of James Shepherd.

— 8. This day visited yᵉ sick, distressed &ᶜ. I pray God to have Compassion on Mary Griswould

— 9. This day in conversation &ᶜ took a Copy of yᵉ doings of yᵉ general Consociation[1]

— 10. This day . . . recᵈ a Letter from Mʳ. Hunn

— 13. Lords day I preached A:M . . . and Mʳ Webster P.M . . . and I baptized Allan yᵉ son of Neil McLean, Moses yᵉ son of James Bicknel George yᵉ son of Cyprian Nickols John yᵉ son of Joseph Alcot

---

[1] The proceedings of the Consociation as a whole have perished. Partial account of them is preserved in Philemon Robbins' *Plain Narrative*. One resolution the Consociation adopted was the following:

"That for a minister to enter another ministers parish, and preach or administer the seals of the covenant, without the consent of, or in opposition to, the settled minister of the parish, is disorderly: notwithstanding if a considerable number of people in the parish are desirous to hear another minister preach, provided the same be orthodox and sound in the faith, and not notoriously faulty in censuring other persons, or guilty of any other scandal, we think it ordinarily advisable for the minister of the parish to gratify them, by giving his consent upon their suitable application to him for it, unless neighbouring ministers should advise him to the contrary."

This action of the Consociation was made by the General Assembly at its Session in the May following, the basis, in connection with the statute of 1708 establishing the Saybrook System of Church Discipline, of some most stringent legislative enactments, of which there will be occasion hereafter to notice.

— 14. This day visited a sick child I pray God to spare its life. cumbred with secular business.

— 15. I pray y^t god would direct the woman with whom I have had serious discourse this night

— 16. Visiting ye sick, at night reckoned with ye Com^{ttee} due to me £42. 11s. 7d

— 18. This day some Good. this day was buried Moses ye Son of James Bicknel who died yesterday.

— 19. . . . Sent a letter to my uncle James by Doct^r. Fitch.[1]

— 20. Lords day I preached A:M: from 2 pet. 2. 9. at M^r. Whitmans meeting and P.M at my own . . . and baptized Sarah ye daughter of Abraham Cadwell

— 21. . . . at night Capt. Wyllys taken with an appoplectick fit.

— 25. This day some study reading, visiting ye sick &^{c}. rec^d M^r. Dickinson Discourses on ye five points[2]

— 26. between four and five o'clock this morning Died Hez: Wyllys Esqr. in ye 70th year of his age, he was seized with an apoplectick fit last monday night. Went to ye East side to preach

— 27. Lords day I preached for M^r. Woodbridge on ye East side . . . cold weather

— 28. This day returned home found my family well, Laus Deo. This day was Interred Capt. Wyllys a good man and a good friend is gone, o y^t god would raise up principle men among us

— 30. This day heard M^r. Edwards preach a Sermon from rev. 14. 3.

January begins [1742]

Jany. 1. This day study &^{c}. Conversed with an uneasy member, visited a sick woman, discoursed an awakened youth . . . god has carried me thro' another year praised be his name

— 3. Lords day I preached A: M. from psal. 12. 1. and P.M. from

[1] Dr. James Fitch "served in the quality of a physician to the souldiers of this Colony garrison'd at Louisbourgh," and subsequently as "Second Surgeon's mate in the expedition against Canada." He had died before May, 1752. Col. Rec., IX: 221, X: 108.

[2] Rev. Jonathan Dickinson's *True Scripture-Doctrine concerning Some Important Points of Christian Faith.* Mr. Dickinson was born at Hatfield, Mass., Apl. 22, 1688; grad. Y. C. 1706; ordained at Elizabeth, New Jersey, Sept. 29, 1709; a warm supporter of Whitefield, and a writer of many tractates of a controversial character; chosen president of the College of New Jersey in May, 1747; died on October 7 of the same year. He was one of the ablest ministers and theologians of his century.

luk. 16. 9. and baptized Hannah y⁰ daughter of Samuel Flagg, this day died Mary y⁰ wife of Thomas Welles

— 4. . . . Mary Welles burried, snowy weather. o Lord Sanctify all thy dealings with me, many of my dear friends are buried out of my sight.

— 7. This day abt. y⁰ Estate &c. Lecture at Mr. Whitmans meeting Mr. Whitman preached . . .

— 10. Lords day I preached pr. totum from luk. 16. 9. Laboured under . . .

— 12. This day went to Durham. found my friends well.

— 14. This day came to Middletown, o Lord . . . direct me . . . under y⁰ present situation of affairs.

— 15. This day returned home, found my family well, blessed be God for it, may yʳ all be his own

— 16. . . . recd. a letter from Mr. Edwards of Northampton, and one of his Sermons [1]

— 17. Lords day I preached pr. totum from Isai. 55. 7.
James Logan owned y⁰ Covenᵗ

— 18. . . . At night died Elizabeth y⁰ daughter of Samuel Talcot

— 20. . . . Elizabeth y⁰ daughter of Samuel Talcot Interred

— 21. This day went to y⁰ West Division preached a lecture from Hos. 7. 8.

— 24. Lords day I preached . . . Laboured under . . .

— 26. Went to Weathersfield Mr. Whitman preached from Isai. 32. 2. returned home found my family well Laus Deo

— 27. lecture in y⁰ afternoon at Mr. Whitmans meeting Mr. Lockwood preached from Eph. 2. 8. at night I married Jacob Kellogg and Abigail Wadsworth.

— 28. At night preached a lecture at Mr. Churches from Joh. 1. 29.

— 29. This day in study &c. recd. a letter from Mr. Worthington,[2] another from Mr. Knot [3] with a copy of Tenants letter to Mr. Lord [4] and also of some of y⁰ principles of Count Zenzendorf

---

[1] Probably Mr. Edwards' sermon on *The Distinguishing Marks of a Work of the Spirit of God*, which he had preached at New Haven, September 10, 1741, and which had been printed at Boston late in that year.

[2] Rev. William Worthington, born in Hartford Dec. 5, 1695; grad. Y. C. 1716; ordained at the western part of Saybrook, now called Westbrook, June 29, 1726, where he remained till his death Nov. 16, 1756. He preached the Election Sermon May 10, 1744; which shows strong sympathy with the Conservative side in the Whitefieldian Controversies.

[3] Probably Rev. Abraham Nott, mentioned *ante*, p. 24.

[4] The celebrated evangelist and supporter of Whitefield, Gilbert Tennent (born in Ireland, minister in Philadelphia, died about 1765) to Rev. Benjamin Lord of Norwich. Mr. Lord was born at Saybrook May 31, 1694; grad. Y. C. 1714; ordained at Norwich (explicitly renouncing the Saybrook Platform) Nov. 20, 1717. He was a supporter of Whitefield but disapproved of the excesses of

and y* moravian brethren; I pray God to Save us from error.
keep and guide us in this difficult day

— 31. Lords day I preached per totum from Eph. 1. 13.   .
Less difficulty than at sometimes. Thanks be to God.
        Feb: begins

Feby. 2. This day went to Windsor, association met &*.

— 3. This day lecture at Windsor. M*. Colton preached from
Josh. 24, returned home found my family well

— 4. This day lecture M*. Colton preached from Joh. 1. 29.
at night I preached a Lecture at M*. Churches from luk. 14. 17.

— 5. Study &*. finished reading Doct*. Watts his improvment of
y* mind, or supplement &*. An excellent book, in w*. he Con-
siders y* five methods of improvment which are 1 observation.
2. reading. 3. Instruction by lectures. 4. Conversation, and
5. Study.

— 7. Lords day I preached per totum from Zech. 6. 12. and administred y* Sacraments. Joseph Shepherd Jun*. and Mary y*
wife of W™. Nickols were taken into y* chh.

— 8. reading Neals History of New=England &*.

— 9. reading Neal &*. rec*. a letter from M*. Sergeant

— 10. Lecture M*. Lockwood preached from Job. 36. 13. and from
rev. 2. 21.

— 14. Lords day I preached   I pray god to bless w* I
have spoken . . .

— 18. Kept a fast at Eb. Williamsons on acc* of his wife who is
sorely visited and distressed. preached a sermon from 1 pet.
5. 8.   at night preached at M*. Churches from heb. 3. 7.

— 21. Lords day I preached . . . and baptized Joseph y* son
of Thomas Croswell and Nathaniel y* son of Diostheus
Humphreys.

— 22. This day visiting y* Sick &*. . . . o y* I might know
thy mind and will with respect to our religious affairs . . .

— 25. This day a lecture I preached from rom. 8. 1.

— 28. Lords day I preached . . and baptized Elizabeth y*
daughter of Nehemiah Smith.
        March begins

Mch. 3. This day spent in business about Dividing y* Gove™
Estate.

— 4. This day as y* former. I find it very uncomfortable to be
thus busied about y* world

some of his followers. He was trustee of Y. C. from 1740 to 1772; published many sermons, among
them the Election Sermon May 12, 1751. He died March 31, 1784.

— 5. This day reading Caldwells Sermons French prophets' &ᶜ.

— 7. Lords day I preached A:M: . . . and administred yᵉ Sacrament and P.M: Mʳ. Burr preached . . Mary yᵉ daughter of Mʳ. George Wyllys was baptized.

— 8. Visited a poor distressed woman. Mʳ. Clap here. a comet appeared in northeast about a fortnight ago.

— 9. . . nil remarkable occurs. Mʳ. Williamson in great distress

— 10. At night preached a lecture to yᵉ Negroes. I pray God to bless it to yᵐ.

— 11. This day study, had a lecture in the afternoon Mʳ. Newel preached from Joh. 21. 22.

— 12. This day study &ᶜ. Conversed with two uneasy persons at night

— 14. Lords day I preached A:M. at Mʳ. Whitmans meeting and P.M at my own . . .

— 15. . . . Visited by some zealous men. o yᵗ god would teach me my duty and establish me in it

— 17. This day visited Mʳ. Woodbridge found him no better . . returned in safety Laus Deo.

— 19. . . . yᵉ Widow Goodwin Interred. great is yᵉ noise and talk about religion. o yᵗ wee might practice it as well as talk about it.

— 20. . . . Laboured under darkness and discouragement, much discouraged in my work . . .

— 21. Lords day I preached A:m: from Col. 3. 6. and P.M: from Joh. 7. 37. . . .

— 22. This day reading, visiting Mʳ. Woodbridge &ᶜ.

---

[1] Rev. John Caldwell, a minister belonging to the Presbytery of Boston (a body whose date of origin and extinction are alike unknown) but which had at this period a considerable membership. Mr. Caldwell did some work in Derry, New Hampshire, and apparently some in Boston. This sermon was entitled *The Scripture Character or Masks of False Prophets or Teachers.* It was shortly followed by another called *The Nature, Folly and Evil of rash and uncharitable Judging.* Both sermons were preached in what was known as the French Church in School Street in Boston, an organization whose pastor, Rev. Mr. Lemercier, was connected with the Presbytery. The church became extinct about 1748. Rev. James Robie of Kilsyth, Scotland, in his preface to the *Christian Monthly History.* dated Nov. 15, 1743, accuses this James Caldwell as an imposter, a thief and a man who under his real name Thompton, was under ministerial disgrace in Ireland. Mr. Robie's allegations suffer some measure of discredit, however, by his immediately coupling with this statement respecting Caldwell a certainly unjustifiable reflection upon Rev. Samuel Mather of Boston, "a Known Enemy to this Work," who was, he affirms, "dismissed by the Majority of his own Congregation because his Character was such both in regard to Life and Principles, as he could be no longer useful among them." Mr. Mather's honorable ministry in England after his most incorrectly represented dismission from Boston, is a sufficient answer to this insinuation. The fact is, partisans on both sides of the Revival question were too ready to asperse, not the opinions only, but the character of their opponents.

— 23. . . . Mʳ. Hart¹ of S:brook here. recᵈ. a letter from Mʳ. Worthington.

— 24. . . . preached a lecture at night at Thomas Ensigns from luk. 14. 17.

— 25. Mʳ. Edwards preached a lecture at Mʳ. Whitmans meeting from heb. 5. 7. 8. and Mʳ. Rogers at our meeting from luk. 7. 47.

— 26. . . . Visited Anne Williamson, found her something more rational. I pray God to restore her to her right mind.

— 28. Lords day I preached per totum from rom 6. 11. and baptized Marianne yᵉ daughter of Mʳ. Wᵐ. Keith. . . .

— 29. This day yᵉ Association met at Mʳ. Whitmans. Discoursed upon yᵉ business &ᶜ. One Grant complained of Mʳ. Collins² for teaching yᵗ Crist was yᵉ Son of God by eternal generation

— 31. This day Mʳ. Steel preached from Isai. 53. 3. yᵉ association broke up.

April begins

Apl. 1. When people murmur agᵗ. and chide with yʳ rulers and teachers, yʸ should go to god, ask help and direction of him Exod. 17 Numb. 20.

— 2. . . . o Lord I pray thee support me under all my difficulties. . . .

— 4. Lords day I preached and administred yᵉ Sacrament . . . , baptized John yᵉ son of Timothy Biggelow

— 6. Nil remarkable occurs, save yᵗ I saw a man in a very uncomfortable condition. I Intend to reprove him if God give me opportunity.

— 7. a day of fasting and prayer in yᵉ forenoon I preached from Isai: 26. 9. and P:M Mʳ. Whitman from Exod. 33. . . .

— 11. Lords day I preached A:M: from luk. 12. 5. and P:M. from luk. 12. 31. . . .

— 12. This day Freemans meeting. I preached from 2 Sam. 23, 3. Joseph Pitkin & Joseph Buckingham were chosen Deputies. yᵉ Lot is Cast into yᵉ Lap but yᵉ disposing of yᵉ matter is yet of yᵉ Lord.

— 13. This day visiting &ᶜ. brother Lewis and sister here. recᵈ. a letter from Mʳ. Nott. .

¹ Rev. William Hart of Saybrook, born in East Guilford, May (or March) 9, 1713; grad. Y. C. 1732; ordained at Saybrook, Nov. 17, 1736; died in that pastorate July 11, 1784. A conservative "Old Light" theologian and a powerful controversialist, publishing many pamphlets on current questions.

² Rev. Timothy Collins, born at Guilford, April 13, 1699; grad. Y. C. 1718; ordained at Litchfield, June 20, 1723; dismissed Nov. 15, 1752; continued to live at Litchfield engaged in medical practice and civil duties till his death in February, 1777. He was an "Old Light," and his dismission from his parish was said to be largely owing to intrigues against him by Dr. Bellamy.

11

— 14. . . . At night married Sam^ll. Welles and Susanna Dickenson.

— 17. This day in Study. one informed me y^t one of ye Itinerant preachers desired him to tell me y^t I preached nothing but myself. if it be true y^t I do so, I pray God to shew it me & teach me to preach christ & him crucified; if it be false, as it is, if I know my own heart, I pray God to give y^t man grace to repent of his rash censure

— 18. Lords day I preached A:M: from 1 tim: 2. 19. and P.M: from Hoz. 8. 12. went thro my work with some difficulty. Sarah Spencer propounded for admission to communion with ye church.

— 23. The news of S^r. Robert Walpoles resigning his posts and ye change of ye ministry at home comes vouched.

— 25. Lords day I preached . . . and baptized Abigail ye daughter of John Turner.

— 26. Went to visit M^r. Woodbridge &^c. I pray God to deal graciously with him . . .

— 29. Lecture in ye afternoon at M^r. Whitmans meeting. M^r. Marsh preached from Matt. 5. 6.
      May begins.

May 2. Lords day I preached . . . and administred ye Sacrament, and admitted Sarah Spencer and Jerusha Andrews to communion with ye chh. . . .

— 3. This day reading Rutherford ag^t ye Antinomians &^c. I pray God . . . preserve me, my people & ye people of this Land from y^r. errors

— 4. . . . at night a refreshing conversation with M^r. Hopkins . . .

— 6. This day in Study. o Lord God appear I pray for ye help of this Town. Save us from Contention and Confusion.

— 9. Lords day I preached . . Laboured under much weakness . . .

— 11. Went to ye West Division &^c ye ministers begin to meet

— 12. This day visited M^r. Woodbridge I pray God to heal him. I thank him y^t he has bro't so many of my friends here in safety

— 13. This day Election &^c. ye Govern^r. Jonathan Law^1 Esqr.,

---

1 Jonathan Law, born at Milford, Aug. 6, 1674; grad. H. C. 1695; died in office as Governor Nov. 3, 1750. He was opposed to the Itinerators and forward in promoting the repressive legislation enacted at this session.

Roger Wolcot[1] Esq'. Dep. Gov: assistants as in y* year past with the addition of Roger Newton Esq'.   M'. Stiles[2] preached from psal. 147. 2.

— 14.   This day . . .   news y' a ship Load of Moravians lay of at Fishers Island.

— 15.   This day . . .   wearied with y* fatigues of y* week.   O that I might have rest in God

— 16.   . . .   being Lords day M'. Stiles preached for me A: M. from Isai. 55. 3. and M'. Campbell P. M: from Eph. 2: 12.

— 23.   Lords day I preached p'. totum from 1. Joh. 2. 6.   a hot day.   Laboured under considerable difficulty.   O Lord help a poor worm.

— 24.   This day prayed at Court . . .   there is news y' Mason is arrived.   May this Gov'. be guarded ag'. his unrighteous . pretentions.

— 25.   M'. Nott here.

— 27.   This day little Study; great disturbance in y* country by Davenport and other Itinerant preachers.

— 28.   . . .   this day y* general assembly passed a bill to restrain Itinerant ministers, and another to apprehend James Davenport and Ben: Pumroy and bring y^m before y* assembly[3]

— 30.   Lords day I preached A: M: from act. 24. 16. and P: M: from 25. 17. . . .

— 31.   This day some reading, visiting and visited; at night y* Sheriff bro't. Davenport and Pumroy to Town   W' God is about to do with us I know not.

June 1742.

June 1.   This day M'. Davenport preached at Daniel Bulls, or

[1] Roger Wolcott, born in Windsor Jany. 4, 1679; member of Council, Judge, Lieut.-Governor, Governor from 1750 to 1754, commander of the Connecticut forces in the Louisburgh expedition of 1745, with the rank of Major-General, writer of "Poetical Meditations" and a defence of the Consociated system of Church government. He died in East Windsor, May 17, 1767.

[2] Rev. Isaac Stiles of North Haven, born in Windsor July 30, 1647; grad. Y. C. 1722; ordained at North Haven Nov. 11, 1724; died in office May 14, 1760. He was a zealous Old Light; and his sermon on this Election occasion was decidedly polemic in its references to holders of opposing views, and is credited with having considerable influence in promoting the stringent legislation adopted by the Assembly at this session against the Itinerating Evangelists.

[3] This extraordinary Bill proceeded upon the wholly unjustifiable assumption that the Saybrook system (accepted by the Assembly in 1708, for such churches as agreed thereto, as a system established by law) was binding upon all churches irrespective of such agreement. And it went on to apply its assumption to the existing state of affairs by sundry stringent enactments, limiting the right of individual ministers to preach anywhere out of their immediate parishes without consent of the settled pastor; punishing any minister who did so by depriving him of all power to collect his salary in his own lawful parish; while, respecting any foreigner or person from outside Connecticut who should preach in any parish without the minister's consent, it provided for his summary arrest as a "vagrant" and expulsion from the Colony. Col. Rec., VIII: 454-457.

rather railed there if I am Informed right. in y⁰ afternoon Davenport and Pumroy were bro't before y⁰ generall assembly. y⁰ assembly adjourned after sunset when there was a great tumult occasioned by D: and P. w⁰. with much difficulty was quelled by the authority.

— 2. This day went to Wintonbury to y⁰ association there. Mʳ. White preached from psal. 45. 2. Mʳ. Colton and myself chosen Delegates to go to y⁰ general assocⁿ. at New London. Davenport sentenced by y⁰ Court as an Enthusiast, a breaker of y⁰ peace, teaching doctrines destructive to y⁰ peace and order of y⁰ government and ordered to be transported out of y⁰ Governmᵗ.[1]

— 3. This day Davenport was shiped for transportation. y⁰ genˡˡ. assembly adjourned without day; I pray God to bless y⁰ endeavours to settle and secure peace to this people

— 4. . . . had a lecture in y⁰ afternoon, preached from psal. 104. 34. I pray God to bless . . .

— 6. Lords day I preached . . . and administred y⁰ Sacrament, and baptized Joseph y⁰ son of William Pratt

— 7. . . . in y⁰ night its said yᵗ Pomroy preached at T: Seymours

---

[1] Mr. Davenport (see *ante*, p. 70 note) and Mr. Pomroy (p. 61 note) were brought before the Assembly on a complaint from Ripton parish in Stratford, alleging that Davenport and Pomroy were there collecting assemblies of people, mostly children and youth, and under pretence of religious exercises were inflaming them with doctrines subversive of law and order.

The hearing occupied two days and was in Mr. Wadsworth's meeting house. The town was in a great state of excitement. As the arrested ministers came out on to the meeting-house steps, at the end of the first day's hearing, Davenport commenced a violent harangue to the crowds about the door. The sheriff took hold of his sleeve to lead him away. "He instantly fell apraying, Lord, thou knowest somebody's got hold of my sleeve. Strike them Lord! strike them!" Mr. Pomroy also called out to the sheriff, "Take heed how you do that heaven-daring action; the God of heaven will surely avenge it on you."

For awhile it looked as if the prisoners would be taken out of the sheriff's hands. The night was little less than a riot. The house where the ministers were lodged was surrounded by an angry multitude, with difficulty dispersed by the magistrates. In the morning forty militia men were ordered under arms to preserve the peace.

At the conclusion of the second day's hearing the Assembly adjudged that though Mr. Davenport's doctrines and behavior had "a natural tendency to destroy the peace and order of the government," yet as it appeared that he was "disturbed in the rational faculties of his mind" he was to be "pitied and compassionated and not treated as he otherwise might be." The Assembly, therefore, under the provisions of the act respecting "strangers and foreigners" just passed, ordered Mr. Davenport to be sent to Southold, out of the jurisdiction. And so about four o'clock in the afternoon, between "two files of musketiers," Mr. Davenport was marched down from the meeting house to the Connecticut river, and put aboard the vessel of one Mr. Whitmore, who, having received his charge, set sail immediately. There will be occasion to notice Mr. Davenport's later history hereafter.

Mr. Pomroy was discharged without penalty. Indeed, it will be observed by Mr. Wadsworth's entry in his Diary, five days later, that Mr. Pomroy was still in town and holding a meeting at the house of Mr. Thomas Seymour.

— 8. M^r. H: of meriden here. Visited a distracted woman and an erroneous man. M^r. Eliot here at night, a pleasant conversation

— 10. . . . nil remarkable occurs, at night married Levi Jones and Elizabeth Cook.

— 13. Lords day I preached . . . and baptized Jonathan y^e Son of Benjamin Richards and catechised y^e children.

— 14. This day set out for New.London went as far as Colchester, a comfortable Journey. . . .

— 15. This day went to New=London   much pleased and I hope edified with y^e good Conversation of y^e grave and venerable M^r. Adams.[1] Y^e Gen^ll. Association formed. M^r. Adams moderator. M^r. Colton Scribe

— 16. A Lecture M^r. Colton preached from Col: 4. 12. Lat. part. Somethings uncomfortable happened after y^e Exercise was over. I pray y^t it may be overruled for good

— 17. ye Gen^ll Association brake up[2] ye next is to be at Fairfield on ye 3^d Tuesday of June next, at M^r. Hobarts. returned as far as Colchester.

— 18. This day got home, found my family well, for w^e I magnify & praise ye great and glorious God

— 20. Lords day I preached . .   and baptized John ye son of John Bidwell

— 21. This day reading Conversation &^{c}. great is ye talk about religion, O y^t wee might practice it as well as discourse about it

— 22. This day went to ye Association on ye East Side of ye River at Hartford   advised ye people to settle a Colleague with M^r. Woodbridge & honourably to support M^r. Woodbridge.[3]

---

[1] Rev. Eliphalet Adams of New London. He was born at Dedham, Mass., March 26, 1677 ; grad. H. C. 1694 ; ordained at New London Feb. 9, 1708 9. A trustee of Y. C. from 1720 to 1738 ; published several sermons, among which are two Election Sermons, 1710 and 1733. He died Oct. 4. 1753.

[2] This meeting of the General Association put on record its " Thankfulness to God the Father of Mercies " for his grace in " Stirring up Great Numbers among us to a Concern for their Souls " ; but expressed its conviction that " the Great Enemy of Souls who is ever ready with his Devices to Check, Damp & Destroy if possible the Work of God, is very busy for that purpose." Wherefore it felt constrained to exhort, among other things, " That seasonable and due testimony be borne against such Errors and Irregularities as doe already prevail among some persons, As Particularly the Depending upon & following Impulses & impressions made on the mind as tho' they were Immediate Revelations of Some truth or Duty that is not Reveal'd in the Word of God – Laying too much Weight upon bodily agitations, Raptures, Extacies, Visions &c — Ministers disorderly intruding into other Ministers' parishes Laymen taking it upon them in an unwarrantable manner publickly to teach and Exhort — Rash Censuring & Judging of others," etc., etc.

[3] Rev. Samuel Woodbridge had now for a good while been unable to discharge the duties of his office by reason of his invalidism. Several ministers had already preached in East Hartford temporarily ; and the Association now advised a colleagueship. Propositions were accordingly made to several persons successively, but for one reason or other in vain.

— 23. This day advised y⁰ people on y⁰ East Side to invite Mʳ. Chauncey Whittlesey to preach on probation and in case he cant be obtained then to apply to Mʳ. Willᵐ. Adams.¹ Mʳ. Whitman preached a Lecture from Eph. 1. 13. returned home found my family well for which I bless god. . . .

— 27. Lords day I preached . . . and in y⁰ Evening to y⁰ negroes at y⁰ School house² from Mark 8. 36. . . .

— 29. . . . went to Farmington. Saw my friends in usual health. Laus Deo. recᵈ. of my brother Jno' £20. 10.

— 30. this day returned home, found my wife not well I pray god to heal her ; found Mʳ. Chaunceys Sermon this day upon y⁰ outpouring of y⁰ Spirit, an excellent discourse.³ May it be blessed to me and others ; o yᵗ God would put a stop to the Enthusiasm yᵗ prevails in y⁰ Land.

  July begins.

July 1. This day paied Capt: Hooker £10: 11ᵇ: o which I borrowed of him May 30ᵗʰ.

— 2. This day spent much of it in a hurry of worldly business, blessed be God yᵗ has carried mee so well thro' it. in y⁰ afternoon Mʳ. Whitman preached a lecture from rev. 1. 12.

— 4. Lords day I preached A:M: from rev. 1. 5. and administred y⁰ Sacrament of y⁰ Lords Supper and P:M: from Jam. 2: 8.

— 5. This day went to Salmon brook   found y⁰ people in very uncomfortable circumstances. I pray God to heal yʳ divisions⁴

— 6. This day finished y⁰ Salmon brook affair and returned home.
          . . .

— 9. The news comes of Davenport being excluded y⁰ pulpits in Boston. I hope it will be a means of stopping him in his mad career

— 11. Lords day I preached pʳ. totum from Eph. 2. 10 . . .

— 12. . . . O Lord God Almighty I pray thee prevent

---

¹ William Adams, son of Rev. Eliphalet of New London. Born Oct. 7, 1710; grad. Y. C. 1730; tutor there 1732–34 ; a preacher for more than sixty years, but never ordained and never married, saying he could not have the burthen of a parish or a wife. His work was done chiefly in the vicinity of New London, on Shelter Island, and the Eastern end of Long Island, though his latest years found him in New London, where he died Aug. 25, 1798.

² "The School house" stood in what is now called Main Street, then a hundred feet wide, in front of what is now known as the "Linden" building.

³ Rev. Charles Chauncey of the First Church of Boston ; born Jan. 1, 1705; grad. H. C. 1721 ; ordained at Boston First Church Oct. 25, 1727 ; died Feb. 10, 1787, æ. 82.

⁴ The Salmon brook Society in Simsbury had called Rev. Eli Colton, son of Rev. Benjamin Colton of West Hartford, sometime in 1740 or 41. But difficulties arose, the Society would not pay him the stipulated salary ; and at the advice of the Association given in October, 1742, Mr. Colton withdrew. He was afterward settled at Stafford, where he was called Sept. 14, 1744, and died there in office June 8, 1756. He was born at West Hartford Aug. 8, 1716, and grad. at Y. C. in 1737.

ye unhappy division and separation y^t is threatened in this Town. Calm ye minds and turn ye hearts of those y^t may be attempting of it. Let y^m see ye sin and danger of it, and be diverted from it, if it may be thine holy will:[1]

— 14. This day visited M^r. Woodbridge found him better than usual . . . o y^t God would prevent any unhappy divisions in this Town w^e wee seem to be in danger of. . . . This day Jonah Gross came Home, he was taken by ye Spaniards May 30. 1741 and carried to Porto Valla from there to Leguvia, from thence over Land to Crokus and kept in prison there till sometime in april Last and then released. May god give him a thankful heart for his deliverance

— 15. This day . . . rejoyced at the return of one of my people from Captivity.

— 16. This day in study, ye news paper informs y^t a warrant was Issued in Boston to apprehend one Sam^{ll}. Green a noted enhab. for blasphemy.

— 18. Lords day I preached per totum from Col. 1. 28. and at night to ye negroes at ye school house. . . .

— 19. This day reckoned with M^r. Austin ye whole of my account with him was £16. 7. 1. . . . I am still in his debt 12 shillings.

This day also four men from Colchester were bro't to prison for breach of ye Law Lately made for Restraining and Correcting abuses in ecclesiastical affairs — but I since hear it was for holding a Separate meeting upon ye Sabbath Contrary to y^r old

---

[1] The present writer has undertaken no responsibility for the defence of Mr. Wadsworth's views and anxieties about the condition of things in his parish or in Connecticut generally. But it is only fair to him to remember certain incontestable facts. Not only had Mr. Whitefield in his journey through New England publicly inveighed against a majority of the ministry as unconverted men, and deliberately recorded in his Journal that "many, perhaps, most that preach, I fear do not experimentally know Christ," and that the colleges, Harvard and Yale, had "become darkness — darkness that may be felt," but a large number of Mr. Whitefield's followers had exceeded him in denunciation of the settled ministers and in counseling separation from them. Rev. Gilbert Tennent, who had preached with great impression at Boston a few months after Mr. Whitefield's first visit, indulged in similar censures. Indeed, in his sermon dedicated to the people of Nottingham, Pennsylvania, he represents the body of the "Clergy of this generation" as "varlets," "the seed of the Old Serpent," "men whom the devil drives into the ministry," "blind and dead men," "rebels and enemies to God," "dead drones," "dupes," "children of Satan."

Such preachings as these could not be without divisive results. Almost every town in Connecticut was actually in a turmoil. Every parish had its sympathizers with the itinerating revolutionists. Many parishes were disrupted and permanently divided. Many ministers were harried out of their pulpits and their livings by parties raised up against them among those they had baptized and welcomed to church fellowship. The signs of such possible results were visible wherever Mr. Wadsworth could turn his eyes. His own Society and those of his neighbors Whitman and Colton were sorely disquieted. Whether a different course on his part would have averted any of these tribulations is at least an open question. That the tribulations were actual and ominous of lasting calamity there can be no dispute.

Law ye penalty for w^c. is 20s. y^y were fined but wo'd not pay it and so ye authority was obliged to send y^m to Jail

— 20. This day visiting &^{c}. Uncle Thomas here. I pray God mercifully to prevent any divisions or Sinfull Separation in this Town.

— 22. This day reading &^{c}. ye Snake in the grass.[1] O y^t god would Save us from a spirit of blindness, delusion and enthusiasm

— 23. This day in Study. I thank God y^t has given me of late so much Calmness and serenity of heart and mind under ye melancholly prospect of our religious affairs, verging toward enthusiasm and Confusion. I pray God y^t I may be directed to and kept stedfast in ye way of my duty, and y^t my people may be saved from error, enthusiasm and Confusion, be converted & built up in holiness.

— 25. Lords day I preached . . . and baptized Dorothy ye daughter of Daniel Goodwin. Staied ye church and Chose a Com^{ttee}. with me to admit preachers.[2]

— 26. . . M^r. White of B here, refreshed with his company.

— 27. . . . M^r. Merrick[3] of Sp: here. a very warm day, I pray God to save from divisions his churches in this Town.

— 28. . . . visited some of my people: I pray God to bless and direct y^m Save y^m from error, prevent their being Led astray by such as creep into houses to Lead captive ye Silly

— 29. This day went to ye West division, returned and visited some uneasy people, I pray God to save y^m from an unchristian temper and practice . . .

August begins

Aug. 1. Lords day I preached A:M: . . . and P.M: M^r. Morison preached for me from heb. 13. 1. . . .

— 2. This day . . read M^r. Chaunceys Sermon[4] upon &^{c}. I

---

[1] *The Snake in the Grass, or Satan Transformed into an Angel of Light*, a tractate by Charles Leslie, "Discovering the deep and unsuspected subtlety which is Couched under the pretended simplicity of many of the principal leaders of the people called Quakers." First published in 1696, but having several subsequent editions.

[2] With characteristic caution Mr. Wadsworth brought the question of the determination of what preachers should (under the existing state of the law and of popular sentiment) be allowed to preach in his parish before the Church and secured the appointment of a committee to divide the responsibility with him.

[3] Rev. Noah Merrick, born at West Springfield, Aug. 6, 1711; grad. Y. C. 1731; preached awhile at Brimfield and Hadley; ordained at Springfield Mountains (now Wilbraham) June 10, 1741; died in office Dec. 22, 1776.

[4] Probably Chauncey's sermon on *Enthusiasm Described and Cautioned Against*, published this year. This sermon was in criticism and discouragement of the extravagances which had followed the early stages of the revival period; and was a forerunner of Dr. Chauncey's larger work published the following year, entitled *Seasonable Thoughts on the State of Religion*.

pray God it may be blessed to all into whose hands it may
come and be a happy means of Stemming the torrent of enthusiasm and disorder y' has been prevailing in y' Land. heard
y' Georgia was taken by y' Spaniards

— 4. . . . Sister Hooker delivered of a Son. the news of
Georgia being taken further confirmed.

— 5. At night I heard y' Amos Munson ' was Committed to prison
for holding forth at Colchester contrary to Law. pag. 511.

— 6. This day in Study. at night Amos Munson held forth in y'
Goal,² many people to hear him, o y' God would appear for our
help and deliver us from these delusions.

— 8. Lords day I preached A:M: from rev. 3. 1. and P.M: from
heb. 4. 3. o that god would bless w' I have spoken . . .

— 9. This day in Secular business &c. visited M'. Woodbridge
in y' afternoon. This day an Itinerant preacher came to
Town, preached at night at y' west side of y' Town.

— 10. This day in Study and other affairs Two men from Colchester committed to Goal for holding a separate meeting on
y' Sabbath contrary to Law page 290. Y' is for refusing to
pay y' penalty in that Case provided

— 11. Visited Amos Munson in prison, find him tho' zealous yet
wildish and scatter brained. I pray God to restore him to a
sound mind

— 13. M'. little³ here; much confusion in y' Country. o Lord
appear for our help I pray. Lord guide and direct magistrates,
ministers and people in their duty o god I Intreat, and
especially afford Guidance unto me thine unworthy servant

— 14. Laboured under a considerable disquiet Last night my rest
much broken by reason of y' confusions of y' present times.
Lord god almighty support and strengthen me I pray, prepare
me for y' duties of thine holy sabbath

— 15. Lords day I preached A:M: from Col. 1. 12 and P.M. from
2 Cor. 5. 10 and baptized Elijah y' son of Samuel Andrews,
and Moses y' son of Joseph Shepherd Jun'.

---

¹ Amos Munson, born at New Haven, April 9, 1719; grad. Y. C. 1738; licensed to preach by
the New Haven Association, Sept. 30, 1740, but so embraced the new measures that the Association remonstrated with him as preaching "in a manner which we think disorderly." He was never
ordained, and became in May, 1742, one of the original members of the Separatist Church in New
Haven. He died at 29 years of age, in 1748.

² The jail at this time stood on the north side of Court House Square, a little easterly from
the present *Courant* building.

³ Rev. Ephraim Little of Colchester, born at Scituate, Mass.; grad. H. C. 17..; ordained at
Colchester Sept. 20, 1732, died in office June, 1787. An Old Light in the present tribulations.

— 18. This day went to a Councel at ye West Division. entered upon ye Case.[1]

— 18. Spent at ye West Division in Councel &^c. returned home, found my family well. Laus Deo.

— 20. This day . . . toward night a Court at Coln'. Stanleys, Seth Youngs sentenced to be bound to his good behaviour for exhorting contrary to Law, but refusing to give bond was in ye evening committed to Goal

— 22. Lords day I preached . . . and baptized Elizabeth ye daughter of John Skinner and Lois ye daughter of Michael Burnham: catechised ye children at night

— 23. This day . . . saw a poor distressed creature, a sick man &^c. I pray god have mercy on y^m both according to y^r necessity. this day ye conjunction of Saturn and Jupiter in Leo so much talked of .

— 24. . . . Considerable tumults and commotions are still among us an ugly squabble happened last night at ye Goal. . . .

— 27. This day in Study. ye news from Boston comes y^t James Davenport is imprisoned there.[2]

— 28. This day . . nil remarkable occurs, save y^t M^r. Woodbridge of Simsbury[3] died very suddenly in the forenoon as I heard at night.

— 29. Lords day I preached p^r. totum from luk. 21. 36. and in ye evening at the school-house from Deut. 32. 29

— 30. This day went to Symsbury. M^r. Marsh preached a funeral Sermon from Matt. 24. 46. ye Rev^d. M^r. Woodbridge was Interred.

---

[1] This was but one of several councils which the disturbed condition of matters in the West Hartford parish caused to be summoned. Rev. Dr. Nathan Perkins in his *Half Century Sermon*, preached in 1822, says: "During the Rev. Mr. Colton's ministry, the church and parish, as appears from authentic documents, had a most unhappy period, for four or five years, of very great and cruel divisions and contentions, which could not be healed and adjusted but by calling in two whole Consociations, that of Hartford County and Litchfield County."

[2] Mr. Davenport was interviewed by the Boston ministers on his arrival, June 28, but they received no satisfaction and united in a Declaration disapproving his course. This led to violent denunciations by him in his street preaching, and these to his apprehension and imprisonment, August 21. On examination, however, he was adjudged insane, and sent home. Mr. Davenport continued his erratic course, and with increasing extravagances, sometime longer. A providential illness, however, put a pause to his travels, and this, with expostulations from Revs. Messrs. Solomon Williams and Eleazer Wheelock, availed to secure from him a public Confession and Retraction published in the Boston *Gazette* in August, 1744. His later ministerial services were performed in New York and New Jersey, interrupted by a missionary tour in Virginia. He died the 10th of November, 1757. He was doubtless a good man, but of an excitable and unbalanced judgment.

[3] *Ante*, p. 48.

— 31. This day Doct^r. Chauncey at my house a pleasant conversation. . . .

September, 1742.

Sept. 2. This day . . . in ye afternoon preached a Lecture from John 6. 33. . . .

— 3. This day . . . visited M^r. Woodbridge found him better Laus Deo.

— 5. Lords day I preached . . . and administred ye Sacrament . . . felt weak and indisposed.

— 6. This day set out on a Journey to N: Haven. Lodged at Wallingford, a refreshing conversation there.

— 7. This day got to New-Haven safe and in health Laus Deo.

— 8. This day Commencement. ye affairs of it conducted with considerable order and decency.

— 9. This day returned as far as Wallingford a kind entertainment.

— 10. This day got home I found my family well, blessed be god for it and y^t he has bro't me home in safety.

— 12. Lords day I preached A: M: from tit. 2. 10. and P.M. from gen. 39. 9. . . .

— 15. This day spent much of it at Court, hearing Trial of Richardson for putting of Counterfeit money.[1] ye Jury bro't him in guilty. poor man pray God to give him repentence

— 16. This day prayed at Court. . . . Edward Aldridge found guilty of Counterfeiting money &^{c}.

— 18. This day went to Symsbury to take my turn in preaching to ye bereaved chh.[2]

— 19. Lords day preached at Symsbury from Ecclesiastes 12. 5.

— 21. This day freemans meeting Capt. Marsh and M^r. Buckingham chosen Deputies. rainy weather.

— 22. Went to Farmington M^r. Marsh preached from Deut. 33. 2.

— 23. . . . Last night I hear was a sad tumult at ye goal occasioned by Munson and his adherents

— 25. . . . M^r. Sewal[3] here.

---

[1] Richardson and Aldridge (mentioned as tried the next day) were by the next Assembly, in October following, allowed to depart out of the jurisdiction, on payment of costs of trial, board at the prison, and forty pounds " premium paid to the informer against them."

[2] According to a current usage of the time, designed not only to express the fellowship of the churches, but to continue awhile to the family of the deceased minister the salary which his death, without such continued supply of his pulpit, might at once interrupt.

[3] Probably Rev. Joseph Sewall of Boston, born Aug. 15, 1688; grad. H. C. 1707; ordained colleague with Rev. Ebenezer Pemberton at the Old South Church, Boston, Sept. 16, 1713; died June 27, 1769.

— 26. Lords day I preached A: M: from rom. 5. 12. and P.M: from
Col. 4. 12. Went thro' my work with less difficulty than at
sometimes. Laus Deo. . . .

— 27. This day . . . reading Pickerings letters. Caldwells
Sermon upon uncharitable Judging[1] &ᶜ. &ᶜ.

— 28. This day Timothy Biggelow first came to school to me
. . . Visited Mʳ. Woodbridge, found him better Laus Deo

— 29. This day yᵉ afternoon spent in prayer with Mⁿ. Williamson
at night married Job Marsh and Rebecca Pratt

— 30. This day . . . in yᵉ afternoon a Lecture at Mʳ. Whitmans meeting   Mʳ. Whitman preached from 2 Cor. 8. 9.
        October begins

Oct. 1. This day . . . nil remarkable occurs, Saving yᵉ Tergi-
versation and Sophistry of some men. See yᵉ Evening post
for monday Last.[2]

— 3. Lords day I preached   . and administred yᵉ Sacrament . . .

— 5. This day went to Litchfield, to yᵉ association[3] there.

— 6. This day Lecture at Litchfield Mʳ. Marsh preached from
rev. 11. 10. a stormy tempestuous day

— 9. This day . . recᵈ. a letter from my uncle James with
an accᵗ of yᵉ affairs of yᵉ East

— 10. Lords day I preached . . . Laboured under weakness
. . . George Alcot owned yᵉ Covenant his son George
was baptized.

— 12. Mʳ. Eliot here at night.

— 13. This day went to Farmington, preached from Eph. 2. 10.
. . .

— 14. This day went to yᵉ west Division to a wedding, Daniel
Skinner & Jerusha Whiting married —

— 17. Lords day I preached . . . and at night from rom. 5.
12. to yᵉ negroes.

— 23. This day . . brother Lewis here from Boston.

---

[1] *Ante*, p. 80, note.

[2] The *Evening Post*, published in Boston, began to be issued under that title in August, 1735, succeeding to a paper called the *Weekly Rehearsal*. The article in the *Post* to which Mr. Wadsworth refers was a letter by Rev. Gilbert Tennent in partial disavowal of the extravagancies of some of the revivalistic itinerants ; a disavowal, however, which, in view of many of Mr. Tennent's own and frequent utterances, not unreasonably occasioned the use by Mr. Wadsworth of the epithets above employed.

[3] This Association at Litchfield among other "resolves" passed this one respecting troubles at Goshen : "This Association having heard that some difficultys have arisen in Goshen by Reason of the singing of Doctr. Watts psalms in publick Worship, wee advise that for the present they use only our common Version of the psalms of David in publick worship."

— 24. Lords day I preached . . . and baptized Frances y^e
daughter of Daniel Brace. rec^d at night a letter from uncle
James &^{c}.

— 27. M^r. Marsh of Kent here at night.

— 30. This day . received a letter from uncle James by
Capt. Marsh.

— 31. Lords day I preached A:M: from heb. 12. 1. and P.M. from
1. Joh. 3. 10. Went thro' my work with some difficulty.
November begins

Nov. 2. This day County Court. Visited poor Anne Williamson
a distracted crazy creature I pray God to relieve and help
her and restore to health and soundness of body and mind.

— 3. . . . M^r. Hopkins of Springfield here.

— 4. This day . . in ye afternoon a lecture. I preached
from rev. 1. 5.

— 7. Lords day I preached A:M: from Cant. 1. 3. and administred ye Sacrament, and P.M: from 1 Cor. 6. 1.

— 10. This day . . . saw somewhat very disagreeable in a
friend. o y^t God would save him from ye destroyer

— 11. This day a publick thanks giving throughout Connecticutt.
I preached from psal. 118. 29. a very cold day . . .

— 12. A very cold day. nil remarkable occurs. ye great river
shut.

— 14. Lords day I preached A:M: from Ezk. 22. 14, and P.M:
also. at night preached to ye negroes at ye school house from
Eph. 2. 3.

— 15. This day I went to Farmington found my friends in usual
health. Laus Deo. The great river froze over last friday
which is earlier I suppose than it was ever known to do

— 16. I returned from Farmington found my family well Laus
Deo. I hear y^t last Sabbath was a Conventicle at D. Bulls,
present of my people D. B. and J. S. I pray god to shew y^m
ye evil of so doing

— 21. Lords day M^r. T. Woodbridge of Hatfield preached for me
A.M. from phil. 3. and M^r. McChinstry[1] P.M: from matt:
11. 28.

— 22. . . . at night visited by some uneasy members, I pray
y^t god would prevent y^m going astray, Save y^m from disorder

---

[1] Rev. John McKinstry of Ellington, born in Scotland ; graduated at University of Edinburg
1712 ; awhile at Sutton, Mass.; installed at Ellington about 1733, though he had been resident
there three years previous ; dismissed 1749 ; died January, 1753.

and confusion, dispose y^m to hearken to advice, give me grace to behave aright under all trials and temptations

— 28. Lords day I preached . . . and at night to ye negroes in ye school house. . . .

    December begins

Dec. 1. This day went to ye West Division to visit M^r. Colton. a pleasant conversation   o Lord appear, I pray to heal the Divisions of this poor Town.

— 2. This day a lecture P.M. M^r. Whitman preached from 2. Cor. 14. 15.

— 3. This day . . . M^r. Burr of Worcester here. . . .

— 8. This day was buried Susanna McLean ye wife of M^r. Allan McLean.

— 12. Lords day I preached . . . and at night to ye Negroes at ye school house from 2 Cor. 5. 10. . . .

— 14. This day . . reckoned with ye Societies Com^{ttee}. due to me £62. 7^s. 3^d.

— 15. . . . discoursed and prayed with a sick woman, I pray god y^t her awakening may prove a saving conversion

— 19. Lords day I preached pr. totum from Eph. 2. 4. 5. . . . went thro' my work with less difficulty than at many other times . . .

— 22. This day visited M^r. Woodbridge I pray god to heal him and to restore him to usefulness again

— 26. Lords day I preached . . . and in ye evening at ye school house to ye negroes from 1 thes. 5. 2. . . .

— 27. This day I paied to M^r. John Lawrence 7–0–6. on acc^{tt}. of John Fowler of Symsbury and £5–0–0 in money on my own acc^{tt}. I yet owe him eight pound. visited a sick child and prayed with it.

— 28. . . . M^r. Collins here at night.

— 30. This day . . . a lecture. I preached from Eph. 5. 1.

— 31. This day in study. ye month and year concludes. god give me a happy entrance upon another

    January begins [1743]

Jany. 2. Lords day I preached A: M. from rev. 5. 9. administred ye Sacrament and P.M. from luk. 13. 8. May thy blessing o god attend thy word.

— 4. reading magazines &c. nil remarkable at night discoursed with an uneasy member I pray god to convince him I cant.

— 7. This day little Study. much visited. under great perplexity and trouble.

— 9. Lords day I preached A:M: from luk. 13. 14. and P.M. from heb. 2. 6. and at night at y' school house from rom. 5. 1. went thro' my work with great difficulty. y' Lord bless his word.

— 13. Study. Conversing with an offender, I pray God to bring him to his duty, Lord thou canst turn y' hearts of y' children of men, change I pray and turn his heart.

— 14. this day was buried y' son of Edward Cadwell Jun'. y' was born on Wednesday night last

— 16. Lords day I preached   Laboured under much difficulty . . .

— 17. . . . This day M". Waters was interred, aged 88

— 20. This day . . . visited an aged disciple indisposed. I pray god to heal him and prolong his Life

— 23. Lords day I preached A:M: from Joh. 12. 38. and P.M: from Joh. 12. 38. and at night from col. 4. 5. at y' School house . . .

— 25. at night conversed with an uneasy dissatisfied person I pray god to rectify his mistakes, to give him a right spirit, and me grace to discharge my duty to him and all others under like circumstances y' I may be concerned with.

— 27. This day . . . I married Isaac Clark and Ruth Spencer

— 28. My daughter Abigails birth day. thanks to god for her life

— 30. Lords day preached A:M. from Joh. 12. 38. and P.M. from Job. 31. 14.

          Feb. 1742/3

Feby. 1. This day y' Association met at my house. advised Symsbury to M'. Estabrook &'.

— 2. This day lecture   M'. White of Bolton preached from Isai. 55. 1. y' association broke up.

— 4. This day Study. conversation in y' evening with one called a new light.

— 6. Lords day I preached .   . and administred y' Sacrament and at night from Eph. 2. 17. at y' school house.

— 7. This day Laboured under indisposition of body, did little business, writ a letter at night to go to Doct'. Chauncey

— 8. . . . rec'. a letter from an uneasy member of our church, I pray God to open his eyes to show him wherein he is in a mistake and assist and direct me to discharge my duty faithfully to him.

— 9. . . . visited a distressed parishoner. I pray god to heal
and restore to soundness of body and mind. and o y' god
would put a stop to y° growth of intemperance among us.

— 10. . . . Conversed with a man under suspicion of Scandal,
and also another y' has withdrawn from y° publick worship, I
pray god to bring y™ both to y'. duty.

— 13. Lords day I preached pr. totum from Gal. 19. 20. 21.

— 15. This day spent at Southington &°. the Councel unani-
mously agreed it was not expedient to dismiss M'. Curtis.[1]

— 16. This day as before at Southington, M'. Colton preached,
y° result of the Councel published &°. returned home found
my family well Laus Deo.

— 18. This day dejected, little study. I pray God to direct me
to a suitable and seasonable text on which to make a sermon
tomorrow if I am bro't to see y° light of y' day.

— 20. Lords day I preached A: M: from psal. 112. 7 and P.M:
from heb. 10. 24. 25. and in y° evening at y° School house
from Eph. 2. 10.

— 22. This day visiting &°. at night discoursed with some uneasy members but to little purpose

— 24. This day went to west Division to Consult &°. advised
Symsbury people to wait patiently on god in y° way of his
providence &°. at night discoursed with 2 members of the
Church y' are wandering out of y° way.

— 27. Lords day I preached . . . o Lord heal our divisions.

— 28. . . . O Lord god direct and guide me in this difficult
day . . .

        March begins

Mch. 2. This day at Court, visiting &°. rec⁴ a letter from Doct'.
Chauncey &°.

— 3. This day prayed at Court, lecture in y° afternoon at M'.
Whitmans meeting, he preached from rom. 5. 10.

— 6. Lords day I preached A.M. from rev. 19. 9. and administred
y° Sacrament, and P.M. M'. Burr of Worcester preached for
me . . . and I baptized Hannah y° daughter of Sam".
Graham and Mary y° daughter of Daniel Badger Jun'.

— 7. A stormy Tempestuous day. visited and prayed with a sick
child, and a young woman y' is Languishing, and that never
had but little if any reason

<hr>

[1] Difficulties had arisen at Southington owing to the attitude of Mr. Curtis toward the New
Measures of the Awakening. He took, like the Hartford ministers, a conservative position, and
incurred the dislike of a majority of his congregation. The trouble was smoothed over for awhile,
but resulted in his dismission in 1755.

— 9.　Bethia the daughter of Sam^ll. Shepherd was interred.　She died on monday night last.

— 11.　little study, rec^d. M^r. Calamys caveat against ye new prophets from M^r. Ruggles.[1]

— 13.　Lords day I preached A: M: from luk. 8. 12. and P.M: from rom. 6. 1.

— 14.　This day . . . reading concerning ye french prophets

— 15.　This day visited M^r. Woodbridge found him better than I expected.　Saw a Letter directed to him, M^r. Ozias Pitkin, and M^r. William Pitkin, ye most abominable thing y^t almost ever I saw.[2]

— 17.　This day not very profitably spent, Little Study, diverted by Various affairs — rec^d. a letter from Govern^r. Law desiring me, if M^r. Steel fails to preach ye Election Sermon[3]

— 20.　Lords day I preached . . . and baptized Jerusha ye daughter of M^r. James Bicknel, and at night preached at the school house from heb. 4. 13.

— 21.　This day to little profit.　M^r. Stiles of N. Haven here.

— 23.　This day in Study &^c.　M^r. White of Bolton here in ye afternoon. . . .

— 24.　This day went over ye river, Lecture there, M^r. Hunting[4] preached from psal. 73. 27.　Lord have Compassion on that people and provide for them

— 27.　Lords day I preached . . . Stephen Turner and his wife owned ye Covenant.

— 29.　This day Study &^c. received a letter from my uncle James Dated at Norwich March 25. 1743. o Lord look with Compassion on this Land, save us from error, heresy & confusion

— 31.　Lecture in ye afternoon I preached from heb. 12. 2.　may the blessing of god attend what has been spoken.

[1] Rev. Thomas Ruggles of Guilford, born in that place Nov. 27, 1704; grad. Y. C. 1723; ordained at Guilford March 26, 1729; Fellow of Y. C. from 1746 till his death Nov. 20, 1770. He was an Old Light; a man of considerable scholarship; published several sermons, and left a manuscript history of Guilford, since printed.

[2] Troubles in East Hartford growing out of Mr. Woodbridge's disability and the unsuccessful attempts to settle a colleague pastor had been increasing for a good while. In connection with some phase of this affair Roger Bidwell wrote the letter above referred to. Upon which he was by complaint brought before the General Assembly charged with "making and publishing a false, scandalous, infamous libel against Ozias Pitkin, William Pitkin Esquires and the Rev. Mr. Samuel Woodbridge in particular." Bidwell pleaded guilty; was adjudged disabled of voting in any public meeting, or acting on any jury, and was bound over to keep the peace under penalty

[3] Mr. Steel as before noticed (p. 14, note) kept the appointment, and spared Mr. Wadsworth the necessity.

[4] Jonathan Huntting; one of the several candidates recommended as colleagues to Rev. Mr. Woodbridge at East Hartford. He was born at East Hampton, L. I., in October, 1714; grad. Y. C. 1735; failed early in health, and "became a small merchant in his native town," dying ther Sept. 3, 1750, in his 36th year.

April 1743

Apl. 3. Lords day I preached A.M. . . . and administred yᵉ Sacrament and P.M. Mʳ. Marsh¹ of Kent preached . . . at night I preached at yᵉ school house from luk. 12. 31.

— 4. This day visiting &ᶜ. hardly best to Invite Mʳ. E:² to preach &ᶜ.

— 6. This day a lecture at Farmington Mʳ. E. Whitman preached from Cant. 1. 3.

— 6. This day brother John and myself finished yᵉ partition of our Land, returned home found my family well. Laus Deo.

— 8. Mʳ. Eliot of Boston here, Mʳ. Graham³ also.

— 10. Lords day I preached from heb. 12. 2. per totum, and baptized mary yᵉ daughter of Wᵐ Nickols. at night at yᵉ School house

— 11. This day lecture Mʳ. Colton preached from psal. 122. 8. 9. Freemans meeting Capt. Marsh and Mʳ. Buckingham chosen deputies.

— 13. This day publick fast. I preached A.M. from Ezk. 7. 5. and Mʳ. Whitman P.M. from pr. 3. 25. may yᵉ prayers of gods people be heard.

— 16. I am exercised with many thoughts about yᵉ times, I pray God direct assist and strengthen me in this difficult day, o Lord in thee do I trust.

— 17. Lords day I preached pʳ. totum from Matt. 22. 32. 38. 39. 40. baptized Elizabeth yᵉ daughter of Thom. Loree. O Lord appear for and help and relieve me I pray under all my difficulties.

— 20. This day overseeing business, workmen &ᶜ. pleasant weather; wearied with yᵉ affairs of this present evil world.

— 21. This day reading yᵉ christian History study &ᶜ.

---

¹ Rev. Cyrus Marsh, born in Plainfield March 14, 1718-19; grad. Y. C. 1739; ordained over a new church gathered at Kent, May 6, 1741. He was Old Light in his sympathies and in some trouble with his congregation thereabout. He left the ministry under something of a cloud, but represented the town in the General Assembly in May, 1761, and for twelve or more sessions afterward. He died June 9, 1771.

² Probably the Mr. Eliot spoken of two days later. He was Rev. Andrew Eliot, born about 1710; grad. H. C. 1737; ordained at Boston, as colleague with Mr. Webb at the New North Church, April 14, 1742. Mr. Wadsworth's hesitation about inviting him to preach was probably owing to apprehension respecting his position on the New-Measures question of the day; an apprehension which his companionship with Rev. John Graham tended to increase.

³ Rev. John Graham, born in Edinburgh, Scotland, in 1694; educated as a physician at Glasgow; came to America in 1718; ordained at Stafford, May 25, 1723; dismissed for inadequate support 1731; installed at what is now Southbury, Jan. 17, 1733; died in office Dec. 11, 1774. He was an ardent advocate of Whitefield and the New-Measures generally.

— 24. Lords day I preached from rom. 6. 17. per totum I pray god bless his word . . .

— 25. This day reading Baxters Saints everlasting Rest. Messr⁹. Steel and White here

— 28. In yᵉ afternoon a Lecture at Mʳ. Whitmans meeting he preached from Eph. 1. 6.

May, 1743.

May 1. Lords day I preached pʳ. totum from heb. 2. 17. and administred yᵉ Sacrament. baptized Levi yᵉ son of Elisha Pratt. preached at night at yᵉ school house from Joh. 9. 4.

— 2. This day reading in Flavel &ᶜ. a little rainy weather. dies fere sine linea.

— 3. This day some Study. a Comᵗᵉᵉ. of the east here. yᵉ association Comᵗᵉᵉ. advised them to Mʳ. David Judson¹ to preach for yᵐ.

— 6. This day Study. god be pleased to grant me his gracious assistance in finishing yᵉ discourse I have begun upon a future Judgment, yᵗ it may be an instructive, awakening discourse and if I have opportunity to deliver it may it be accompanied with thy blessing, o Lord.

— 8. Lords day I preached A: M: from heb. 2. 17. and P.M. from rom. 1. 18. I pray God to bless what was spoken . . .

— 10. visited Mʳ. Woodbridge, found him much in yᵉ same state as to health he has for some time been in.

— 11. This day little Study. Several good friends visited me. may yᵉ blessing of God rest on yᵐ

— 12. This day Election &ᶜ. yᵉ Governʳ. Dep: Governʳ. and Assistants as in yᵉ year past saving yᵗ Colonᶦ. Bulkley was chosen in yᵉ room of Col: Huntington.

— 15. Lords day Mʳ. Webster preached for me A.M. from Matt. 27. 37. and P.M. I preached from act. 17. 31. and baptized Susannah yᵉ daughter of Stephen Turner

— 16. This day little Study. rainy weather. more news of yᵉ awfull outbreakings of gross sin in yᵉ Land

— 18. This day . . . recᵈ a letter from Mʳ. Hunn.

— 20. This day Study &ᶜ. discoursed with a person under Considerable concern yᵉ general assembly resolved to call Mʳ.

¹ Rev. David Judson, born in Stratford, Sept. 26, 1715; grad. Y. C. 1738; ordained at Newtown, Sept. 21, 1743; died in office Sept. 24, 1776. Under his leadership and in consequence of sermons preached and published by him the major part of his church and society in 1773 rejected that part of the Saybrook Platform relating to church discipline, and renounced connection with Fairfield Consociation.

Owen [1] to an account for his opprobrious expressions relating to yᵉ Civil authority

— 22. Lords day I preached A: M from heb. 13. 9. . . . and P.M: from act. 17. 31. and at night from heb. 10. 31. Laboured under much indisposition

— 25. This day indisposed, read something in Baxter &ᶜ. visited at night by some gentlemen of yᵉ general assembly.

— 26. This day visited yᵉ prison &ᶜ. discoursed yᵉ negroe woman committed on suspicion of murdering her child. She denies yᵉ fact.

— 27. This day under some perplexity and difficulty. yᵉ genˡˡ. Court adjourned I prayed at yᵉ close of yᵉ Court.

— 29. Lords day I preached . . . and baptized Anne yᵉ daughter of Daniel Butler and Hannah yᵉ daughter of Thomas Welles Junʳ. o Lord bless I pray my poor Labours.

— 30. Visited Mʳ. Colton. . . . yᵉ man yᵗ was drowned on yᵉ 13 instant found this day

        June begins

June 2. lecture P.M. I preached from rom. 4. 25. . . .

— 4. Lord prepare my heart for yᵉ duties of yᵉ Sabbath, to approach to yᵉ table of yᵉ Lord

— 5. Lords day I preached A.M. 1. Cor. 11. 23. 24. 25. and administred yᵉ Sacramᵗ. and P:M. from act. 3. 26. and in yᵉ evening at yᵉ school house from luk. 12. 5. I pray God succeed my weak Labours.

— 7. This day went to yᵉ assocⁿ. at Bolton.[2]

— 8. This day Lecture at Bolton, Mʳ. Whitman of Hartford preached from Ezekiel 36. 26.

— 9. returned from Bolton, found my family well, Laus Deo. heard yᵗ a man was killed yesterday at Wethersfield with yᵉ thunder, may I be prepared for my own great and Last change.

— 10. . . . yesterday a Negro fellow was committed to prison for committing a rape between Middletown and Haddam; great are yᵉ outbreakings of sin in yᵉ Land.

---

[1] Rev. John Owen of Groton. He was a native of Braintree, Mass.; grad. H. C. in 1723; ordained at Groton in November, 1727, and died in 1753. The occasion of Mr. Owen's "defamatory and invective speeches Against the laws and authority of this government" was probably his dislike of the stringent legislative enactments against the itinerants and kindred measures. He acknowledged his fault, asked "pardon for what he had done amiss" and promised "to teach and yield due obedience" for the time to come. Whereupon the Assembly accepted his confession and ordered him dismissed on payment of costs, which amounted to £4. 11s. 6d.

[2] One of the questions raised at this meeting of the Association was: "Whether males under the age of Twenty one years and slaves that are members in full communion with a church are to be allowed to give their Vote in matters of Discipline in the church? Resolved in the Negative."

— 12. Lords day I preached   baptized Thomas ye son
of Thomas Andrews Junr.

— 13. This day reading M^r. Fishers pamphlet relating to ye religious commotions in Scotland.

— 19. Lords day I preached   Laboured under weakness
and difficulty in speaking

— 22. This day reading &^{c}. M^r. Edwards of Scantick and his
wife here on a visit.

— 26. Lords day I preached p^r. totum from luk. 19. 27. Catechised ye children in ye afternoon as I did also ye last Sabbath:
at night preached at ye School house from 2 rev. 21. 22

— 28. Visited M^r. Woodbridge in ye afternoon   .   .   .

— 30. A lecture in ye afternoon at M^r. Whitmans meeting he
preached from Cant. 1. 4.

      July 1743

July 3. Lords day I preached A.M. from Matt. 16. 21. and administred ye Sacrament and P.M. from Act. 20. 21. went thro'
my work with great difficulty, my strength seems to fail me,
speaking hurts me exceedingly: Lord may thy blessing attend on my weak Labours

— 5. This day reading M^r. Hookers book entitled ye doubting
christian drawn to Christ.[1]

— 6. This day visited M^r. Colton &^{c}. read a sermon of Doct^r.
Doddridges on the character of ye unregenerate

— 7. reading Doct^r. Doddridges Sermons on regeneration. May
I be enabled to make a due improvment of y^m.

— 9. This day I was exercised with great pain. .   disabled
from business

— 10. Lords day my illness abated, but not able to go out I
pray god to be with my people and bless ye means y^y enjoy.

— 11. This day almost recovered to usual health, blessed be God
for it. read something in Doct^r Doddridges Sermons.

— 12. This day reading &^{c}. in ye afternoon my wife was delivered of a son.[2] blessed be god for it. God grant she may be
raised up to health and strength and ye life of ye child be preserved and wee have grace to bring it up in his fear.

— 17. Lords day I preached A.M. from Act. 20. 21. and P.M.
from 2 pet. 3. 9. and baptized my son Jeremiah and Olive y^e

[1] Ante, p. 69, note.

[2] Jeremiah; afterward Commissary General of the Continental Army; delegate 1786-8 to
the Continental Congress; representative from 1789 to 1795 in the National Congress; died in
Hartford April 30, 1804.

daughter of Moses Cadwell. I laboured under great weakness and bodily indisposition.

— 19.   in ye afternoon visited M^r. Woodbridge

— 21.   This day reading Baxter &^{c}. in the afternoon visited M^r. Bissell of Wintonbury. a thunder storm at night   will god prevent ye awfull effects y^t sometimes attend such storms

— 24.   Lords day I preached . .   and propounded Daniel Skinner to own ye Covenant.   . . at night preached at ye School house from luk. 8. 12.

— 31.   Lords day M^r. Morison preached for me, A: M: from psal. 65. 9. and P.M from Job. 13. 15.   Daniel Skinner owned the Covenant and his daughter Jerusha was baptized

   August begins

Aug. 1. This day visited and prayed with a sick woman in ye forenoon, in the afternoon visited ye criminals in prison and prayed with y^m.   .   .   .

— 2. This day in ye morning visited a poor woman adying, she died before I left ye house.   .   .   .

— 3.   This day   ye wife of Thomas Andrews Junr. was buried.

— 4. This day . . . visited ye prisoners; in the afternoon preached a lecture from 1. cor. 5. 8.

— 5. This day . .   an Infant born before its time   buried. viz. Isaac Clarks.

— 7. Lords day   I am by and by to administer ye Sacrament, God permitting, and what now is the state of my soul, art thou at peace with God. I humbly hope I am I think if I know myself and w^t faith is I have believed on Christ; Lord I believe help mine unbelief.   preached A.M. from rom. 5. 6 and administred ye Sacrament, in ye afternoon from psal. 39. 9. and baptized Christian ye daughter of Abraham Cadwell. at night preached at ye School house from luk. 13. 24.

— 8. . . . in ye afternoon visited and prayed with poor Ann Williamsson. . . .

— 9. This day entred into a serious examination of my state which I have written and purpose to transcribe into this Diary[1]

— 10. This day went over ye river to visit M^r. Woodbridge and

---

[1] A purpose, happily, left unfulfilled. That Mr. Wadsworth was a devout, sincere Christian, no one who reads this Diary can doubt. The narrower "examination" he inflicted upon himself if recorded would have pained others besides himself.

to Scantick to visit M\'. Edwards, returned home found my family well Laus Deo.

— 11.   This day visited y* Negroes in prison   found one of y\'\" something penitent, the other pretty far from being so

— 14.   Lords day I preached per totum from 1 pet. 1. 15. and baptized Samuel the son of Barzillai Clark, went thro' my work with difficulty.   Labouring under much weakness. . . .

— 15.   This day dejected   . read something in Baxters Saints everlasting rest.

— 17.   This day went to Durham, found my friends well Laus Deo.

— 18.   This day returned home found my family well Laus Deo. blessed be God that has preserved me in my outgoings and returning.   . . .

— 19.   This day visited y* negroes in prison, one of y** seems to be considerably penitent.

— 21.   Lords day preached p\'. totum from luk 8: 21. and at night in y* school house from phil. 3. 18. 19.

— 22.   Visited y* sick &*.   M\'. White here at night

— 23.   This day visited M\'. Colton.   Visited a sick man and prayed with him &*.

— 24.   Visited M\'. Woodbridge in y* forenoon.   in y* afternoon visited the negroes in prison.   one of y** seems to be much affected and concerned.

— 25.   This day reading Edwards history of errors[1] &*.

— 26.   this day is eleven year since I came to live in this Town. hitherto y* Lord has preserved me blessed be his name.

— 28.   Lords day I preached   . .   Laboured under great difficulty in speaking.   . . .

— 30.   This day visited a sick man & prayed with him twice, y* Last time apprehended him to be adying, but he revived.   I pray God to raise him up to health.

— 31.   Went to the west Division to a meeting of y* association Com***, returned home safely Laus Deo.

        September begins

Sept. 1.   This day in y* forenoon visited a woman in great distress. in y* afternoon Lecture at M\'. Whitmans meeting.   M\'. Whitman preached from 1 Joh. 3. 5.   Visited y* negroes and prayed with y**.

---

[1] *Gangraena, or a Catalogue and Discovery of many of the Errors, Heresies, Blasphemies and pernicious Practices of the Sectaries of this time*, by Thomas Edwards, a Presbyterian minister of England, published in 1646.

— 4. Lords day I preached A: M. from heb. 7. 26. and administred y⁰ Lords Supper and P. M: from Isai. 65. 2. and baptized
Aaron y⁰ son of Lieu⁰. John Cook.

— 5. y⁰ forenoon spent in prayer for M⁰. Austin grievously sick,
with a number of christians, in y⁰ afternoon visiting y⁰ sick in
my own parish. . . . at night M⁰. John Austin died.

— 6. This day visited a sick woman in y⁰ forenoon, in y⁰ afternoon prayed at Court visited y⁰ negroes in Goal read Doct⁰.
Chaunceys book upon y⁰ times[1] &⁰

— 7. . . . M⁰. John Austin Interred. this day died y⁰ widow
Clark in 71 year of her age

— 8. This day prayed at Court &⁰. M⁰. Eliot of Kellingsworth
here in y⁰ forenoon, and M⁰. Eliot of Boston at night. y⁰
widow Clark Interred at night

— 9. . . . y⁰ Grandjurors found y⁰ bill against y⁰ 3 negroes in
prison. I pray God to give y⁰ poor criminals repentence

— 11. Lords day I preached A: M: from Job 16. 22 and P.M. from
Isai. 65. 2. I pray God to bless his word . . .

— 12. This day M⁰. Hancock and M⁰. Smith here in y⁰ forenoon.
Kate a negroe wench Tried this day for y⁰ murder of her child
and found guilty

— 14. Commencement at N. Haven, the affairs of y⁰ commencement conducted with decency and order

— 18. Lords day I preached A.M. from rev. 21. 8. and P.M. from
Act 10. 43. and baptized John y⁰ son of Thomas Croswell

— 19. . . . Visited y⁰ condemned prisoners. found one y⁰
very stupid.

— 20. This day Freemans meeting Capt: Marsh and M⁰. Buckingham chosen Deputies

— 21. This day visited y⁰ condemned prisoners. found one of
y⁰ very stupid, and in an undesirable condition.

— 25. Lords day I preached per totum from luk. 13. 3. and baptized Susannah y⁰ daughter of Samuel Flagg and at night
preached at y⁰ school house from rev. 7. 14.

— 27. This day visited y⁰ condemned Negroes found y⁰ but little
affected with y⁰ condition

— 29. This day lecture in y⁰ afternoon I preached from psal.
73. 28

---

[1] Dr. Charles Chauncey's *Seasonable Thoughts on the State of Religion in New England*,
now just published. Among the Hartford subscribers for this celebrated volume are to be found
Rev. D. Wadsworth, Rev. Elnathan Whitman, Rev. Benjamin Colton, Mrs. Abigail Woodbridge
(three copies), Mr. John Cook, Mr. David Ensign, Mr. John Whiting, Mr. Stephen Steel. Rev.
Samuel Whitman of Farmington subscribed for two copies.

October 1743

Oct. 1. This day in Study. visited ye negroe man condemned to die, prayed with him.

— 2. Lords day I preached . . . admitted Agnes Humphreys into ye church and adminstred ye Sacrament .

— 3. . . . visited ye prisoners condemned to die

— 4. This day went to ye association at Southington, M^r. Adonijah Bidwell[1] and M^r. Noah Welles[2] were examined and Licensed to preach.

— 5. This day Lecture at Southington M^r. Collins preached from prov. 12. 26. ye next association to be at ye West Division on ye 1st Tuesday in Feb. M^r. Bartholomew to preach. ye next at Farmington M^r. Steel to preach, ye 1st Tuesday in June, ye next at Wellington, I am appointed to preach.

— 9. Lords day I preached . . and at night at ye school house from rom. 1. 18.

— 10. Visited ye sick. in ye afternoon visited M^r. Woodbridge found him much better than usual

— 11. This day visited ye negroes under sentence of death in ye forenoon. in the afternoon visited a sick man.

— 12. . . . M^r. Merrick[3] of Branford here at night.

— 13. This day writing a letter to a friend in England . . . Wrote a letter also to a friend at New-Haven

— 14. . . . Visited also ye negroes in goal. o y^t god would give y^m repentence unto salvation.

— 16. Lords day I preached per totum from Deut. 5. 29. ye Lord bless his word and make it effectual.

— 18. Visited prisoners under sentence of death. Lord give y^m repentence unto salvation

— 19. This day went to ye West Division to visit M^r. Colton. returned found my family well, Laus Deo.

— 21. Visited ye prisoners .

---

[1] Born in Hartford, Oct. 18, 1716; grad. Y. C. 1740; ordained Oct. 5, 1744; chaplain of the Connecticut fleet in the Cape Breton expedition of 1745; installed at Tyringham now Monterey, Mass., Oct. 3, 1750; died in office June 2, 1784. His journal of the Cape Breton expedition is printed in the N. E. Historical and Genealogical Register, volume xxvii, pp. 153 59.

[2] Born in Colchester Sept. 25, 1718; grad. Y. C. 1741; teacher of Hopkins Grammar School in Hartford while studying theology; recommended by Hartford North Association in 1742 to the troublesome East Hartford pulpit to aid Mr. Woodbridge; ordained at Stamford Dec. 31, 1746; died in office of jail-fever contracted while ministering to British prisoners Dec. 31, 1776. He was Fellow of Y. C. 1744 to his death; preached the Election Sermon May 10, 1764; and published several Anti-Episcopalian tracts in defence of Presbyterian ordination.

[3] Rev. Jonathan Merrick, born in Springfield, Mass., Aug. 13, 1700; grad. Y. C. 1725; ordained at North Branford at a date not precisely determined; died June 27, 1772. A Fellow of Y. C. from 1763 to 1769, and in the divisions of the time an Old Light.

— 23. Lords day I preached A; M. from rev. 22. 12. and P.M; from Matt. 13. 44 . . .

— 24. . . Visited ye prisoners . . .

— 27. . . . M^r. John Skinner died aged [blank] in ye afternoon visited ye negroes in prison . . ye Lord prepare those poor creatures for y^r great change.

— 28. . . . in ye afternoon was Interred M^r. John Skinner

— 30. Lords day I preached p^r. totum from psal. 90. 12. and admitted Ruth Clark to full communion with ye church. at night preached at ye school house from rev. 3. 18.

November begins

Nov. 1. Study &^c. Visited ye prisoners &^c.

— 3. . . . in ye afternoon a lecture at M^r. Whitmans meeting M^r. Marsh preached from Jam. 1. 15.

— 4. . . . rec^d. a letter from uncle James.

— 6. Lords day I preached A.M. from rev. 5. 21. and administred ye Sacrament and P.M. from 1 tim. 6. 6.

— 7. . Visited ye sick. and in ye afternoon ye prisoners . . . and prayed with y^m

— 10. This day publick thanksgiving in Connecticutt. I preached from psal. 116. 12. blessed be ye Lord y^t has preserved me thro' another year and spared ye lives of my wife, children and servant. o y^t wee might all live to ye glory of God our preserver

— 11. . . . Visited ye prisoners . o Lord have pity on those poor creatures

— 13. Lords day preached A.M. from Ezek. 18. 30 and P.M. from 1 tim. 6. 6. and baptized Nathaniel ye son of Daniel Goodwin.

— 14. Visited ye prisoners . . .

— 15. James Logan was buried who died last Lords day about noon.

— 16. This day a lecture at our meeting house M^r. E. Whitman preached from psal. 15. previous to ye execution of Jack and Kate two negroes ye one condemned to die for a rape ye other for murdering her child. y^y were executed about 3 o'clock P.M. may it be a warning to all others.

— 19. . . . Went over ye river at night

— 20. Lords day I preached on ye East Side of ye River A.M. from Deut. 13. 11. and P.M: from rom. 5. 1.

— 21. This day returned home found my family well. Laus Deo.
read the American Magazine[1] for yᵉ month of Sept. 1743.

— 23.   reading Rutherfords sermons

— 24. . . .   writing a letter to Scotland &ᶜ.

— 27. Lords day I preached A.M. from Deut. 13. 11. and P.M.
from Eph. 4. 29. and baptized James yᵉ son of Samuel Andrus

December 1743

Dec. 1. . . .   in yᵉ afternoon a lecture   I preached from phil.
2. 8, at night married Hezekiah Marsh and Christian Edwards.

— 4. Lords day I preached   and administred yᵉ Sacrament. . .

— 8. This day   recd. a letter to go to a Councel at Wos-
tershire

— 11. Lords day I preached . . .   and baptized Susanna yᵉ
daughter of Nehemiah Cadwell. yᵉ Lord bless his word and
make it effectual

— 13. Went to Weathersfield &ᶜ. Wrote a letter to Doctʳ. Doddridge, by Mʳ. Rod: Morison[2]

— 14. This day . . .   delivered a letter to Mʳ. Rod: Morison
to go to Doctor Doddridge. Mʳ. Morison set out in order to
embark at New London

— 15. . . .   at night Elijah Cadwell and Rebecca Burr were
married

— 18. Lords day I preached pʳ totum from gal. 22. 21, and baptized William the son of Mʳ. Samuel Talcott, yᵉ Lord bless
him and make him a blessing.

— 20. This day visiting &ᶜ. recd. a letter at night to go to a
Councel at Southington the first Tuesday in January next

— 21. . . .   reckoned with yᵉ Societies Comᵗᵗᵉᵉ. at night

— 25. Lords day I preached pr. totum from rom. 2. 14. I pray
God to bless his word . . .

— 28. This day reading yᵉ Christian History &ᶜ. snowy weather

— 29. This day reading &ᶜ. in yᵉ afternoon a lecture at Mʳ.
Whitmans meeting   Mʳ. Whitman preached from rev. 7. 14.
at night I preached at yᵉ school house from rom. 10. 4.

---

[1] This was the first number of the *American Magazine and Historical Chronicle.* The
work was issued three years and four months, at Boston, by Samuel Eliot and Joshua Blanchard,
and then discontinued.

[2] Roderick Morison, a brother of Dr. Normand and Rev. Evander Morison. He died in
Hartford in 1751.

January 1743/4.

Jany. 1. Lords day. I preached A.M. from 1. pet. 18. 19. and administred yᵉ Sacrament and P.M. from Jam. 4. 14. and yᵉ
church chose Deacⁿ Edwards a messengʳ to go to a Councel at
Southington [1]

— 3. This day went to Southington to a Councel. yᵉ Councel
opened &ᶜ.

— 4. This day yᵉ Councel finished and I returned home, found
my family well, Laus Deo.

— 5. This day reading &ᶜ. I pray God to direct me to a Suitable subject on which to prepare a Sermon. Dreamed I saw
D. L. wᵗ does it portend.

— 8. Lords day I preached pʳ. totum from heb. 12. 25. I pray
yᵗ god would bless his word . . .

— 9. .   wrote a letter to Mʳ. Eliot at Boston

— 10. . . . Mʳ. Collins here in yᵉ morning.

— 12. This day in Study. at night preached at yᵉ School house.
. . . direct o Lord and assist me I pray in preparing sermons for yᵉ Sabbath

— 13. This day in study. at night discoursed with a member of
yᵉ church under difficulty, yᵉ Lord bring to a sense of his duty.

— 15. Lords day I preached pʳ. totum from rev. 2. 4. and baptized Levi the son of James Shepard.

— 19. . . . in yᵉ afternoon married Return Strong of Windsor
to Sarah Nickols of Hartford.

— 22. Lords day I preached pʳ. totum from Deut. 32. 28. and
baptized Sarah yᵉ daughter of John Lord

— 24. This day visited a poor distressed woman Mʳ. Hunn here.

— 25. This day went to Farmington with my good friend Mʳ.
Hunn, heard Mʳ. Adams[2] preach from Eph. 2. 8.

— 27. This day . . . Brᵗʰʳ. Cowles[3] here at night

— 29. Lords day I preached per totum from Matt. 24. 42. and
baptized John yᵉ son of Mʳ. Niel Mᶜ.Lean and Obadiah yᵉ son
of Daniel Spencer.

[1] Doubtless on some phase of the long controversy in the parish of Rev. Jeremiah Curtis
(ante, p. 31) growing out of the Whitefieldian difficulties. A previous council in the year 1743 had
been made the subject of great local wrangle and of appeal to legislative aid.

[2] Probably Joseph Adams, who about this time was recommended by the Hartford North
Association to the church in New Cambridge, now Bristol. He was born in Lebanon Aug. 26, 1717;
grad. Y. C. 1740; preached, apparently, at various places in 1744-45, but settled in New Haven as
an attorney and innkeeper, and died Oct. 16, 1782.

[3] Husband of Mr. Wadsworth's sister Sarah.

— 29. This day reading ye plain account[1] &^c. visited M^r. Woodbridge.

— 31. This day reading Christ: Loves[2] Sermons and Firmins
Real Christian &^c.

February begins

Feby. 2. This day lecture in ye afternoon. I preached from psal.
105. 5.

— 4. This day in Study. Lord prepare my heart for ye duties of
thine holy day   O blessed Saviour may I meet thee at thine
holy supper tomorrow. give me a devout frame, and help to
lead in ye services of ye day as becomes a minister of thine

— 5. Lords day I preached pr. totum from John 21. 17. and administred ye Sacrament. ye Lord bless his word and make it
effectual.

— 6. This day   reading Tailor on ye doctrine of original
sin[3]

— 7. This day went to ye association at y^r west division.

— 9. . .   at night preached at ye school house from prov.
23. 26.

— 12. Lords day I preached per totum from psal. 106. 40. 41.

. . .

— 18. This day in Study. the Comet y^t appeared in y^r west has
bin seen of late in ye east particularly as I am Informed on
wednesday morning this week, and on this day its said to
have bin seen about ye middle of ye day about an hour before
ye sun.[4]

---

[1] Probably Bishop Benjamin Hoadly's *Plain Account of the Nature and End of the Sacrament of the Lord's Supper*, published in 1735.

[2] An English Presbyterian divine (1618-1651) executed under charge of treason against the
Commonwealth. A voluminous and evangelic writer, who seems to have been made the victim perhaps of some personal indiscretions but more of the political exigencies of the turbulent hour of
Charles Second's invasion of England at the head of a Scottish army. His books have been characterized as full of "plain practical doctrine, old divinity, sound, solid and conscience-searching
truths."

[3] *The Scriptural Doctrine of Original Sin*, a treatise by Rev. Dr. John Taylor, a Unitarian
minister of Kirkstead in Lincolnshire, England. The book made a great impression on both sides
the Atlantic, and drew forth elaborate answers both from John Wesley and Jonathan Edwards.

[4] The great comet of 1743-44 attracted the attention of European astronomers from its appearance Dec. 9, 1743, to its evanishment in April or later, 1744. It was seen at noonday by observers in
England, and all the countries to Italy. At Bologna it was observed seven successive days in full
sunshine, being at some periods of the brightness of Sirius. Its most distinguishing feature, however, was its multiple tail, being at different stages of its history apparently supplied with from
three to five of these appendages. J. B. Hind, F. R. S., says of its course: "If elliptic at all, it
will be a very remote posterity indeed that will be interested in its return. It is by no means improbable that the appearance of this splendid comet in 1743-44 constituted its first visit to this part
of the universe." In Ames' Almanack for 1745 he gives a metrical table of important chronological
events in which he records it as one year:

"Since in our Skies there blaz'd an awful Star, Presaging Earthquake and a General War"

— 19. Lords day I preached per totum from luk. 14. 19. y⁵ Lord
bless his word and may it be a word in season. at night
warned a church meeting to be on Tuesday next at 2 oclock
P.M.

— 20. This day Study. in y⁵ morning about half an hour before
sun rise I saw y⁵ comet in y⁵ east about 3 quarters of an hour
high.

— 21. This day had a Church meeting. y⁵ Church voted y' James
Shepard be called to an account for going to y⁵ separate meeting &ᶜ. and for absenting from y⁵ publick worship, and y' Jos.
Wadsworth Junʳ. appear before y⁵ church y' y⁵ church may
hear what he has to say as to the objections made agᵗ. his
owning y⁵ covenant.

— 23. . . . in y⁵ evening preached at y⁵ School house from
psal. 41. 4

26. Lords day I preached per totum from Col. 1. 18. I pray
god to bless it . . .

- 28. This day a chh meeting heard Joseph Wadsworth and
James Shepards case   adjourned y⁵ meeting to y⁵ 3ᵈ Tuesday in March.

- 29. This day study &ᶜ. I pray God to assist and direct me in
y⁵ way of my duty   heal y⁵ difficulties and division in y⁵ chh
o Lord support me I pray under all y⁵ reproaches and injurious
treatment I meet with, may I bear it with a christian spirit
March begins

March 1. This day Lecture at y⁵ S. meeting   Mʳ. Whitman
preached from Joh: 19. 34. in y⁵ evening I preached at y⁵
School house from Matt. 6. 29.

— 4. Lords day I preached A:M. from rom. 5. 8. and administred
y⁵ Sacrament and P.M: from phil. 4. 18. Pricilla negro propounded to own y⁵ covenant.

- 6. This day . . . Mʳ. Steel here, Uncle James at night.

— 7. This day uncle William here. in y⁵ afternoon I attended a
meeting of y⁵ proprietors of Hartland.¹

— 11. Lords day I preached . . . and baptized Nathaniel y⁵
son of Joseph Olcot and Ruth y⁵ daughter of Jedediah
Richards. God bless his word   .

¹ The territory now known as Hartland was part of those lands granted by the General Court
in 1687 to the towns of Windsor and Hartford "to make a plantation or villages thereon." Controversy subsequently arising, it was in 1726 agreed that the lands should be divided and a half of
them confirmed to Hartford and Windsor. By deeds of partition in 1732 " four parcels of land lying
within said tract were set out to the patentees of the town of Hartford," and one of them was
named Hartland, i. e. Hartford land. The first proprietors' meeting was held in Hartford, July 10,
1733. Others followed as above.

— 13. This day   Mr. White of Bolton here.

— 15. This day . . . in yᵉ afternoon Joined Edward Dod and Rebecca Barnard in marriage

— 18. Lords day I preached A: M. from Deut. 32. 15. And P. M: from Amos 5. 6. God grant that his word may take deep root

. . .

— 20. This day a church meeting. the church voted Joseph Wadsworth Junᵣ. not to be admitted to own yᵉ covenᵗ. and James Shepard to render satisfaction &ᶜ. or be censured

— 25. Lords day Mr. Morison preached A: M: from Josh. 24. 15. and I preached P. M. from psal. 32. 5. and baptized Rachel yᵉ daughter of Joseph Shepard Junᵣ. Pricilla a negro woman made a publick confession &ᶜ. owned yᵉ Covenant and was baptized.

— 28. This day in Study. Rector Clap here at night.

— 29. This day lecture in yᵉ afternoon   I preached from 1. Cor. 15. 3.

— 30. This day Mr. Clap went from hence.
        April begins

April 1. Lords day I preached . . . and administred yᵉ Sacrament and . . . had a contribution for Richard Seymour and Samˡˡ. Jones of Canaan [1]

— 5. This day went to Weathersfield preached at night at yᵉ School house from Jam. 4. 14.

— 6. This day   .   nil remarkable occurs

— 7. This day . . . nil remarkable occurs.

— 8. Lords day I preached per totum from 1 Cor. 15. 58. yᵉ Lord bless his word and make it powerfull

— 9. This day lecture in yᵉ forenoon Mr. Whitman preached from psal. 78. 72. freemans meeting Capt. Marsh and Mr. Buckingham chosen Deputies.

— 11. This day a publick fast. I preached A. M. from Jer. 2. 19. and Mr. Whitman P. M. from Jer. 18. 7. 8. yᵉ Lord hear our prayers and accept our humiliations.

— 15. Lords day I preached pr. totum from Matt. 26. 41. yᵉ Lord accompany it with his blessing.

— 16. This day went to Farmington   saw my friends in usual health Laus Deo.

— 17. This day returned from Farmington, found my family well Laus Deo.

---

[1] The people of Canaan were struggling with a church-building enterprise in their but newly commenced settlement. The contribution was probably in aid of this effort, though possibly it had a more personal character.

— 22. Lords day I preached per totum from luk. 12. 58. 59. . . .

— 25. . . . at night Daniel Eggleston and Mary Ashley were married

— 26. This day visited Mr. Woodbridge & Mr. Edwards, returned &c.

— 29. Lords day I preached per totum from prov. 4. 23. And baptized Elizabeth ye daughter of Diostheus Humphreys, went thro' my work with great difficulty by reason of a great cold.

— 30. This day reading Neals History of the Puritans &c.

May 1744

May 3. This day reading Neal &c. in ye afternoon a lecture at Mr. Whitmans meeting. Mr. Whitman preached from Matt. 27. 51.

···· 6. Lords day I preached A.M. . . . and administred ye Sacrament and P.M . . . ye Lord bless his word .

7. This day .   nil remarkable occurs

8. This day . .   nil remarkable occurs

9. This day . . . at night Jonathan Catlin of Harwinton and Thankfull Collier of Hartford were Joined in marriage

— 10. This day Genll. election   Mr. Worthington preached from psal. 77. last verse &c. Gov. Dept. Gov. and assistants as in ye year past.

— 13. Lords day Mr. Whittelsey preached for me. A:M: from luk. 12. 54   and P.M: from luk. 13. 3.

— 15. This day went to Litchfield.

— 16. The Councel convened at Litchfield.[1] determined ye business

— 17. This day returned home, found my family well. Laus Deo.

— 20. Lords day I preached per totum from 2 pet. 3. 14 ye Lord bless his work . . .

— 24. This day little study   Spent some time at Court

— 27. Lords day I preached pr. totum from 1 Cor. 9. 24 And baptized Hannah ye daughter of Jonathan Olcot. . .

28. This day reading Shepards Sound believer

---

[1] Rev. Timothy Collins (ante, p. 81) had been a good while in difficulties in his parish. The trouble was partially about the raising of his salary and had manifested itself as far back as 1728. This year, however, 1744, the town voted "not to make any rate for Mr. Collins under present difficulties"; and the following year voted to appoint a committee to "eject Mr. Collins from the parsonage right." Underlying any salary difficulty, however, was the ecclesiastical one. Mr. Collins was an Old Light, and the consociation of that region was dominated by Dr. Bellamy and New Light sympathies. Mr. Collins was engineered out of his pulpit by their combined influences in 1752; but continued to reside in Litchfield, practice medicine, and serve in public office with the apparent approval of his townsmen till his death. Probably the council to which Mr. Wadsworth went on this occasion was on some phase of Mr. Collins' protracted church tribulations.

— 30. This day visited a poor distressed creature.   Some reading &c.

— 31. This day Study.   lecture in yᵉ afternoon Mʳ. Welles preached from heb. 10. 20

     June begins.

June 1. This day in study.   yᵉ Genˡˡ. Assembly broke up in yᵉ afternoon

— 3. Lords day I preached pr. totum from Matt. 12. 18. and administred yᵉ Sacrament   .   in yᵉ morning about 10 o'clock was an earthquake

— 4.   .   .   .   in yᵉ afternoon comes news yᵗ war with France was proclaimed in Boston Last Saturday.   a paquet comes to our Governʳ. with orders for yᵉ same

— 5. This day went to Farmington   the association met there

— 6. This day Lecture at Farmington, Mʳ. Steel preached from Ezk. 5. 8.   returned home found my family well

— 10. Lords day I preached pʳ. totum from Eccles. 12. 1.   .   .   . in yᵉ afternoon catechised yᵉ children.   in yᵉ forenoon yᵉ Councel of war sat to concert measures to go to Albany to deal with yᵉ Indians.   Commissioners to set out tomorrow morning[1]

— 11. This day Dep: Gov. Wolcot & Col: Stanly set out with a guard for Albany to treat with yᵉ Indians, and in yᵉ afternoon a declaration of war against yᵉ French King was published here.

— 13. This day indisposed.   yᵉ heat of yᵉ weather exceeding great.

— 14.   .   .   .   Mʳ. Rector Clap here at night.   I pray yᵉ Lord to bless him

— 16.   .   .   .   went over yᵉ river

— 17. Lords day preached at yᵉ East side, from rom. 5. 12. A.M. and from Eccl. 2. 17. P.M., returned home found my family well Laus Deo.

— 19. This day went to Durham to the general association[2]

---

[1] The declaration of war by France against England which had been made on March 4th of this year (1744) had awakened alarm as to the attitude of the Indians of the Northwest border.   It was deemed necessary to treat with them to neutralize the French influence always so easily operative in stirring up hostility to the English interests.

[2] The General Association at this Durham meeting answered the following questions :

"Whither a minister or a number of ministers Entring into any Established parish in this Government & then Gathering a Ch of members that had before disorderly separated themselves from the Ch to which they belonged, and some of them actually under Ecclesiastical Censure, be not matter of offence.   Voted in the Affirmative.

Whither to require persons particularly to promise to walk in Communion with this Ch of Christ into w'ch they Seek admission concienciously attending and upholding the Public worship of God in this place till regularly dismist therefrom be a hard or unreasonable term of Communion. Resolve in the negative."

— 20. This day at Durham at ye Gen^ll Association, M^r. Hall preached from Joh. 17. 21.

— 21. This day returned home, found my family well, Laus Deo.

— 22. . . . brother Lewis here from Boston

— 23. This day reading Shackfords Connection: magazine &^c.

— 24. Lords day I preached per totum from psal. 50. 22. and catechised ye children . . .

— 26. This day reading . . Doct^r Colmans Sermon on ye death of Gov. Holden[1]

— 27. This day reading Shackfords Connection, Sir Isaac Newtons Chronology &^c.

— 29. This day . . . in ye afternoon a lecture at ye South meeting house   M^r. Whitman preached from rev. 19. 9.
        July begins

July 1. Lords day I preached pr totum from 2 tim. 2. 8. and administred ye Sacrament of ye Lords Supper

— 3. This day went to ye West Division   Col: Stanley returned from Albany recovered of his indisposition

— 7. This day reading, Prince, Penhallow &^c   Thomas Clap died

— 8. Lords day I preached p^r. totum from 1 pet. 5. 9. and baptized Isaac and Isaiah Twin sons of Moses Ensign   Thomas Clap was buried.

— 12. This day visited ye sick ye Gov. & Councel I hear have appointed a fast on ye 3^d Wednesday of August next.

— 15. Lords day I preached pr. totum from psal. 81. 11. 12. . . . .

— 17. This day went to ye West Division examined and approved M^r. Mills.[2] examined M^r. Webster,[3] adjourned his examination to ye 1st Tuesday in September

— 18. This day visited ye sick. in ye afternoon M^r. Gay[4] of Suffield and his wife here

— 20. This day   . Isaiah ye son of Moses Ensign was buried.

— 21. . went over ye river in ye afternoon

---

[1] Samuel Holden, Governor of the Bank of England, had been a benefactor of the Province of Massachusetts, and his death in 1740 was made the occasion of a discourse by Dr. Benjamin Colman of Boston before the General Court there. "Holden Chapel" at Cambridge, Mass., was built in his memory and by gifts supplied by his widow and daughters.

[2] Doubtless the Gideon Mills ordained the following fifth day of September at Simsbury, *q. v.*

[3] David Webster (see Oct. 11th, *seq.*) born at Glastonbury, Jan. 29, 1721; grad. Y. C. 1741; became a lawyer failing in ability to become a minister; died in Berlin May 12, 1806.

[4] Rev. Ebenezer Gay; born in Dedham, Mass.; grad. H. C. 1737; died at Suffield in 1796, after a ministry of fifty-three years.

— 22. Lords day preached at y[e] East Side from rom. 10. 3. per totum and baptized Rebecca y[e] daughter of Solomon Gilman. returned in y[e] evening found my family well, Laus Deo.

— 24. This day in y[e] afternoon went to Farmington. Sister Ruth sick [1]

26. This day went to Farmington. my sister Ruth sick.

- 27. This day returned from Farmington, my sister Ruth somewhat better Laus Deo

— 29. Lords day I preached A.M: from heb. 12. 10. & P.M. from Matt: 13. 22. and baptized Eunice y[e] daughter of John Shepard.

— 30. This day . . . in y[e] afternoon died John Cole very suddenly in the meadow.

— 31. . . . John Cole Interred

August begins

Aug. 2. This day . . in y[e] afternoon Lecture, I preached from 1. pet. 3. 18

— 4. This day . in y[e] afternoon Robert Webster was Interred.

— 5. Lords day I preached A:M: from 1. pet. 3. 18 and administred y[e] Sacrament and P.M. from Eccles. 8 8. I pray god to bless . . .

— 6. This day visited y[e] sick &[c]. nil remarkable occurs

— 12. Lords day I preacht . . and baptized William y[e] son of Capt. George Wyllys.

— 14. This day studying a sermon for y[e] fast. heard a sorrowfull account of y[e] wickedness of one of my parishoners. o God I pray thee restrain and reform him. direct and assist me in y[e] discharge of my duty to him.

— 15. This day a publick fast on acc[t]. of y[e] war I preached A:M: from 2 chron. 20. 3. 4. and M[r]. Whitman P:M: from Deut. 20. 3. 4.

— 19. Lords day I preached . . .

— 22. This day went to Farmington, saw my friends in usual health. returned home Laus Deo.

— 25. . . . Lord prepare me I pray for thine holy Sabbath.

— 26. Lords day I preached . . . and baptized Rachel y[e] daughter of Stephen Turner

— 28. This day in y[e] afternoon visited M[r]. Woodbridge

— 30. This day in Study: in y[e] afternoon a lecture at M. Whitmans meeting. M[r]. Whitman preached from Dan. 9. 24.

---

[1] Wife of Elisha Lewis of Farmington.

— 31. This day in Study.   Europe in a Tumult
         September begins

Sept. 2. Lords day I preached pʳ. totum from Ezek. 9. 9. and ad-
         ministred yᵉ Sacrament, admitted Isaac Clark into yᵉ church.

— 5. This day went to Symsbury.   Mʳ. Gideon Mills¹ ordained
         there.   I began yᵉ solemnities with prayer, the Revᵈ. Mʳ. Whit-
         man of Farmington preached from Eph. 4. 11.   Mʳ. Colton
         made yᵉ prayer before yᵉ charge   Mʳ. Whitman of Farmington
         gave yᵉ charge   Mʳ. Bissel made yᵉ next prayer, Mʳ. Whitman
         of Hartford gave yᵉ right hand of Fellowship. a very rainy
         day.

— 6. This day returned home found my family well Laus Deo.
         Saw a sorrowfull spectacle by yⁿ way.

— 8. This day in Study.   Mʳ. Townsend and Mʳ. Allyn² here from
         Boston

— 9. Lords day I preached pʳ. totum from Matt. 3. 8. 9. and
         baptized Jerusha yᵉ daughter of Hezekiah Marsh.

— 10. This day travelled to Wallingford.

— 11. This day went to New-Haven   Saw many of my friends
         there

— 12. This day commencement at New-Haven, yᵉ affairs of it
         conducted with decency and order

— 14. This day returned home found my family well, Laus Deo.

— 16. Lords day I preached per totum from rom. 3. 16. and
         baptized Isaac yᵉ son of Isaac Clark

— 18. This day reading Edwards preacher³   Mʳ. Carpenter⁴ of
         Hull here in yᵉ afternoon.

— 23. Lords day I preached pʳ. totum from 1 Cor. 15. 34. and
         baptized Daniel yᵉ son of Capt. John Talcot.

— 24. This day reading Edwards preacher

— 25. This day reading Edwards preacher visiting &ᶜ.

— 28. This day is twelve year since my ordination, blessed be
         god yᵗ has preserved me alive thus Long

¹ Rev. Gideon Mills was born at Windsor, Aug. 15, 1715; grad. Y. C. 1737; taught the Hopkins Grammar School in New Haven in 1738; ordained at Simsbury, Sept. 5, 1744; dismissed in
August, 1754; installed at Canton, Feb. 18, 1761; died in office Aug. 4, 1772. He was a younger
brother of Rev. Jedidiah Mills, and like him a New Light.

² Perhaps the Jeremiah Allen mentioned *ante*, p. 40.

³ *The Preacher*, a book by Rev. Dr. John Edwards, a Calvinist divine (1637–1716) of Colchester and Cambridge, England. The book was published in three parts, successively in 1705,
1706, and 1709.

⁴ Rev. Ezra Carpenter, grad. H. C. 1720; died 1785. He sympathized with the Whitefieldian
revival, but objected to the itinerating habits of Whitefield's followers.

— 30. Lords day I preached pr. totum from psal. 4. 4. I pray
God to bless his word   .

October 1744

Oct. 1. This day visiting ye sick, in ye morning died Capt. John
Marsh, very suddenly aged 75 and in ye afternoon Thomas
King aged 59.

— 2. . . . in ye afternoon Capt. Marsh was Interred

— 3. . . . in ye afternoon Thomas King was Interred.

— 5. This day . . . in ye afternoon a lecture I preached
from heb. 1. 68. 69. under great indisposition

— 6. This day . . . heard ye ships are arrived from England &c.

— 7. Lords day I preached . . . and administred ye Sacrament, in ye morning died Richard Burnham said to be in ye 90th
year of his age

— 8. This day . . . Richard Burnham Interred.

— 11. This day went to ye West Division to finish ye examination
of David Webster, find him Insufficient, would not license him.[1]
Last night died ye widow Mason

— 12. the widow Mason buried in ye 90th year of her age

— 13. Lords day I preached   and baptized Josiah ye son
of Daniel Brace

— 16. This day some reading &c M^r. Chickley[2] of Boston here:
nil remarkable occurs

— 18. This day   brother Lewis and Sister here from
Boston

— 21. Lords day I preached per totum from 1 thes: 5. 6 . .

— 23. This day went to Farmington, saw my friends in usual
health, Laus Deo

— 24. This day returned from Farmington found my family well
Laus Deo.

— 25. This day Study, visiting &c. received a letter from Uncle
James.

— 28. Lords day I preached pr. totum from psal. 28. 5. I pray
God would bless his word and pardon my imperfections

— 31. This day went to Stafford to ye ordination there
November begins

Nov. 1. This day M^r. Colton[3] was ordained M^r. B. Colton preached
from 1 Cor. 4. 1. 2.

---

[1] Ante, July 17th.

[2] Rev. Samuel Checkley, pastor of the New South church in Boston; grad. H. C. 1715;
died 1769.

[3] Rev. Eli Colton, ante, p. 86, note.

— 2. This day returned home found my family well Laus Deo.

— 4. Lords day Mr. Welles preached for me A:M: from Isai. 55. 6. and I administred ye Sacrament. and P.M. I preached from gal 1. 4. Lord bless thy word

— 7. This day . . . visited and prayed with a sick man. Samuel Marshal died

— 8. This day publick Thanksgiving I preached from psal. 31. 21. I bless ye Lord for all ye Instances of his kindness to me in ye year past, that he has preserved my life, ye lives of my wife children and family and for ye health wee have been favoured with, for any fruit in my ministry

— 9. This day . . . Samuel Marshal buried

— 11. Lords day I preached . . . I pray God to bless his word

— 14. This day visited Mr. Woodbridge &c. my birth day.

— 16. This day in Study. at night finished ye settlement of ye Governors Estate

— 18. Lords day I preached pr. totum from 1 pet. 1. 17. . . .

— 20. This day went to Farmington. saw my friends well, returned home safe Laus Deo

— 25. Lords day I preached per totum from 2 thes. 1. 7. 8 . . . pardon o Lord w'ever thou hast seen amiss in me.

— 29. This day . . . in ye afternoon a lecture, I preached from Col. 1. 19.

December 1744

Dec. 2. Lords day I preached pr. totum from 1 Cor. 3. 11. and administred ye Sacrament . . .

— 8. This day Study. read an excellent Caution against Itinerants

— 9. Lords day I preached per totum from psal. 100. 13. . .

- 10. This day visiting ye sick &c. Mr. Collins here at night

— 12. This day went to Farmington. Ye Comtee. of ye Association met advised New Cambridge to Mr. Newel

— 14. . . . At night Joined Doctr. Daniel Lathrop[1] and Mrs. Jerusha Talcot in marriage.

— 15. . . . Mr. Marsh of Kent here in ye afternoon. . . .

— 16. Lords day I preached A.M. from phil. 2. 15. and P.M. from heb. 3. 12. I pray God to bless . . .

:- 17. This day visited a sick child &c. Nil remarkable occurs

---

[1] Of Norwich. He was born May 1, 1712; grad. Y. C. 1733; studied medicine in London; established the first drug store in Connecticut; became by his marriage Mr. Wadsworth's brother-in-law. He died in Norwich, Jan. 8, 1782; his widow died at the same place, Sept. 14, 1805.

— 23. Lords day I preached . . . I pray y' Gods word might be accompanied with y' operations of his Spirit

— 26. This day . recd. a letter from M'. Hunn dated Dec. 3. 1744

— 27. This day in Study. blessed be god that has disposed my people to contribute so liberally to my support. may I be excited and encouraged to serve y'" faithfully and be abundantly assisted therein

— 30. Lords day I preached A.M: from matt. 7. 22. 23. and P.M. from Matt. 5. 8 I pray god to make his work awakening and convincing and Instructive to them y' heard it.

January begins [1745]

Jan. 2. This day Study &'. went to y' west division sent a letter to Doct'. chauncey p' M' Butler

— 3. . . . Sent a letter to M'. Hunn p'. M'. Day. in y' afternoon a lecture at M'. Whitmans meeting. M'. Whitman preached from heb. 9. 15

— 6. Lords day I preached per totum from Johs 13. 34 and administred y' Sacrament Elijah Cadwell owned y' Covenant and Elijah his son was baptized

— 10. This day study, visiting &'. remember o Lord y' poor Lame person I have visited this day, relieve and heal her.

— 13. Lords day I preached per totum from psal. 96. 9. I pray God to bless his word and make it effectual

— 16. This day in Study. M'. Marsh and M'. Mills here

— 17. This day . . . in y' afternoon visited M'. Woodbridge.

— 19. This day in Study. a weighty case propounded to me, I pray god assist and direct me in y' resolution of it

20. Lords day I preached pr. totum from luk. 5. 32. Thomas Burr Jun'. owned the Covenant and Samuel y' son of Thomas Burr Jun'. was baptized

— 21. This day in visiting &'. reading magazine, Dr. Chaunceys Sermon &'.

— 22. This day Travelled to Bolton Lodged at M'. Whites.

— 23. This day travelled to Norwich

— 24. This day spent at Norwich in the afternoon a lecture M'. Lord preached from Joh. 12. 57.

— 25. This day set out for home. came to East-hartford, snowy in y' afternoon

— 26. This day got home found my family well, Laus Deo.

— 27. Lords day I preached A: M: from luk. 5: 32 & P.M. from
prov. 11. 21. I pray God to bless his word . . .

— 30. This day in Study, wrote a letter also to M^r. Whittlesey[1]

— 31. This day . in ye afternoon preached a lecture from
rev. 14. 4.

February

Feb. 3. Lords day I preached per totum from rev. 14. 4. and administred ye Sacrament. . . .

— 5. This day went to ye association at Windsor. ye association
agreed upon a Testimony ag^t. M^r. Whitefield[2]

— 6. at ye association &^c. M^r. Whitman of H. preached a lecture
from Joh. 15. 5.

— 7. This day . . . rec^d. a letter from M^r. Clap

— 10. Lords day I preached A: M: from prov. 11. 21 and P.M:
from rom. 6. 22. . . .

— 17. Lords day I preached A.M. from rom. 6. 22. and P.M. from
prov. 1. 24. 25. 26. . . .

— 19. This day Study, visiting &^c. a negro committed to prison
for a Rape.

— 22. This day in Study. 2 delinquents here to discourse
about confessing &^c.

— 24. Lords day I preached A: M: from prov. 1. 24. 25. 26. and
P.M: from prov. 28. 13. Moses Barnard his wife owned y^e
Covenant

— 25. This day went to Kensington to visit my friends

[1] Probably Rev. Samuel Whittlesey of Wallingford, or his son, Rev. Samuel Whittlesey of
Milford; both were "Old Lights." The father was born at Saybrook in 1686; grad. Y. C. 1705;
ordained at Wallingford May 17, 1710; Fellow of Y. C. from 1732 onward; preached the Election
Sermon May 13, 1731; died April 15, 1752.
The son was born at Wallingford July 10, 1713; grad. Y. C. 1729; ordained at Milford Dec.
9, 1737; died in office Oct. 22, 1768.

[2] A second journey of Mr. Whitefield was now anticipated. In view of it the Association of
Hartford County, like many other similar bodies, adopted a Testimony against his methods. It
will suffice to quote only a portion of this document.

"As the Errors, Disorders and Confusions which for some years past have so generally
prevailed through the Churches of this Land, had their Rise (as we apprehend) from the Preaching and Management of the Rev. Mr. *George Whitefield* in his former visit to *New England*
. . . we the associated Ministers in the Northern Part of the County of *Hartford* think it
needful to bear a publick Testimony against him and his conduct . . . hereby declaring that
under the present Circumstances of Things we shall by no Means admit him into any of our
Pulpits, and in Faithfulness to the People under our respective Charges we would solemnly warn
and caution them to take Heed and beware of Him."

The Testimony was signed by the following named pastors: Benjamin Colton, [West] Hart-
ford; Stephen Steel, Tolland; Thomas White, Bolton; Elnathan Whitman, Hartford; Daniel
Wadsworth, Hartford; Stephen Heaton, Goshen; Jonathan Marsh Jr., New Hartford; Samuel
Whitman, Farmington; Samuel Woodbridge, [East] Hartford; John McKinstry, Ellington; Timo-
thy Collins, Litchfield; Daniel Fuller, Willington; Andrew Bartholomew, Harwinton; Eli Colton,
Stafford; Elisha Webster, Canaan; Cyrus Marsh, Kent.

— 26. This day went to New-Haven

— 27. This day spent at New=Haven visiting &c.

— 28. This day returned from N. Haven found my family well, Laus Deo.

> March begins

Mch. 3. Lords day I preached pr totum from act. 5. 31. and administred yᵉ Sacrament. yᵉ Lord bless his word.

— 5. This day   . . prayed at yᵉ Court, yᵉ Superior Court opened

— 10. Lords day I preached pr. totum from psal. 22. 27. I pray God to forgive w'soever he has seen amiss in me .

— 12. This day sold Stafford Land

— 13. This day spent mainly at Court, Pomp a negro man tried for a rape

— 14. This day .   yᵉ Genˡˡ. Assembly met, prayed at Court in yᵉ afternoon

— 15. This day . . . reckoned with Capt. Hooker paied him in full, £83. 16s. 0d.

— 17. Lords day I preached pr. totum from luk. 18. 21. 22. 23. .   .   .

— 19. This day prayed at Court, visited yᵉ sick &c. the Court break up

— 20. . . . in yᵉ afternoon went over yᵉ River on a visit. I pray God to direct me to a suitable subject to preach upon

— 24. Lords day I preached per totum from prov. 3. 6.

— 28. . . . This day Deputy Governour Wolcot set out for N: London in order to embark for yᵉ Expedition agᵗ Cape Breton [1]

— 31. Lords day I preached pr totum from psal. 18. 6.

> April begins — 1745

Apr. 3. This day a publick fast, I preached A: M: from Deut. 23. 9. and Mʳ. Whitman P.M. from psal. 20. 7. . . .

— 4. This day visiting &c. prayed with Capt Church his company, which set out for New-London in order to embark upon

---

[1] A special session of the Assembly had been called at New Haven on the 26th of February and "concluded and resolved, (relying on the blessing of Almighty God,) to joyn with the neighboring governments in the intended expedition against his Majesty's enemies at Cape Breton and parts adjacent." It was further resolved "That the number of five hundred able-bodied, effective men for the land service be suitably encouraged to inlist" by wages, premiums, and "equal share in all the plunder." The "Colony Sloop *Defence*" was immediately put in readiness, and suitable and "sufficient transports hired." Lt.-Gov. Roger Wolcott was appointed Commander-in-Chief; Maj. Andrew Burr, Colonel; Capt. Simon Lathrop, Lieutenant-Colonel; Capt. Israel Newton, Major; while eight Captains, including James Church of Hartford, were designated for the enterprise.

y͏ᵉ Expedition ag͏ᵗ Cape Breton   I pray y͏ᵉ Lord of hosts go
with them

— 7. Lords day I preached A:M. from Cant. 1. 4. and administred y͏ᵉ Sacrament and P.M. from eph. 5. 6. and baptized Abigail y͏ᵉ daughter of William Nickols.   John Spencer Jun͏ʳ.
owned y͏ᵉ Covenant.

— 8. This day Freemans meeting   I preached a Lecture from
rom. 13. 4. and M͏ʳ. Buckingham and M͏ʳ. Joseph Talcot were
chosen Deputies.

— 9. This day reading Windhams Letter, Willisons Catechism
&͏ᶜ.

— 10. This day . . . in y͏ᵉ afternoon visited M͏ʳ. Woodbridge

— 14. Lords day I preached pr totum from rom. 5. 10. and baptized John y͏ᵉ son of Edward Dod and Elizabeth y͏ᵉ daughter
of John Spencer Jun͏ʳ.

— 15. This day visiting &͏ᶜ. Nathaniel Andrus, who died yesterday, Interred.

— 16.   . . . heard that our forces sailed from N: London last
Lords day for Cape Breton

— 18. This day Study, received a letter from M͏ʳ. Clap.

— 21. Lords day I preached per totum from gen. 18. 19. and
baptized Ruth the daughter of Edward Cadwell Jun͏ʳ.

— 23. This day in Study. this morning died M͏ʳˢ. Mary Ham
very suddenly

— 24. This day Publick fast. I preached A:M: from Eccles. 9.
18, and M͏ʳ. Whitman P.M: from 2 Chron. 6. 34. 35. at night
M͏ʳˢ. Ham buried

— 25. This day in Study. Eleazer Peck and Sarah King Joined
in marriage

— 26. This day .   . wrote a letter to M͏ʳ. Clap

— 28. Lords day I preached pr. totum from psal. 39. 4.

— 29. This day visiting &͏ᶜ. rec͏ᵈ. a letter from Doct͏ʳ. Chauncey.
May begins.

May 3. This day in Study, nil remarkable occurs. (my creatures
went to y͏ᵉ West Division to pasture this day).

— 5. Lords day I preached A:M: from Jam. 1. 21. and P.M. from
Jer. 2. 19 and baptized Elizabeth y͏ᵉ daughter of Moses Burr

— 7. This day y͏ᵉ Superior Court opened here I prayed at Court

— 9. This day Election. M͏ʳ. Whitman preached from 2 Sam.
23. 4. Gov. Dep: Gov. and assistants as in y͏ᵉ year past.

— 11. This day . . . a man y͏ᵗ was drowned in y͏ᵉ great river
some time ago buried

— 12. Lords day M^r. Hunn preached for me from 1 Cor. 15. 58.

— 13. This day . . . M^r. Hunn went from hence

— 15. This day prayed at Court   the upper house passed ye new Charter for ye College [1]

— 17. This day in business Relating to the college

— 19. Lords day I preached p^r. totum from heb. 12. 4. and baptized James ye Son of Timothy Biggelow

— 20. This day reading Present State of great Brittain &^{c}.

— 21. This day news from Cape Breton that y^e royal Battery is taken, y^e english army encamped before y^e Town

— 26. Lords day I preached A: M: from Joh. 4. 10. and P.M: from Joh. 5. 25. and Baptized Mabel y^e daughter of Abraham Cadwell. . . .

— 28. This day Study &^{c}. at night y^e Post Returned from Boston, no news from Cape=Breton

— 30. This day in Study. Y^e general assembly adjourned without day.

— 31. This day .   in y^e afternoon had a lecture preached from Joh. 5. 25.

       June begins

June 2. Lords day I preached per totum from Eph. 5. 2. and administred y^e Sacram^t. . . .

— 4. This day went to Tolland, y^e assoc^n. Sat there

— 5. This day lecture at Tolland I preached from Col. 1. 28. came to Bolton much indisposed.

— 6. This day returned home   found my family well Laus Deo.

— 9. Lords day I preached p^r. totum from rom. 13. 12.   . .

— 12. This day Study, visiting &^{c}. M^r. Reynolds [2] here.

— 13. This day .   nil remarkable

— 14. This day . . nil remarkable

— 15. This day . . . nil remarkable

— 16. Lords day I preached p^r. totum from phil. 1. 27. had a brief [3] or collection for Thom: Hudson.

---

[1] This was an act for the enlargement of the powers of the corporation of the Collegiate School and an alteration of the corporate name to that of "The President and Fellows of Yale College in New Haven." Mr. Wadsworth was one of the corporators at this time (and one of the petitioners for the enlarged powers of the new charter), having been chosen into the body in September, 1743, to succeed Rev. Samuel Woodbridge of East Hartford, who at that time resigned.

[2] Probably Rev. Peter Reynolds of Enfield. He was born in Bristol, R. I.; grad. H. C. 1720; ordained at Enfield, 1724; died 1768.

[3] A letter, in English use, authorizing a charitable contribution. "This day in o^r Church was read the Briefe for a collection for the relief of ye Protestant French." Evelyn's Diary, April 8, 1686.

— 19. This day went to Newington. M^r. Woodbridge preached a lecture from 2. tim. 2. 19.

— 20. . . . Broth^r. Lewis from Boston. news from Cape Breton of the death of Major Newton[1]

— 23. Lords day I preached p^r. totum from Isai. 55. 6. and Catechised ye Children

— 24. This day visiting, reading &^{c}. M^r. Nott here at night

— 26. This day much indisposed, ye soldiers sent from here toward New-london in order to embark for Cape-Breton: M^r. Clap here at night.

— 27. . . . Lieut^{nt}. Root[2] came home from Cape Breton ·

— 29. . . . M^r. Clap here this day

— 30. Lords day I preached pr. totum from 1 pet. 4. 7. And baptized Timothy the son of Caleb Spencer.

    July

July 4. This day   . . in ye afternoon lecture at M^r. Whitmans meeting   M^r. Whitman preached from 2 Cor. 5. 18.

— 5. . . . at night comes news y^t Cape Breton is taken

— 7. Lords day I preached per totum from heb. 9. 4. and administred ye Sacrament and baptized Timothy ye Son of Barzillai Clark and Moses ye son of Moses Burr and Rebecca ye daughter of Samuel Andrews.

— 8. This day visiting &^{c}. in ye afternoon publick rejoycing on account of ye Taking of Cape Breton.

— 12. This day in Study, ye news of ye Reduction of Cape Breton confirmed.

— 15. Lords day I preached per totum from rom. 16. 17. and baptized Lois the daughter of Moses Cadwell

— 18. . . . Last night died William Keith

— 19. This day study, W^m. Keith Interred

— 20. . . . at night heard y^t Major General Wolcott and Doct^r. Farnsworth[3] are got home from Cape Breton

— 21. Lords day M^r. Welles preached for me from prov. 3. 17. . . . and P.M. I preached from psal. 94. 12.

— 22. This day visited Doct^r. Farnsworth who Returned last Saturday from Cape Breton.

---

[1] *Ante*, p. 121, note. Maj. Newton was from Colchester.

[2] Timothy Root was from Farmington.

[3] Dr. Joseph Farnsworth appointed by the Assembly in March "to be improved as Physician and Surgeon's-Mate in the expedition against Cape Breton." He was born in Hartford ; baptized by Rev. Timothy Woodbridge of the First Church, April 28, 1717 ; grad. Y. C. 1736 ; settled at Wethersfield, but removed about 1790 to Vermont, where he died in July, 1804.

— 25. This day publick thanksgiving on y⁰ account of y⁰ success of our army in reducing Louisburgh. I preached from 1 Sam. 17. 12.

— 28. Lords day I preached A:M: from psal. 94. 12. and P.M: from Deut. 6. 11. 12. and baptized Nathaniel y⁰ son of John Skinner and Daniel y⁰ son of Daniel Goodwin

— 30. This day Major General Wolcot passed thro' this Town in his way home from Cape Breton. God be praised for his safe Return. Visited M⁰. Woodbridge.

— 31. . . . Y⁰ widow Andrus died in y⁰ morning.
        August begins

Aug. 1. . . . y⁰ widow Andrus Interred.

— 3. Lords day I preached A:M. from Tit. 2. 14 and administred y⁰ Sacrament. in y⁰ afternoon Indisposed and went not out.

— 6. this day went to Farmington   Saw my friends well.

— 7. this day returned home found my family well Laus Deo

— 9. . . . This day Capt. Church returned from Cape Breton

— 11. Lords day I preached   and baptized Ruth y⁰ daughter of Isaac Clark

— 12. This day   rec⁰. a letter from Doct⁰. Morison at lewisburgh

— 18. Lords day I preached   and baptized Daniel y⁰ son Daniel Skinner.

— 19. This day much indisposed.

— 21. This day . . . much indisposed

— 22. This day in Study. nil remarkable

— 23. This day in Study. nil remarkable

— 24. This day in Study. nil remarkable

— 25. Lords day I preached pr totum from Joh. 1. 12. . . .

— 26. This day in secular business. news y⁰ y⁰ Duke of Tuscany is elected Emperor of Germany.

— 28. . . . at night died Cyprian Nickols Jun⁰.

— 29. . . . M⁰. Whitman preached a lecture from psal. 118. 20.

— 30. . . . Cyprian Nickols Jun⁰. Interred
        September Begins

Sept. 1. Lords day I preached . . . and administred y⁰ Sacrament . . . and baptized James y⁰ son of M⁰. Samuel Talcot, and Jonathan y⁰ son of Sam¹. Flag.

— 7. . . . ye Widow Hopkins and y⁰ wife of Deacon Sheldon were Interred

— 8. Lords day I preached per totum . .   and baptized Martha the daughter of John Spencer Jun⁰.

— 9. This day set out for New-Haven   Lodged at Wallingford
— 11. Commencement at New-Haven.   26 graduated A. B.
— 15. Lords day M^r. Wells preached for me A: M: from phil. 2.
   12. and P.M. I preached from rev. 3. 1. and baptized Timothy
   ye son of Timothy Shepard
— 18. This day visited ye sick.   M^r. Day married in y^r afternoon.
— 20. This day . . . at night died Abigail ye daughter of
   Thomas Hopkins
— 21. . . . Thomas Hopkins his daughter Interred
— 22. Lords day I preached . .
— 23. This day visiting ye sick &^{c}. in ye afternoon wrote Jonathan Ashleys will.
— 25. .   Joseph Shepards child died
— 26. . . . Joseph Shepards son buried
— 29. Lords day I preached . . .
    October begins
Oct. 1. This day went to Wintonbury. the association met there
— 2. This day lecture at Wintonbury M^r. Colton preached from
   act. 8. 39. M^r. Belden[1] was examined and licensed to preach.
— 4. This day .   . in ye afternoon had a lecture, preached
   from phil. 2. 5.
— 5. This day . . . heard ye Sorrowfull news of ye death of
   my kinsman Samuel Wadsworth of Farmington
— 6. Lords day I preached per totum from luk. 24. 46. and administred ye Sacrament   after ye afternoon service Jedidiah
   Atwood made publick confession of sin in ye disturbance he
   made sometime ago in ye meeting house reviling ye minister
   &^{c}.
— 10. . . . President Clap here at night. news y^t General
   Pepperel is made a Baronet, M^r. Warren an admiral & Govern^r.
   of Cape Breton[2]
— 13. Lords day I preached .   and baptized Thankfull y^e
   daughter of Daniel Butler
— 16. Some study, received a letter from uncle James

---

[1] Joshua Belden, born at Wethersfield July 19, 1724; grad. Y. C. 1743; ordained at Newington Nov. 11, 1747; discharged the duties of his office till Nov., 1803; died after ten years of increasing feebleness, July 23, 1813, aged 89.

[2] These awards to William Pepperell and Peter Warren of the Massachusetts contingent of
the army were not, perhaps, envied by the Connecticut branch. Still it was not without annoyance
that they saw the representations made in behalf of the Connecticut troops practically ignored in
the distribution of honors. Dr. Benj. Trumbull, writing long afterward, says: "Notwithstanding
these humble and earnest solicitations, I believe no officer except captain, afterward general Woos-
ter, who went on business to England, and was honoured with a lieutenancy and half pay during
life, received any appointment or emolument from the crown."

— 20. This Lords day preached pr. totum from rom. 6. 23. baptized Nathaniell the son of Moses Burnham. Moses Burnham owned yᵉ Covenant   James yᵉ son of Mʳ. Samuel Talcot died an Infant about two months old

— 21. This day   James Talcot buried.

— 26. This day . . . recᵈ. a letter from Mʳ. Clap.

— 27. Lords day I preached pr. totum from psal. 78. 34. 35. 36. 37. . . .

    November.

Nov. 3. Lords day I preached pr. totum . . . Levi Jones owned the Covenant, Julius yᵉ son of Levi Jones was baptized.

— 4. This day visiting yᵉ sick &ᶜ. received a Letter to go to a Councel at N. cambridge

— 6. . . . heard yᵗ yᵉ duke of Tuscany is elected Emperor &ᶜ. The Pretenders son in Scotland makes progress.

— 7. This day publick thanks giving preached from psal. 126. 6. blessed be god yᵗ has carried me and my family thro' another year.

— 10. Lords day I preached per totum from heb. 2. 3. . . . .

— 13. This day went to New-cambridge, advised Mʳ. Newel¹ not to settle, returned home

— 17. Lords day I preached A:M: from Jam. 4: 17. & P:M from 2 tim. 3. 4 . . . .

— 23. This day in Study. news yᵗ yᵉ french and Indians have made an irruption on our western borders.

— 24. Lords day I preached per totum from psal. 94. 19.

— 28. This day lecture, I preached from Joh. 3. 14. 15.

    December begins

Dec. 1. Lords day I preached per totum from Joh. 3. 14. 15. James Shepard made a publick confession &ᶜ. Benjamin yᵉ son of Samˡˡ. Graham and Ruth yᵉ daughter of Daniel Spencer were baptized

— 8. Lords day I preached A.M. from rom. 13. 14. P.M. indisposed went not out.

— 11. This day reading yᵉ September testimony²

— 15. Lords day preached A:M. from rom. 13. 14. and P:M. from Matt. 9. 2.

— 16. This day some study. at night reckoned with yᵉ Commᵗᵉ

---

¹ *Ante*, p. 60, note.

² The Association's Testimony against Whitefield, mentioned *ante*, p. 120.

— 22. Lords day preached A: M. from Matt. 9. 2. & P.M. from Col. 3. 5. Joseph Wadsworth Junr. and his wife owned ye Covenant

— 23. . . . news of a great number of Indians near ye upper Towns

— 29. Lords day I preached per totum from heb. 2. 14. 15.

January [1746.]

Jany 2. . . . in ye afternoon Lecture at ye South Meeting house M^r. Whitman preached from Matt. 20. 28.

— 5. Lords day I preached per totum from rom. 6. 21. I pray God to bless his word . . .

— 12. Lords day I preached per totum from Col. 1. 10. ye pretenders cause [1] earnestly prayed against

— 17. This day   reading [illegible] History of ye rebellion

— 19. Lords day I preached pr. totum from psal. 90. 12.   .

— 20. This day visited M^r. Woodbridge and M^r. Colton

— 26. Lords day I preached pr. totum from psal. 20. 4

— 28. This day went to Farmington and returned.

— 30. in ye afternoon lecture I preached from 1. Cor. 11. 26.

— 31. This day in study   I^s. Field here
        February begins

Feby. 2. Lords day I preached .   . and adminstred ye Sacrament.

— 4. This day went to ye association at Windsor

— 5. This day lecture at M^r. Marsh at Windsor   I preached from 1 Joh. 3. 9. & returned home

— 9. Lords day I preached pr. totum from luk. 18. 3 and baptized Neil ye son of Doct^r. McLean and Timothy ye son of Joseph Wadsworth

— 12. This day went to ye west division nil remarkable occurs read y^t ye pretender was taken

— 15. Lords day I preached pr. totum from 2. Cor. 6. 2. I pray God to bless . . .

— 18. This day visited M^r. Woodbridge

— 19. This day . . . nil remarkable occurs, save y^t Thomas Croswell died very suddenly in ye evening

---

[1] Prince Charles Edward, grandson of James II, had just landed in Scotland, gained a victory at Preston Pans, reduced Carlisle, and advanced into England. On the following 16th of April he was defeated at Culloden and the Stuart cause finally lost.

— 22. . . . ye news of the defeat of ye pretenders army confirmed

— 23. Lords day preached A:M: from Eccl. 9. 12. and P.M. from
2. Cor. 4. 18

— 25. This day went to New-Haven   severe cold

— 26. This day spent at N-Haven

— 27. This day as ye former

— 28. This day returned home, found my family well Laus Deo
March begins

Mch. 2. Lords day I preached A:M from 2 cor. 4. 18 and P:M:
from Col. 1. 13. I pray God to bless his word

— 4. This day study &^{c} prayed at Court, ye Superior Court opened
in this Town

— 9. Lords day preached A.M from Eph. 6. 11. & p.m. from Col.
3. 16.

— 11. This day spent at Court . . . at night died Ensign
Nathaniel Goodwin a good old man and full of daies

— 13. This day . . . Ensign Nathaniel Goodwin Interred, a
good old man, full of daies, aged about 78 or 79.

— 16. Lords day I preached per totum from psal. 73. 26. I pray
God . . . pardon what has been amiss in me.

— 19. This day . . . reading Walls history of Infant Baptism

— 23. Lords day I preached . . and baptized Daniel ye son
of M^r. Daniel Edwards

— 24. This day went to Farmington, Saw my friends in usual
health. Laus Deo

— 25. This day returned home, found my family well, Laus Deo

— 29. This day in study, M^r. President Clap here

— 30. Lords day I preached . . . and baptized Elizabeth y^e
daughter of John Sheldon.
April begins

Apl. 2. This day went to Weathersfield, Study &^{c}. M^r. Clap went
from hence

— 3. This day . . . in ye afternoon a lecture M^r. M^c.Clenachan [1]
preached from Amos 4. 11.

— 6. Lords day I preached pr. totum from phil. 3. 8 and administred ye Sacrament . . .

— 7. This day freemans meeting. M^r. Colton preached from
Isai. 1: 26. M^r. Buckingham and M^r. Joseph Talcot chosen
Deputies

---

[1] Probably some friend of the Scotch brothers Morison, particularly it may be of Rev. Evander. The name has been vainly sought in the usual finding-places of ministers of the period.

— 9. This day publick fast. I preached A: M. from lev. 26. 3. 6. & Mr. Whitman P.M. from Joshua 24. 20.

— 11. This day . . . Samuel Benton Interred

— 13. Lords day I preached pr. totum from 1 Cor. 1. 18   And baptized Thankfull ye daughter of Nehemiah Cadwell

— 14. This day went to Durham

— 15. This day went to New=Haven

— 16. This day ye Corporation met   Came into various acts

— 17. This day returned to Durham

— 18. This day returned home, found my family well.   Laus Deo.

— 20. Lords day I preached . . .

— 21. This day visiting &c. Comes news from Louisburg of ye death of Lieutnt. Ashley[1] and others of this Town.

— 25. . . . News of ye destruction of Ashuelot by the Indians but wants confirmation

— 27. Lords day I preached pr totum from Eccles. 7: 14. and baptized Thomas and Joseph sons of Joseph Wadsworth Junr. and Elisha ye son of Elisha Pratt.

    May begins

May 4. Lords day preached   . and administred ye Sacrament . . . rainy day

— 8. This day Genll. Election.   Mr. S: Hall[2] preached from 2 chron. 19. 5. 6.   Governr. Dep: Governr. & Assistants as in ye year past.   Saving Col: Whiting left out and Col. Burr put in

— 11. Lords day Mr. Hall preached for me.

— 18. Lords day I preached . . .

— 19. This day and yesterday marched forth 300 men for ye defence of our frontiers, nil remarkable

— 22. . . . ye soldiers that went to ye western frontiers returned without discovering any enemy[3]

---

[1] Ezekiel Ashley, commissioned at the May session of the Assembly, 1745, as "Lieutenant of one of the companies . . . for the expedition against Cape Breton." Before leaving Hartford Ashley made a will, dated June 28, 1745, in which he leaves his property to his "loving wife Hannah," charging her with some small bestowments upon his son Ezekiel, and his two daughters, Hannah and Griffith, when they come to be of age.

[2] Rev. Samuel Hall of New Cheshire (afterward Cheshire), born at Wallingford, Oct. 5, 1695; grad. Y. C. 1716; ordained at December 9, 1724; died in office February 26, 1776. He preached the Election Sermon (as recorded above) May 8, 1746, and was a vigorous Old Light in current controversies.

[3] The General Assembly "for the encouragement" of those engaged in this border defence enacted at this session that "all such officers and souldiers as shall provide themselves with arms, ammunition, provisions and other necessaries, shall have as a reward for every male prisoner of the Indian enemy sixteen years old and upward the sum of three hundred pounds bills of credit old tenor, and for every scalp of such Indian 16 year old and upward, half so much; and for every female prisoner or *children* under the age of sixteen years of such Indians the sum of one hundred

— 25. Lords day I preached . . and baptized James y' son of James Shepard.

— 26. This day Jonathan Skinner was killed in an Instant by y' accidental firing of a great Gun and John Bunce and Benjamin Gardner grievously wounded.

— 27. This day . . . Jonathan Skinner Interred

— 29. This day study, lecture in y' afternoon

— 31. This day in study. y' General assembly Adjourned June begins

June 1. Lords day I preached pr. totum from Eccl. 7. 2. & baptized Sarah the daughter of William Tyley & Abigail y' daughter of Stephen Turner

— 3. This day Association met at M'. Whitmans.[1]

— 4. This day lecture at M'. Whitmans meeting. M'. Whitman of Farmington preached from 2 Cor. 1. 2.

This morning about 8 o'clock was heard a loud rumbling noise something like thunder, some tho't it an earthquake, to y' southeast but wee since hear that in divers places was seen a Large Ball of fire moving south eastward, and was seen to break, which was presently followed with y' noise above mentioned

— 8. Lords day I preached A.M. from Eph. 6. 4. & P.M. from Matt. 24. 12. .

---

and fifty pounds like bills, and for every scalp of such enemy Indian female or *children* of such Indians half so much, to be paid out of the treasury of this Colony, on an order drawn by said Committee [of War], on the producing to them of such prisoners or scalps."

It is gratifying to notice even so much delicacy on the Assembly's part respecting the above atrocious order, that the "entry on the publick records" of all votes " passed by this Assembly for the encouragement of obtaining Indian enemy prisoners or their scalps," was suppressed till further order.

[1] This meeting of the Association was mainly concerned about the question of the expediency of settling Rev. David S. Rowland in the Northwest Society of Simsbury (now Granby). Mr. Rowland was born in Fairfield in 1719; grad. Y. C. 1743; and after very brief preparation was licensed to preach, in August, 1744, by the "New Light" Fairfield Association. By February, 1745, he was preaching at the Symsbury Northwest Society; but his settlement was delayed by advice of the Hartford Association given in October of that year. At this June meeting the Association appointed a committee, of which Mr. Whitman of Farmington and Mr. Whitman of Hartford and Mr. Wadsworth were members to "see to it," as preliminary to any consent to his ordination, that Mr. Rowland "approve and submit to the Ecclesiastical Constitution established in the churches of Connecticut," as, also, that "the said Rowland will not Countenance and encourage Mr. Whitefield by inviting him to preach or attending his administrations or on any other Itinerant Preachers, or any other of the errors, seperations or disorders prevailing in y' County." As a result of this action Mr. Rowland's ordination at Simsbury failed to take place, though he continued to preach there until August, 1747. He was subsequently some years at Plainfield, where he was ordained, and at Providence, R. I., in both of which places he had an unquiet career, but was finally installed at Windsor (First Church) March 27, 1776, where he died Jan. 13, 1794. He published several sermons, some of which were plainly occasioned by episodes of his rather chequered ecclesiastical experiences.

— 9. This day . . . in yᵉ morning died the Revᵈ. Mʳ. Samuel
Woodbridge Pastor of yᵉ Church on yᵉ East Side of yᵉ River in
this Town.[1]

— 10. This day yᵉ Revᵈ. Mʳ. Samuel Woodbridge was Interred.
The Revᵈ. Mʳ. Ashbel Woodbridge preached a Sermon on yᵗ
occasion from phil. 1. 23.

— 11. . . . Doctʳ. Chauncey & Mʳ. Tailor[2] here

— 15. Lords day I preached A: M: from Joh. 11: 11 & P.M. from
Matt. 24. 12. and catechised yᵉ children

— 19. This day . . . yᵉ Genˡ. Assembly met at New Haven

— 22. Lords day I preached A: M: from Matt. 24. 12 & P.M. from
Eph. 2. 4. 5. and baptized Rebecca yᵉ daughter of Elijah
Cadwell

— 24. This day went to yᵉ West Division upon a certain affair,
returned re Infecta

— 26. This day . . . at Deacⁿ. Sheldon wedding. at night
married Moses Dickinson & Elizabeth Pratt.

— 29. Lords day I preached A: M: from Eph. 2. 4. 5. & P.M.: from
gen. 1. 26.

July 1. This morning about break o' day my wife was safely
delivered of a daughter.[3] Laus Deo.

— 3. . . . in yᵉ afternoon a Lecture at Mʳ. Whitmans meeting
he preached from Joh. 20. 31.

— 4. . . . nil remarkable domestick, from abroad wee hear yᵗ
yⁿ rebels are totally defeated

— 6. Lords day I preached A.M. from Joh. 17. 24. and administred yᵉ Sacrament, and P.M. from Jer. 3. 12 and baptized my
daughter Ruth

— 10. This day went to Glastenbury on a visit to Mʳ. Woodbridge[4] who is going chaplain in yᵉ Army to Canada wᵐ God
prosper

— 13. Lords day I preached A: M: from Jer. 3. 12. & P.M. from
psal. 31. 19. . .

— 15. This day . . . was Interred on Sowerhill a soldier from
Cape Breton and his wife

— 17. . . . the defeat of the Rebels farther Confirmed

---

[1] Ante, pp. 14, 85, and notes.

[2] Probably Rev. John Taylor, born at Boston ; grad. H. C. 1721 ; ordained at Milton, Mass.,
Nov. 13, 1728; died Jan. 26, 1750, aged forty-six.

[3] Ruth, who lived only four years, dying Dec. 27, 1750.

[4] Ante, p. 25, note. As events turned Mr. Woodbridge did not go to Canada, and the regiment was disbanded in October following the present date.

— 20. Lords day I preached A: M: from psal. 31. 19 & P.M: from luk. 12. 15.

— 21. This day study, news y⁴ yᵉ fleet for Canada is not likely to come this year

— 27. Lords day I preached pʳ. totum from heb. 3. 7. 8. . . .

— 31. This day . . . in yᵉ afternoon a lecture Mʳ. Williams preached from Joh. 15. 12.

    August begins

Aug. 3. Lords day I preached from act. 2. 36 pʳ. totum

— 8. This day in study orders come for yᵉ marching troops to N. London

— 10. Lords day I preached A.M. from heb. 12. 11 and P.M. from psal. 97. 1. and baptized Huldah yᵉ daughter of John Shepard

— 12. This day prayed with yᵉ soldiers that marched from here toward New-London going on yᵉ expedition ag⁴ Canada   I pray God to go with & prosper them.

— 15. This day accompanied Col. Talcot, Lᵗ Biggelow & Doctʳ. Morison part of yᵉ way on yʳ Journey to N. London [1]

— 16. This day Study, went over yᵉ river

— 17. Lords day preached on yᵉ East side A: M: from phil. 4. 20. and P.M. from psal. 97. 1.

— 20. This day went to Farmington   returned found my family well Laus Deo

— 24. Lords day I preached A.M from [illegible] 12. 11 and P.M. from act. 2. 36. in yᵉ afternoon a thunder storm

— 25. This day went to Norwich

— 26. This day went to N. London

— 27. This day back to Norwich

— 29. This day returned home   found my family well Laus Deo.

— 31. Lords day I preached pr. totum from phil. 3. 13. 14.   rainy weather

    September—

Sept. 1. This day went to Durham

— 2. This day went to New-Haven

— 3. This day Commencement at N: Haven.

---

[1] At the June session of the General Assembly it had been resolved to raise "as soon as possible in this Colony the number of one thousand able bodied effective men," to be "imployed in his Majestie's service for the reduction of Canada." Samuel Talcott had been designated as Lt.-Colonel; Timothy Bigelow "Second lieutenant of the Colonel's Company"; and Dr. Normand Morrison as "Chief Physician and Chirurgeon." Thirty pounds bounty was offered to every soldier enlisting; and impressment into service could be resorted to if enlistment failed. These preparations were, however, rendered nugatory by events quite outside of Colonial influence, and the regiment did not leave the soil of the Commonwealth.

— 4. This day returned to Wallingford

— 5. This day returned Home found my family well Laus Deo.

— 7. Lords day I preached pr. totum from act. 13. 47

— 9. This day some study. Presdt. Clap here at night

— 11. This day went to Farmington   returned found my family well Laus Deo

— 12. . . . Laboured under indisposition

— 14. Lords day I preached per totum from Col. 1. 21. pardon whatsoever thou has seen amiss in me

— 17. This day some study, wrote my will,[1] visited a prisoner

— 18. This day . . . attended y* funeral of widow Webster

— 21. Lords day I preached . . .

— 23. This day went to Windsor on a visit

— 28. Lords day I preached pr. totum from psal. 50. 11.

— 29. . . . y* talk of a french fleet alarms y* country
October begins

Oct. 2. This day in Study. in y* afternoon preached a lecture previous to y* Sacrament[2] from rom. 10. 4

— 5. Lords day I preached pr. totum from psal. 73. 33 and administred y* Sacrament, and baptized Elizabeth y* daughter of Colonel Talcot.

— 7. This day went to y* Association at Harwinton

— 8. This day association Lecture at Harwinton, lecture preached by M^r. Gid. Mills from Matt. 11. 28. Came to Farmington.

— 9. This day returned Home found my family well.

— 12. Lords day I preached pr. totum from Jam. 5. 19. 20. and baptized Sarah y* daughter of Dan^ll. Goodwin and Dorcas y* daughter of Samuel Andrus

— 15. This day visiting Last night died Dorothy y* wife of Lt. Daniel Goodwin and this day Died Noadiah Phelps a stranger in Town

— 19. Lords day preached per totum from Job 2: 10 and baptized James y* son of Diostheus Humphrys

---

[1] This will was apparently executed Dec. 19 following. Mr. Wadsworth added a codicil, in a noticably feebler hand, on October 3d of the subsequent year, 1747, giving his wife, in addition to former provision made for her, a certain piece of land in Farmington.

The inventory of his property, as proved after his decease, showed real estate in Hartford to the amount of £3,450; and in Farmington of £1,117. A list of his Library may be found in Walker's *History of the First Church of Hartford.* It may be interesting to note that there are specified as items of his personalty also, "1 Black cow, 1 Red Cow, 1 Brindle white-face, 21 Sheep, 1 old negro woman nam'd Rose, 6 Loads of Hay, one Hive bees."

[2] This is the first indication in the First Church history of what has in modern times been familiarly known as the Preparatory Lecture. Such a lecture seems to have been established some time before in several Boston churches; the first one being March 4, 1720, by the cooperate action of the First and the Brattle Street churches, then respectively under the charge of Rev. Thomas Foxcroft and Rev. Benjamin Colman.

— 22. This day . . . M^r. Eliot here

— 26. Lords day preached . . . and baptized Huldah ye daughter of Daniel Brace

— 30. This day study, lecture in ye afternoon at M^r. Whitmans meeting M^r. Whitman preached from psal. 119. 34
    Nov. 1746

Nov. 2. Lords day preached A: M. Joh. 3. 17. P.M. rom. 2. 4.

— 5. This day publick thanksgiving preached from Isai. 25. 1.

— 8. This day . . . received a letter from Thomas Wadsworth of Longbuckby in England

— 9. Lords day preached A: M: from Isai. 65. 12. and P.M: from Job 21. 14

— 11. This day went to Farmington Saw my friends in usual health. returned found my family well Laus Deo

— 12. . . . M^r. John Ellery who died ye 10 Instant, was Interred

— 16. Lords day I preached A: M. from Joh. 9. 4. & P.M. from rom. 12. 1. I pray god to make his word beneficial to y^m y^t heard it

— 23. Lords day I preached per totum from Eph. 5. 8 and Mary Skinner was admitted to Communion with ye Church

— 25. . . . M^r. Hez. Ripley & Mary Skinner married.

— 26. This day without study, rainy weather, no study

— 27. This day writing &^{c}. nil remarkable occurs

— 30. Lords day preached A.M: from 2 pet. 3. 3. 4. and P.M. from Col. 3. 6.
    December begins

Dec. 4. This . . . P.M. preached a Lecture from rev. 1. 5.

— 7. Lords day I preached A: M. from Isai. 53. 5. and administred ye Sacrament and P.M. from Eccles. 1. 2. baptized Abigail ye daughter of Jos: Shepard Junr.[1]

— 8. This day . . . at night reckoned with ye Society com^{tte}.

— 14. Lords day I preached A: M: from Eccles. 1. 2. and P.M. from Ezek. 22. 19.

— 19. This day in ye forenoon I was suddenly seized with a fainting or epileptick fit, ye form^r. I suppose, but thro' gods great goodness I am recovered, praised be his name for it. may I live to his praise

— 20. This day kept house.

---

[1] The baptism of this child is the last act of Mr. Wadsworth recorded by him on his Official Church-Book. It is apparent from his handwriting in this Diary, as well as from more formal expressions, that he had been gradually growing feebler in health.

— 21. Lords day, I went not out by reason of my indisposition
— 23. This day reading. our Society at yᵉ meeting voted me
£340. salary.
— 27. Lords day I preached A:M: from Lam. 3. 22 and P.M.
from Ezek. 22. 14.

January begins [1747.]

Jany. 1. This day a lecture at Mʳ. Whitmans meeting. Mʳ. Willᵐˢ
preached from prov. 13. 13.
— 2. This day study. snowed
— 3. This day in Study, pray God I may be prepared for yᵉ
duties of yᵉ approaching Sabbath
— 4. Lords day 1 preached pr. totum from rom. 6. 11.
— 5. This day went to Weathersfield over yᵉ river &ᶜ.
— 6. This day indisposed, took physick
— 7. This day spent in visiting
— 8. This day in Study &ᶜ.
— 9. This day Recᵈ. a Paquet from Doctʳ. Doddridge with some
pamphlets
— 10. This day in Study nil remarkable occurs
— 11. Lords day I preached A.M. from Eph. 5. 1. and P.M. from
luk. 4. 36
— 12. This day in studying, visiting &ᶜ.
— 14. This day held a fast at Mʳ. Williamsons to pray for his
wife that has been a Long time in a distressed Condition,
Mʳ. Colton preached from psal. 37. 3. 4. 5. 6. 7.   ·
— 15. This day went to Farmington. Saw my friends in usual
health   returned in safety, Laus Deo.
— 16. This day indisposed
— 17. This day had an epileptick fit in yᵉ morning, but thro' gods
goodness was carried thro'
— 18. Lords day I went not out by reason of indisposition
both Societies met at yᵉ South meeting house
— 19. This day visiting and being visited
— 20. This day incapable of study
— 21. This day under indisposition
— 22. As before
— 23. As before
— 24. Advised by a physician not to preach tomorrow
— 25. Lords day went not out in the forenoon in yᵉ afternoon
went to Mʳ. Whitmans meeting he preached from luk. 10. 42

— 26. went to Stepney returned late[1]

— 27. This day at home

— 28. This day as ye former

— 29. This as before

— 30. and this in like manner

— 31. This day visiting and receiving visits

  February begins

Feby. 1. Lords day went to meeting in ye afternoon M^r. Whitman preached from Zech. 9. 10.

— 2. 3. 4. Monday, Tuesday, Wednesday spent chiefly in giving
and receiving visits and preparing for my Intended voyage
unto ye West Indies

— 5. This day went to Farmington. Saw my friends in usual
health, returned safely, Laus Deo

My indisposition incapacitated me about this time to keep a
Diary. I therefore now enter only some remarkables

On ye 10th of Feb. I had a small touch of an Epileptick fit w^c
lasted but a minute or two and did not deprive me of my reason

On ye 16th instant another small touch of a fit

The above is the last entry made by Mr. Wadsworth in his
diary. Whether he carried out his intention to take a sea voyage
cannot, perhaps, positively be stated, but it seems altogether improbable. On March 2d, and on August 4th, votes indicative of
the pastor's continued "indisposition" are recorded in the Society's
minutes; and on the second of those occasions a committee was
instructed "to apply themselves to M^r. Edward Dorr to Continue
to Administer to this Society during M^r. Wadsworths Incapacity,
and as need shall require."

Mr. Wadsworth survived till November 12, 1747, lacking two
days of forty-three years of age, and having filled a pastoral term
of fifteen years and two months.

[1] A meeting of the First Ecclesiastical Society of this date, Jan. 26, took action for the secur-
ing a minister "during Mr. Wadsworth's absence provided he go to Sea for his health."

INDEX.

www.ingramcontent.com/pod-product-compliance
Lightning Source LLC
Chambersburg PA
CBHW021123020726
47500CB00003B/899